BEHOLD THAT STAR

Behold that Star

A Christmas Anthology

Edited by the Bruderhof

Illustrated by Maria Maendel

The Plough Publishing House

© 1996 by The Plough Publishing House
of The Bruderhof Foundation

Farmington PA 15437, USA
Robertsbridge, East Sussex TN32 5DR, UK

First printing	1966
Second printing	1967
Third printing	1974
2nd Edition	1996

Behold that Star: a Christmas anthology/edited by the Bruderhof:
    illustrations by Maria Maendel. --2nd ed.
        p.   cm.
    Includes bibliographical references.
    ISBN 0-87486-084-9 (pbk.)
        1. Christmas stories. I. Bruderhof Communities (Rifton, N.Y.)
    PN6071.C6B77 1996
    808.83'10833--dc20   96-43565
                                                                  CIP

Printed in the USA

CONTENTS

INTRODUCTION   *vii*

    Behold that Star (song)   1

THE ANGELS' POINT OF VIEW   *J. B. Phillips*   2

    Gloria in Excelsis Deo! (song)   10

    Words from an Old Spanish Carol   13

THE SHEPHERDS   *Ruth Sawyer*   14

    Carol of the Seekers (song)   28

THE WELL OF THE STAR   *Elizabeth Goudge*   29

    The Christ-Child Lay on Mary's Lap (song)   64

THE THREE GIFTS   *Jane T. Clement*   66

    Poverty Carol (song)   96

THE CHILDREN'S CRUSADE   *Ernst Wiechert*   97

    One Star above All Stars (song)   146

THE POOR CHILDREN'S CHRISTMAS   *Ernst Wiechert*   147

    Come, Oh Come, Dear Children All (song)   166

THE ANGEL'S SONG   *Marie Onnen*   168

    Heaven's Gate Has Opened (song)   187

HALLELU-NEIN   *Marie Berg*   188

    Mid-Winter (poem)   220

BROTHER ROBBER *Helene Christaller*   222

 Rejoice All the Heavens (song)   232

THE LEGEND OF THE CHRISTMAS ROSE *Selma Lagerlöf* 233

 Lo! A Light Is in the East (song)   260

THE WORKER IN SANDALWOOD *Marjorie Pickthall*   261

 As I Was Watching by My Sheep (song)   274

THE FOREST BEAR *Reimmichl*   275

 Song for a New Baby (song)   290

THE CHESS PLAYER *Ger Koopman*   291

 How Far Is It to Bethlehem? (poem)   306

THE CRIBMAKER'S TRIP TO HEAVEN *Reimmichl*   307

 People, Look East (poem)   322

JOURNEY TO CHRISTMAS *B. J. Chute*   323

 Advent (poem)   352

INTRODUCTION

Christmas is a time of promise, the meaning of which man
has never fully grasped; the joy of it is too deep for our
small hearts, the message too simple and enormous to be simply believed, except by children; the love embodied in God's
gift is so much greater than any love of which we are capable
that we stand helpless before it, and may even turn away in
rebellious cynicism, or embellish and distort the event with
the trimmings of our materialistic culture.

The meaning of Christmas is for every day and every man
and is for the redemption of the whole world. It is like a many-
faceted jewel, and now here, now there, the light strikes the
heart of the jewel and we catch the gleam of it, a bit of its pure
meaning, a glimpse of the glory that lies beyond us.

For those of us who live in the Bruderhof communities, the
time of Christmas brings each year a new longing and a new
joy. We were drawn together originally in Germany after World
War I as a tiny group because we wished to seek to express,
not in words or ideals or principles or exhortations but in the
spontaneous sharing of our daily life, our belief in the promise
and redemption embodied in the Christ Child. Those who

were part of that group left the outward words and the struc-
tures men had made and sought to find together afresh the
deepest meaning of the event in the Stable, and the responsibility it lays upon us.

In the surge of response of that period between the World
Wars, the little group grew, also breaking down national barri-
ers. This growth continued during the time of Nazi persecu-
tion and eventual flight to England. When the community chose
to leave England in order to remain together, a time of com-
parative isolation followed in Paraguay, the country that gave
us asylum. But after World War II we experienced again a
widespread response to our mission, a new wind blowing, a
new yearning for community, and out of this came our deci-
sion to move to the United States, where we still live, in six
growing communities.

We feel, especially in these days, a sense of our own inad-
equacy in the face of the tremendous responsibilites of life in
the present hour; a longing to bring to expression the faith
that we share, to reach out, in however small a way, that men
may feel hope rather than despair, unity rather than separa-
tion, and love rather than fear of one another.

We look forward to Christmas each year as a time when our
daily life is enriched and permeated by the literature, poetry,
and music that has gathered through the ages around the cen-
tral fact of Christ's birth. Some of this has sprung out of our
own life together, and some we have found and have returned
to year after year. The stories, poems, and carols in this book

Introduction

reflect the varied backgrounds from which we have come; they also reflect how we share together not only our material necessities and our common labor, but the enriching and creative response to God's love for men as we have discovered them in literary and musical expression. In reading aloud at common meals, in times of festival such as Christmas, in the life of our school, we use each opportunity to experience the bond that transcends time and distance. We cannot sing "One star above all stars" without a living sense of kinship with those who fought a similar fight no matter how long ago.

This is a book for children and adults alike, and for all who long for the childlike heart. It expresses our longing to give a little of what we know we have received, and to bring to Christmas something other than tinsel and the outward show, perhaps to catch a gleam of the heart of the jewel. And we wish to express deeply our faith that indeed, however dark the hour or desolate the road, "Love – the Lord – is on the way."

Jane T. Clement

behold that star

Thomas Talley   Thomas Talley

behold that star! behold that star up yonder,
behold that star! it is the star of bethlehem.
there was no room found in the inn
for him who was born free from sin.

the wise men travelled from the east
to worship him, the prince of peace.

a song broke forth upon the night
from angel hosts all robed in white.

behold that star! behold that star up yonder,
behold that star! it is the star of bethlehem.

I

THE ANGELS' POINT OF VIEW

by J. B. PHILLIPS

nce upon a time a very young angel was being shown round the splendours and glories of the universes by a senior and experienced angel. To tell the truth, the little angel was beginning to be tired and a little bored. He had been shown whirling galaxies and blazing suns, infinite distances in the deathly cold of interstellar space, and to his mind there seemed to be an awful lot of it all. Finally he was shown the galaxy of which our planetary system is but a small part. As the two of them drew near to the star which we call our sun and to its circling planets, the senior angel pointed to a small and rather insignificant sphere turning very slowly on its axis. It looked as dull as a dirty tennis-ball to the little angel, whose mind was filled with the size and glory of what he had seen.

"I want you to watch that one particularly," said the senior angel, pointing with his finger.

"Well, it looks very small and rather dirty to me," said the little angel. "What's special about that one?"

"That," replied his senior solemnly, "is the Visited Planet."

"Visited?" said the little one. "You don't mean visited by —— ?"

"Indeed I do. That ball, which I have no doubt looks to you small and insignificant and not perhaps over-clean, has been visited by our young Prince of Glory." And at these words he bowed his head reverently.

"But how?" queried the younger one. "Do you mean that our great and glorious Prince, with all these wonders and splendours of His Creation, and millions more that I'm sure I haven't seen yet, went down in Person to this fifth-rate little ball? Why should He do a thing like that?"

"It isn't for us," said his senior a little stiffly, "to question His 'why's', except that I must point out to you that He is not impressed by size and numbers, as you seem to be. But that He really went I know, and all of us in Heaven who know anything know that. As to why He became one of them—how else do you suppose could He visit them?"

The little angel's face wrinkled in disgust.

4

"Do you mean to tell me," he said, "that He stooped so low as to become one of those creeping, crawling creatures of that floating ball?"

"I do, and I don't think He would like you to call them 'creeping, crawling creatures' in that tone of voice. For, strange as it may seem to us, He loves them. He went down to visit them to lift them up to become like Him."

The little angel looked blank. Such a thought was almost beyond his comprehension.

"Close your eyes for a moment," said the senior angel, "and we will go back in what they call Time."

While the little angel's eyes were closed and the two of them moved nearer to the spinning ball, it stopped its spinning, spun backwards quite fast for a while, and then slowly resumed its usual rotation.

"Now look!" And as the little angel did as he was told, there appeared here and there on the dull surface of the globe little flashes of light, some merely momentary and some persisting for quite a time.

"Well, what am I seeing now?" queried the little angel.

"You are watching this little world as it was some thousands of years ago," returned his companion. "Every flash and glow of light that you see is something of the Father's knowledge and wisdom breaking into the minds and hearts of people who live upon the earth.

Not many people, you see, can hear His Voice or understand what He says, even though He is speaking gently and quietly to them all the time."

"Why are they so blind and deaf and stupid?" asked the junior angel rather crossly.

"It is not for us to judge them. We who live in the Splendour have no idea what it is like to live in the dark. We hear the music and the Voice like the sound of many waters every day of our lives, but to them—well, there is much darkness and much noise and much distraction upon the earth. Only a few who are quiet and humble and wise hear His Voice. But watch, for in a moment you will see something truly wonderful."

The Earth went on turning and circling round the sun, and then quite suddenly, in the upper half of the globe, there appeared a light, tiny but so bright in its intensity that both the angels hid their eyes.

"I think I can guess," said the little angel in a low voice. "That was the Visit, wasn't it?"

"Yes, that was the Visit. The Light Himself went down there and lived among them; but in a moment, and you will be able to tell that even with your eyes closed, the light will go out."

"But why? Could He not bear their darkness and stupidity? Did He have to return here?"

"No, it wasn't that," returned the senior angel. His voice was stern and sad. "They failed to recognize Him for Who He was—or at least only a handful knew Him. For the most part they preferred their darkness to His Light, and in the end they killed Him."

"The fools, the crazy fools! They don't deserve——"

"Neither you nor I, nor any other angel, knows why they were so foolish and so wicked. Nor can we say what they deserve or don't deserve. But the fact remains, they killed our Prince of Glory while He was Man amongst them."

"And that I suppose was the end? I see the whole Earth has gone black and dark. All right, I won't judge them, but surely that is all they could expect?"

"Wait, we are still far from the end of the story of the Visited Planet. Watch now, but be ready to cover your eyes again."

In utter blackness the earth turned round three times,

7

and then there blazed with unbearable radiance a point of light.

"What now?" asked the little angel, shielding his eyes.

"They killed Him all right, but He conquered death. The thing most of them dread and fear all their lives He broke and conquered. He rose again, and a few of them saw Him and from then on became His utterly devoted slaves."

"Thank God for that," said the little angel.

"Amen. Open your eyes now, the dazzling light has gone. The Prince has returned to His Home of Light. But watch the Earth now."

As they looked, in place of the dazzling light there was a bright glow which throbbed and pulsated. And then as the Earth turned many times little points of light spread out. A few flickered and died; but for the most part the lights burned steadily, and as they continued to watch, in many parts of the globe there was a glow over many areas.

"You see what is happening?" asked the senior angel. "The bright glow is the company of loyal men and women He left behind, and with His help they spread the glow and now lights begin to shine all over the Earth."

"Yes, yes," said the little angel impatiently, "but how does it end? Will the little lights join up with each other? Will it all be light, as it is in Heaven?"

His senior shook his head. "We simply do not know," he replied. "It is in the Father's hands. Sometimes it is agony to watch and sometimes it is joy unspeakable. The end is not yet. But now I am sure you can see why this little ball is so important. He has visited it; He is working out His Plan upon it."

"Yes, I see, though I don't understand. I shall never forget that this is the Visited Planet."

GLORIA IN EXCELSIS DEO!

MARLYS SWINGER 1964

& PEACE ON EARTH, GOODWILL TO MEN

WORDS FROM AN OLD SPANISH CAROL

SHALL I TELL YOU WHO WILL COME
   TO BETHLEHEM ON CHRISTMAS MORN,
WHO WILL KNEEL THEM GENTLY DOWN
   BEFORE THE LORD, NEW-BORN?

ONE SMALL FISH FROM THE RIVER,
   WITH SCALES OF RED, RED GOLD,
ONE WILD BEE FROM THE HEATHER,
   ONE GREY LAMB FROM THE FOLD,
ONE OX FROM THE HIGH PASTURE,
   ONE BLACK BULL FROM THE HERD,
ONE GOATLING FROM THE FAR HILLS,
   ONE WHITE, WHITE BIRD.

AND MANY CHILDREN – GOD GIVE THEM GRACE,
BRINGING TALL CANDLES TO LIGHT MARY'S FACE.

SHALL I TELL YOU WHO WILL COME
   TO BETHLEHEM ON CHRISTMAS MORN,
WHO WILL KNEEL THEM GENTLY DOWN
   BEFORE THE LORD, NEW-BORN?

13

THE SHEPHERDS

THE OLDEST LEGEND FROM SPAIN

by RUTH SAWYER

ou who keep Christmas, who keep the holy-tide, have you ever thought why a child needs must be born in the world to save it? Here is a Christmas story about God, meaning Good. It begins far back when the world was first created.

In the beginning God had two favorite archangels: one was called Lucifer, meaning Light, and one called Michael, meaning Strength. They led the heavenly hosts; they stood, one on the right hand and one on the left hand of God's throne. They were His chosen messengers.

Now the Archangel Michael served God with his whole heart and angelic soul. There was no task too great for him to perform, no thousand years of service too long. But the Archangel Lucifer chafed at serving any power higher than his own. As one thousand years swept after another thousand years—each as a day— he became bitter in his service and jealous of God.

The appointed time came for God to create the Universe. He made the sun, the moon, the stars. He made earth and water, and separated them. He made trees and flowers and grass to grow; He made creatures to walk the earth and eat thereof; and He made birds for

the air and fish for the waters. And when all else was created, He made a man and called him Adam, and a woman and called her Eve. It took Him six heavenly days to create this Universe; and at the end He was tired and rested.

While the Creation was coming to pass and God was occupied most enormously, Lucifer went stealthily about Heaven. He spoke with this angel and with that, whispering, whispering. He spoke with the cherubim and seraphim—to all and everyone who would give him an attending ear. And what he whispered was this: "Why should God rule supreme? Why should He be the only one to create and to say what shall be created? We are powerful. We are worthy to rule. What say you?"

15

He whispered throughout the six days of Creation; and when God rested Lucifer led a host of rebellious angels against God; they drew their flaming swords and laid siege to God's throne. But the Archangel Michael drew his flaming sword; he led God's true angels to defend Heaven. The army of Lucifer was put to rout and his captains were taken prisoner and led before God's throne. And God said: "I cannot take life from you, for you are celestial beings. But you shall no longer be known as the hosts of light; you shall be the hosts of darkness. You, Lucifer, shall bear the name of Satan. You and those who have rebelled must seek a kingdom elsewhere. But I command you this—leave this Earth, which I have but freshly made, alone. Molest not my handiwork." So spoke God.

So Lucifer was banished with his minions; and henceforth he was known as Satan. He established a kingdom under the Earth and called it Hell. But because God had commanded him to leave Earth untouched, he straightway coveted Earth for his own. He sent his spirits abroad to tempt and make evil those born upon Earth. So it came to pass that the people of Earth knew at last the power of evil as well as of good; they felt the long reach of darkness even while they lifted their eyes to the Face of Light.

And now the years became millions. Earth became peopled in its four corners; and God looked down upon it and sorrowed. He called Archangel Michael to Him and spoke: "It has come to pass that Satan's power upon Earth is great. No longer can my angels prevail. A kingdom of destruction, of greed, of hate, and of false-witnessing has been set up among my people on the Earth I have created. Their hearts have grown dark with evil; their eyes no longer see the light. I must send to Earth my own Spirit that evil may be conquered. He shall be one conceived of Heaven and born of Earth, none less than my own beloved Son." So spoke God.

Earth had been divided into countries, some great and powerful, some small and weak. And the strong reached out even with their armies and took the weak. Now such a one, taken, was called Judea. Within its rolling hills, its olive groves, its high pastures and twisting rivers, men had built a little city called Bethlehem —King David's city. And to this city the conquering Romans had ordered all of the tribe of Jesse to come and render tribute unto Caesar.

Beyond the city, on the high pastures, many shepherds herded their sheep. And it came to pass that God chose Bethlehem to be the place of birth for His Son; and the time to be the taxing time of the year. He chose to reveal the coming to the shepherds, they being men of simple faith and pure hearts. And God sent forth a star to show them the way, and commanded angels to sing to them of the glad tidings.

The night had grown late. High in the pastures the shepherds had built fires to keep themselves warm, to frighten off stray wolves or robbers. All slept but Esteban, the boy. He alone saw the angel, heard the tidings; and straightway he woke the sleeping ones: "Lo, an angel has but now come among us, singing. Wake—wake, all of you! I think this night must have great meaning for us."

Now at this time Satan stood at the gateway of Hell. Of late he had been troubled in mind, a sense of impending doom moved him. And as he gazed abroad upon the Earth he saw the angel appear. Then did his

18

troubled mind grow fearful. He summoned his hosts of Hell, commanding them to make ready: "Tonight I think again we defy God's power over the Universe. We fight, I think, for Earth, to make it ours. I go to it now. Come when I smite the ground."

Swift as his thought Satan reached the Earth. He came as a wanderer, upon his head a wide sombrero, about his shoulders and falling to the ground a cloak, in his hand a staff. Across the Earth he traveled even as the lightning crosses the sky. He was here—he was beyond. And so he came to the high pastures of Judea and stood at one of the fires about which the shepherds watched. Again the angel came, shouting God's tidings: "Fear not! For unto you is born this day in the City of David a Messiah!"

Satan covered his face and spoke: "What means that message?"

The shepherds cowered. "We know not."

"What is that Saviour—that Messiah yonder apparition shouts of?"

"We know not."

Satan dropped his cloak that they might see the fire that damns and burns shining even in his eyes: "I command you to know!"

It was Benito, the oldest shepherd, who asked: "In the name of God, who are you?"

And Satan answered: "In my own name I am a

wanderer. Once I had taken from me a mighty kingdom. I am here to restore it unto myself."

Could this be the Saviour of whom the angels sang? The shepherds drew close—close. They looked. And to each came terror. Here truly was darkness, not light; here was nameless evil, not good. Here was one who had denied the name of God. Together they shouted: "Begone!" They drew brands from the fire and crossed them, making fiery crosses to burn between themselves and Satan.

While they had been talking among themselves Esteban, the boy, had gone far off seeking stray lambs. Now Satan sought him out. "You heard the angel sing. Where is this City of David?"

"I know not."

"Who is this Messiah?"

"You speak of Matías?" The boy was stupid with fear. "You mean my mother's brother, a shepherd, wise and faithful? But he is ill. I tend his sheep."

"Idiot! Dolt! Fool!" The voice of Satan rose like a whirlwind. "In your great stupidness you sin against me, and that is more terrible than sinning against God. For this you die!"

The boy tried to open his mouth to shriek for mercy. Before words could come, before Satan's hand could smite him, there came between them, out of the vast spaces of the Universe, one who thrust a flaming sword

between the Devil and the boy; while through the vast dome of Heaven rang a voice: "Thou shalt not take the innocent!"

It was the voice of the Archangel Michael. He stood now, all in shining armor, beside Esteban, his sword shielding him. And again he spoke: "How dare you break God's command!"

"I dare do more than that." Satan spoke with mockery. "God's Earth is no longer His but mine. My minions rule it. But tonight I shall fight you for it. I shall take it from you by right of sword and mightier hosts."

He stamped the ground. It split asunder, and from its very bowels came forth rank after rank of devils, waving their double-bladed swords forged in Hell's own fires. Then Michael thrust his sword aloft and behold a mighty stairway, even like Jacob's ladder, was built between Earth and Heaven. Down its shining way came rank on rank of the heavenly hosts. Across the sky rang the shout of "Combat!"

Then such a battle was fought between the armies of darkness and the armies of light as had not been waged since the beginning of all things. And Michael's sword pinioned Satan to the ground so that he could not rise; and Michael's hosts put Satan's to rout, so that the Earth's crust broke with them and they were swallowed in belching flames. And when the Earth was rid of them, Michael spoke to Satan: "You have asked of

22

many this night who is the Saviour—the Messiah. I will answer you, defeated. He is God's Son, and Man's. He is Peace. He is Love. He is one against whom your evil cannot prevail. For next to God He is supreme."

The face of Archangel Michael shone with the light of conquering Heaven, all goodness, all strength. And Satan, crawling to his feet, looked upon it and hated it. "I am conquered now. But wait another thousand years, two thousand!"

Meanwhile the boy Esteban watched. And with the crawling of Satan back to Hell, Michael commanded Esteban to lead the shepherds to Bethlehem that they might look upon the face of their Saviour, and worship Him.

And as the boy joined the shepherds about their fires, there came the angel again, the third time; and with it was a multitude of the heavenly host, praising God and singing hallelujahs! While over all shone a star of a magnitude never seen by them before in all the heavens.

But of the many watching their flocks that night only a few heeded. These wrapped their cloaks about them and followed the boy Esteban. As they walked he pointed out the roadsides, guarded by rank on rank of angels in shining armor. But none saw them save the boy.

Yet a great joy welled up in each heart, so that every shepherd needs must raise his voice in song. Benito, the oldest, gave them words for the beginning:

23

Behold That Star

> Yonder star
>> in the skies
> marks the manger
>> where He lies.

Then Andrés caught the air and gave them the second verse to sing:

> Joy and laughter
>> song and mirth
> herald in
>> our Saviour's birth.

Miguel lifted his voice in a great swelling tumult of thanksgiving:

> Now good will
>> unto all men.
> Shout it, brothers,
>> shout again!

Carlos caught from him the song and threw it back to the others with gladness:

> Peace then be
>> among us all;
> upon great nations
> and on small!

It was Esteban who gave the words for the last, singing them down the end of the road, leading them to the stable opening:

> Let each shepherd
>> raise his voice

till the whole world
shall rejoice;
till in one voice
all shall sing—
Glory to our
Saviour—King!

The star overhead lighted the way into the stable. Within they found a young woman, very fair, and on the straw beside her a small, new-born child. Benito spoke the questions that were on the minds of all: "What is thy name, woman?"

"They call me Mary."

"And his—the child's?"

"He is called Jesus."

Benito knelt. "*Nene Jesús*—Baby Jesus, the angels have sent us to worship thee. We bring what poor gifts are ours. Here is a young cockerel for thee." Benito laid it on the straw beside the child, then rose and called: "Andrés, it is thy turn."

Andrés knelt. "I, Andrés, bring thee a lamb." He put it with the cockerel, rose, and said: "Miguel, give thine."

Miguel knelt. "I bring thee a basket of figs, little one. Carlos, thy turn."

Carlos knelt and held out shepherd-pipes. "I have made them. Thou shalt play on them when thou art grown. Juan, what hast thou?"

25

Juan knelt. "Here is some cheese—good goats' cheese."

In turn they knelt, each shepherd, until all but Esteban, the boy, had given his gift. "Alas, *Nene Jesús*, I have little for thee. But here are the ribbons from my

cap. Thou likest them, yes? And now I make a prayer: 'Bless all shepherds. Give us to teach others the love for all gentle and small things that is in our hearts. Give us

26

to see thy star always on this, the night of thy birth. And keep our eyes lifted eternally to the far hills.' "

And having made the prayer, and all having given their gifts, the shepherds departed into the night, singing.

CAROL OF THE SEEKERS

Phillip Britts   Wolfgang Loewenthal

WE HAVE NOT COME LIKE EAST-ERN KINGS, WITH
GIFTS UP-ON THE POM-MEL, LY-ING,
OUR HANDS ARE EMP-TY AND WE CAME BE-
CAUSE WE HEARD A BA-BY CRY-ING.

WE HAVE NOT COME LIKE EASTERN KINGS,
WITH GIFTS UPON THE POMMEL, LYING,
OUR HANDS ARE EMPTY AND WE CAME
BECAUSE WE HEARD A BABY CRYING.

WE HAVE NOT COME LIKE QUESTING KNIGHTS,
WITH FIERY SWORDS AND BANNERS FLYING,
WE HEARD A CALL AND HURRIED HERE, —
THE CALL WAS LIKE A BABY CRYING.

BUT WE HAVE COME WITH OPEN HEARTS
FROM PLACES WHERE THE TORCH IS DYING.
WE SEEK A MANGER AND A CROSS,
BECAUSE WE HEARD A BABY CRYING.

28

THE WELL OF THE STAR

by ELIZABETH GOUDGE

On the road to Bethlehem there is a well called the Well of the Star. The legend goes that the three Wise Men, on their journey to the Manger, lost sight of the star that was guiding them. Pausing to water their camels at the well they found it again reflected in the water.

I

avid sat cross-legged by himself in a corner of the room, separated from the other children, clasping his curly toes in his lean brown hands, and wished he were a rich man, grown up and strong, with bags full of gold and thousands of camels and tens of thousands of sheep. But he was not rich; he was only a diminutive ragged shepherd boy who possessed nothing in the world except the shepherd's pipe slung around

29

his neck, his little pipe upon which he played to himself or the sheep all day long, and that was as dear to him as life itself.

At the moment he was very miserable. Sighing, he lifted his hands and placed them on his stomach, pushing it inward and noting the deflation with considerable concern. How soon would he be dead of hunger? How soon would they all be dead of hunger, and safely at rest in Abraham's bosom? It was a very nice place, he had no doubt, and suitable to grandparents and people of that type, who were tired by a long life and quite ready to be gathered to their fathers, but hardly the place for a little boy who had lived only for a few short years in this world, who had seen only a few springs painting the bare hills purple and scarlet with the anemone flowers, only a few high summer suns wheeling majestically through the burning heavens.

If only it were summer now, instead of a cold night in midwinter! If only mother would light a fire for them to warm themselves by, a bright fire that would paint the walls of the dark little one-roomed house orange and rose color, and chase away the frightening shadows. But there was no light in the room except the flickering, dying flame that came from a little lamp, fast burning up the last of their oil, set on the earth floor close to his mother, where she sat crouched beside her sick husband, swaying herself ceaselessly from side to side, abandoned to her grief and oblivious of the wails of four little cold and hungry children, younger than David, who lay altogether on their matting bed.

If only he were a rich man, thought David, then it would not matter that storms had destroyed the barley, that their vines had failed, or that their father, the carpenter of this tiny village on a hilltop, could no longer ply his trade. Nothing would matter if he were a rich man and could buy food and wine and oil and healing salves; they would be happy then, with food in their stomachs, their father well, and comforting light in this horrible darkness of midwinter.

How could he be a rich man?

Suddenly there came to David's mind the thought of the wishing well far down below on the road to Bethlehem. It was a well of clear sparkling water and it was said that those who stood by it at midnight, and prayed to the Lord God Jehovah from a pure heart, were given their heart's desire. The difficulty, of course, was to *be* pure in heart. They said that if you were, and your prayer had been accepted, you saw your heart's desire mirrored in the water of the well—the face of someone you loved, maybe, or the gold that would save your home from ruin, or even, so it was whispered, the face of God Himself. But no one of David's acquaintance had ever seen anything, though they had wished and prayed time and again.

Nevertheless he jumped up and crept noiselessly through the shadows to the door. He had no idea whether his heart was pure or not but he would give it the benefit of the doubt and go down to the well. He pulled open the door and slipped out into the great cold silent night.

And instantly he was terribly afraid. All around him the bare hills lay beneath the starlight in an awful waiting, attentive loneliness, and far down below, the terraces of olive trees were drowned in pitch-black shadow. But the sky was streaming with light, so jeweled with myriads of blazing stars that it seemed the weight of them would make the sky fall down and crush the waiting earth to atoms. The loneliness, the darkness, the cold, and that great sky above turned David's heart to water and made his knees shake under him. He had never been out by himself so late at night before and he had not got the courage, hungry and cold as he was, to go down over the lonely hills and through the darkness of the olive trees to the white road below where they said that robbers lurked, wild sheep-stealers and murderers who would cut your throat as soon as look at you, just for the fun of it.

Then he bethought him that just over the brow of a nearby hill a flock of sheep were folded, and their shepherds with them. His own cousin Eli, who was teaching David to be a shepherd, would be with them, and Eli would surely be willing to leave the sheep to the other shepherds for a short time and go with David to the well. At least David would ask him to.

He set off running, a little flitting shadow beneath the stars, and he ran hard because he was afraid. For surely, he thought, there was something very strange about this night. The earth lay so still, waiting for something, and overhead that great sky was palpitating and ablaze with triumph. Several times, as he ran, he could have sworn he heard triumphant voices crying, "Glory to God! Glory to God!" as though the hills themselves were singing, and a rushing sound as though great wings were beating over his head. Yet when he stopped to listen there was nothing; only the frail echo of a shepherd's pipe and a whisper of wind over the hills.

He was glad when he saw in front of him the rocky hillock behind which the sheep were folded. "Eli," he cried, giving a hop, skip, and a jump, "are you there? Jacob? Tobias? It's David."

But there was no answering call from the friendly shepherds, though there was a soft bleating from the sheep, only that strange stillness with its undercurrent of triumphant music that was heard and yet not heard. With a beating heart he bounded round the corner and came out in the little hollow in the hills that was the sheepfold, his eyes straining through the darkness to make out the figures of his friends.

But they were not there; no one was there except a tall, cloaked stranger who sat upon a rock among the sheep leaning on a shepherd's crook. And the sheep, who knew their own shepherds and would fly in fear from a stranger whose voice they did not know, were gathered closely about him in confidence and love. David halted in blank astonishment.

"Good evening to you," said the stranger pleasantly. "It's a fine night."

David advanced with caution, rubbing his nose in perplexity. Who was this stranger? The sheep seemed to know him, and he seemed to know David, yet David knew no man with so straight a back and so grand a head or such a deep, ringing, beautiful voice. This was a very great man, without doubt; a soldier, perhaps, but no shepherd.

"Good evening," said David politely, edging a little closer. " 'Tis a fine evening, but cold about the legs."

"Is it? Then come under my cloak," said the stranger, lifting it so that it suddenly seemed to spread about him like great wings, and David, all his fear suddenly

evaporated, scuttled forward and found himself gathered in against the stranger's side, under the stranger's cloak, warm and protected and sublimely happy.

"But where are the others?" he asked. "Eli and Jacob and Tobias?"

"They've gone to Bethlehem," said the stranger. "They've gone to a birthday party."

"A birthday party, and didn't take me?" ejaculated David in powerful indignation. "The nasty, selfish brutes!"

"They were in rather a hurry," explained the stranger. "It was all rather unexpected."

"Then I suppose they had no presents to take?" asked David. "They'll feel awkward, turning up with no presents. Serve them right for not taking me."

"They took what they could," said the stranger. "A shepherd's crook, a cloak, and a loaf of bread."

David snorted with contempt, and then snorted again in indignation. "They shouldn't have gone," he said, and indeed it was a terrible crime for shepherds to leave their sheep, with those robbers prowling about in the shadows below and only too ready to pounce upon them.

"They were quite right to go," said the stranger. "And I have taken their place."

"But you're only one man," objected David, "and it takes several to tackle robbers."

"I think I'm equal to any number of robbers," smiled

36

the stranger. He was making a statement, not boasting, and David thrilled to the quiet confidence of his voice, and thrilled, too, to feel the strength of the arm that was round him and of the knee against which he leaned.

"Have you done a lot of fighting, great lord?" he whispered in awe.

"Quite a lot," said the stranger.

"Who did you fight?" breathed David. "Barbarians?"

"The devil and his angels," said the stranger nonchalantly.

David was momentarily deprived of the power of speech, but pressing closer he gazed upward at the face of this man for whom neither robbers nor devils seemed to hold any terrors, and once he began to look he could not take his eyes away, for never before had he seen a face like this man's, a face at once delicate and strong, full of power yet quick with tenderness, bright as the sky in early morning yet shadowed with mystery. It seemed an eternity before David could find his voice.

"Who are you, great lord?" he whispered at last. "You're no shepherd."

"I'm a soldier," said the stranger. "And my name is Michael. What's your name?"

"David," murmured the little boy, and suddenly he shut his eyes because he was dazzled by the face above him. If this was a soldier, he was a very king among soldiers.

37

"Tell me where you are going, David," said the stranger.

Now that they had told each other their names David felt that they were lifelong friends, and it was not hard to tell his story. He told it all—his father's illness, his mother's tears, the children's hunger, and the cold home where there was no fire and the oil was nearly finished, his longing to be a rich man that he might help them all, and the wishing well that gave their heart's desire to the pure in heart.

"But I hadn't meant to go down to the road alone, you see," he finished. "I thought Eli would have gone with me, and now Eli has gone to that birthday party."

"Then you'll have to go alone," said Michael.

"I suppose the sheep wouldn't be all right by themselves?" hinted David gently.

"They certainly would not," said Michael firmly.

"I'm not afraid, of course," boasted David, and shrank a little closer against that strong knee.

"Of course not," concurred Michael heartily. "I've noticed that Davids are always plucky. Look at King David fighting the lion and the bear when he was only a shepherd boy like you."

"But the Lord God Jehovah guided and protected him," said David.

"And the Lord God will protect you," said Michael.

38

"I don't *feel* as though He was protecting me," objected David.

"You haven't started out yet," said Michael, and laughed. "How can He protect you when there's nothing to protect you from? Or guide you when you don't take to the road? Go on now. Hurry up." And with a gentle but inexorable movement he withdrew his knee from beneath David's clinging hands, and lifted his cloak from David's shoulders so that it slid back with a soft rustling upward movement, as though great wings were folded against the sky. And the winter wind blew cold and chill about the little boy who stood ragged and barefoot in the night.

"Good-by," said Michael's deep voice; but it seemed to be drifting away as though Michael too were withdrawing himself. "Play your pipe to yourself if you are afraid, for music is the voice of man's trust in God's protection, even as the gift of courage is God's voice answering."

David took a few steps forward and again terror gripped him. Again he saw the bare lonely hills, and the shadows down below where the robbers lurked. He glanced back over his shoulder, ready to bolt back to the shelter of Michael's strong arm and the warmth of his cloak. But he could no longer see Michael very clearly, he could only see a dark shape that might have been

39

a man but that might have been only a shadow. But yet the moment he glanced back he knew that Michael was watching him, Michael the soldier who was afraid neither of robbers nor of the devil and his angels, and with a heart suddenly turned valiant he turned and scuttled off down the hill toward the valley.

II

Nevertheless he had the most uncomfortable journey. Going down the hill he cut his feet on the sharp stones, and fell down twice and barked his knees, and going through the olive grove below he saw robbers hiding behind every tree. There were times when he was so frightened that his knees doubled up beneath him and he came out in a clammy perspiration, but there were other times when he remembered Michael's advice and stopped a minute to play a few sweet notes on his precious pipe, and then he was suddenly brave again and rushed through the terrifying shadows whooping as though he were that other David going for the lion and the bear. . . . But all the same it was a most uncomfortable journey and he was overwhelmingly thankful when with a final jump he landed in the road and saw the water of .the well gleaming only a few feet away from him.

He leaned against the stone parapet and looked at it gravely. Water. In this land that in the summer months was parched with drought and scorched with heat, water was the most precious thing in the world, the source of all growth and all purification, the cure of sickness, the preserver of life itself. It was no wonder that men came to water to pray for their heart's desire, to water the comforter and lord of all life. "Comfort ye, comfort ye, My people." It seemed to him that he heard voices singing in the wind among the olive trees, as though the trees themselves were singing, voices that sang not to the ear but to the soul. "He shall feed His flock like a shepherd: He shall gather the lambs with His arm, and carry them in His bosom. Wonderful! Counselor! The mighty God! The everlasting Father! The Prince of Peace!" Surely, he thought, if the Lord God Jehovah cared so for the little lambs He would care also for David's sick father and weeping mother and the little hungry children, and covering his face with his brown fingers he prayed to the Lord God that he might have gold to buy food and wine and oil for that stricken house up above him on the hill. And so hard did he pray that he forgot everything but his own longing, forgot his fears and the cold wind that nipped him through his rags, saw nothing but the darkness of his closed eyes and heard nothing but his own desperate whispering.

Then, sighing a little like a child awaking from sleep, he opened his eyes and peeped anxiously through his fingers at the water in the well. Would he have his heart's desire? Had he prayed from a pure heart? Was that something glittering in the well? He dropped his hands from his face and leaned closer, the blood pounding so in his ears that it sounded like drums beating. Yes, it was gold! Circles of gold lying upon the surface of the water, as though the stars had dropped down from heaven. With a cry of joy he leaned nearer, his face right over the water, as though he would have touched with his lips those visionary gold pieces that promised him his heart's desire. And then, in an instant of time, his cry of joy changed to a cry of terror, for framed in those twinkling golden points of light he saw the reflection of a man's face, a bearded, swarthy face with gleaming teeth and eyes, the face of a foreigner.

So the Lord God had not protected him. So the robbers had got him. He stared at the water for a long minute, stark with terror, and then swung round with a choking cry, both his thin hands at his throat to protect it from the robber's knife.

"Do not cry out, little son. I will not hurt you." The man stretched out a hand and gave David's shoulder a reassuring little shake. "I but looked over your shoulder to see what you stared at so intently."

The voice, deep toned, kindly, strangely attractive with its foreign inflexion, chased away all David's fears.

This was no robber. His breath came more evenly and he wiped the sweat of his terror off his forehead with his tattered sleeve while he looked up with bulging eyes at the splendid stranger standing in front of him.

He was tall, though not so tall as that other splendid stranger keeping the sheep up on the hill, and he wore a purple robe girdled at the waist with gold and a green turban to which were stitched gold ornaments that shook and trembled round his proud hawk-nosed face. David had one pang of agonized disappointment as he realized that it was only the reflection of these gold ornaments he had seen in the water, and not God's answer to his prayer, and then amazement swept all other thoughts from his mind.

For the star-lit road to the well that a short while ago had been empty was now full. While David prayed, his ears closed to all sounds, a glittering cavalcade had come up out of the night. There were black men carrying torches, richly caparisoned camels, and two more splendid grave-faced men even more richly dressed than his friend. The torchlight gleamed on gold and scarlet, emerald green and rich night blue, and the scent of spices came fragrant on the wind. This cavalcade might have belonged to Solomon, thought David, to Solomon in all his glory. Surely these men were kings.

But the camels were thirsty and the first king drew

43

David gently away from the well that they might drink. Yet he kept his hand upon his shoulder and looked down upon him with kindly liking.

"And for what were you looking so intently, little son?" he asked.

"For my heart's desire, great lord," whispered David, nervously pleating his ragged little tunic with fingers that still shook from the fright he had had.

"So?" asked the stranger. "Is it a wishing well?"

"They say," said David, "that if you pray to God for your heart's desire from a pure heart, and if God has granted your prayer, you will see a vision of it in the water."

"And you saw yours?"

David shook his head. "You came, great lord," he explained. "I saw you."

One of the other kings, an old white-bearded man in a sea-green robe, was listening smiling to their talk.

"We three have lost a star, little son," he said to David. "Should we find it again in your well?"

David thought it must be a joke, for what could three great lords want with a star? But when he looked up into the fine old eyes gazing down into his he saw trouble and bewilderment in them.

'If your heart is pure, great lord."

A shadow passed over the old man's face and he turned back to the third king, a young man with a boy's smooth skin and eyes that were bright and gay.

"Gaspar," he said. "You are young and pure of heart; you look."

Gaspar laughed, his white teeth flashing in his brown face. "Only an old wives' tale," he mocked. "We've lost the star twenty times in the blaze of the night sky and twenty times we have found it again. Why should we look for it now in a well?"

"Yet pray," said the old man sternly. "Pray and look."

Obediently Gaspar stepped up to the well, his scarlet robe swirling about him and the curved sword that he wore slapping against his side, bowed his head in prayer, then bent over the well.

"I can see only a part of the sky," he murmured, "and each star is like another in glory—no—yes." He paused and suddenly gave a shout of triumph. "I have found it, Melchior! It shines in the center of the well, like the hub of a wheel or the boss of a shield."

He straightened himself and flung back his head, his arms stretched up toward the sky. "There! There!" he cried, and David and the elder kings, gazing, saw a great star blazing over their heads, a star that was mightier and more glorious than the sister stars that shone around it like cavaliers round the throne. And as they gazed it suddenly moved, streaking through the sky like a comet.

46

"Look! Look!" cried David. "A shooting star!" And he danced out into the middle of the road to follow its flight. "Look! It is shining over Bethlehem!"

The three kings stood behind him, gazing where he pointed, and saw at the end of the road, faintly visible in the starlight, slender cypress trees rising above the huddled roofs of a little white town upon a hill, and above them the blazing star.

Gaspar, young and excited, suddenly swung round and began shouting to the servants to bring up the camels, but the two older kings still stood and gazed.

"Praise be to the Lord God," said the old king tremulously, and he bowed his head and crossed his hands upon his breast.

"Bethlehem," said the king who was David's friend. "The end of our journey."

His voice was infinitely weary, and for the first time it occurred to David that these great lords had come from a long way off. Their beautiful clothes were travel-stained and their faces drawn with fatigue. They must, he decided suddenly, be lunatics; no sane men, he thought, would come from so far away to visit an unimportant little place like Bethlehem; nor be in such a taking because they had lost sight of a star. Nevertheless he liked them and had no wish to lose their company.

"*I'll* take you to Bethlehem," he announced, and flung back his head and straddled his legs as though it

47

would be a matter of great difficulty and danger to guide them the short way along the straight road to a town that was visible to the naked eye.

"And so you shall," laughed his friend. "And you shall ride my camel in front of me and be the leader of the caravan."

David jigged excitedly from one foot to the other. He had never ridden a camel, for only well-to-do men had camels. He could not contain himself and let out a shrill squeak of joy as a richly caparisoned beast was led up and made to kneel before them—a squeak that ended rather abruptly when the camel turned its head and gave him a slow disdainful look, lifting its upper lip and showing its teeth in a contempt so profound that David blushed hotly to the roots of his hair, and did not recover himself until he was seated on the golden saddle cloth before his friend, safe in the grip of his arm, rocking up toward the stars as the camel got upon its feet.

III

It was one of the most wonderful moments of that wonderful night when David found himself swaying along toward the cypresses of Bethlehem, the leader of a caravan. Because he was so happy he put his pipe to his lips and began to play the gay little tune that shepherds have played among the hills since the dawn of the world, and so infectious was it that the men coming behind began to hum it as they swung along under the stars.

"It is right to sing upon a journey, great lord," said David, when a pause fell, "for music is the voice of man's trust in God's protection, even as the gift of courage is God's voice answering."

"That is a wise child you have got there, Balthasar," said old Melchior, who was riding just behind them.

"I didn't make that up for myself," David answered truthfully. "A man up in the hills told it to me. A man who came to mind the sheep so that Eli and the other shepherds could go with their presents to a birthday party in Bethlehem."

"Does all the world carry gifts to Bethlehem tonight?" questioned Balthasar softly. "Wise men from the desert with their mysteries, shepherds from the hills with their simplicities, and a little boy with the gift of music."

"Do you mean that we are all going to the same place?" asked David eagerly. "Are *you* going to the birthday party too? And am I going with you? Me too?"

"A King has been born," said Balthasar. "We go to worship Him."

A king? The world seemed full of kings tonight, and kings doing the most unsuitable things, too, keeping sheep on the hills and journeying along the highway travel-stained and weary. On this wonderful topsy-turvy night nothing surprised him, not even the news that the birthday party was a King's; but desolation seized him as he realized that he wouldn't be able to go to it himself. For how could he go inside a grand palace when his clothes were torn and his feet were bare and dirty? They wouldn't let him in. They'd set the dogs on him. . . . Disappointment surged over him in sickening waves. He gritted his teeth to keep himself from crying, but even with all his effort two fat tears escaped and plowed two clean but scalding furrows through the grime on his face.

They were at Bethlehem before he realized it, for he had been keeping his head bent for fear Balthasar should see his two tears. Looking up suddenly he saw the white walls of the little town close in front of him, the cypress trees like swords against the sky and that star shining just ahead of them, so bright that it seemed like a great lamp let down out of heaven by a string. The gate of the town was standing wide open and they clattered through it without hindrance, which surprised David until he remembered that just at this time Bethlehem would be full of people who had come in from the country to be taxed. They would not be afraid of robbers tonight, when the walls held so many good strong countrymen with knives in their girdles and a quick way with their fists. The visitors were still up and about, too, for as they climbed the main street of the little hill

town David could see lines of light shining under doors and hear laughter and voices behind them. And a good thing, too, he thought, for at any other time the arrival of this strange cavalcade in the dead of night might have caused a disturbance. The Lord God, he thought, had arranged things very conveniently for them.

"Which way are we going?" he whispered excitedly to his king.

"We follow the star," said Balthasar.

David looked up and saw that the star must have been up to its shooting tricks again, for it had now moved over to their right, and obediently they too swerved to their right and made their way up a narrow lane where houses had been built over caves in the limestone rock. Each house was the home of poor people, who kept their animals in the cave below and lived themselves in the one room above reached by its flight of stone steps.

"The king can't be *here*!" said David disgustedly, as the cavalcade, moving now in single file, picked its way over the heaps of refuse in the lane. "Only poor people live *here*."

"Look!" said Balthasar, and looking David saw that the star was hanging so low over a little house at the end of the lane that a bright beam of light caressed its roof.

52

"The star is making a mistake," said David firmly, "if it thinks a king could be born in a place like that."

But no one was taking any notice of him. A great awe seemed to have descended upon the three kings, and a thankfulness too deep for speech. In silence the cavalcade halted outside the house at the end of the lane, and in silence the servants gathered round to bring the camels to their knees and help their masters to the ground. David, picked up and set upon his feet by a sturdy Nubian whose black face gleamed in the torchlight like ebony, stood aside and watched, something of the awe that gripped the others communicating itself to him, so that the scene he saw stamped itself upon his memory forever. The torchlight and starlight lighting up the rich colors of the kings' garments and illumining their dark, intent faces as though they were lit by an inner light; the stir among the servants as three of them came forward carrying three golden caskets, fragrant with spices and so richly jeweled that the light seemed to fall upon them in points of fire, and gave them reverently into their masters' hands. The birthday presents, thought David, the riches that Balthasar had spoken of, and he looked hastily up at the poor little house built above the stable, incredulous that such wealth could enter a door so humble.

But the door at the top of the stone steps was shut fast and no line of light showed beneath it or shone out

53

in welcome from the window. The only light there was showed through the ill-fitting door that closed in the opening to the cave below, and it was toward this that Melchior turned, knocking softly on the rotten wood and standing with bent head to listen for the answer.

"But that's the *stable!*" whispered David. "He couldn't be there!"

But no one answered him for the door opened and the three kings, their heads lowered and their long dark fingers curved about their gifts, passed into the light beyond, the door closing softly behind them, shutting David outside in the night with the strange black servants and the supercilious camels.

But his curiosity was too strong for him to feel afraid. There was a hole quite low in the door and kneeling down he pressed his dirty little face against the wood and squinted eagerly through it.

Of course there was no king there; he had said there wouldn't be and there wasn't; looking beyond the kings he saw there was nothing there but the stable and the animals and a few people, poor people like himself. The animals, a little donkey with his ribs sticking through his skin and an old ox whose shoulders bore the marks of the yoke they had carried through many hard years, were fastened to iron rings in the wall of the cave, but both of them had turned their sleepy heads toward the rough stone manger filled with hay, and toward a gray-

bearded man who held a lighted lantern over the manger and a woman with a tired white face, muffled in a blue cloak, who lay on the floor leaning back against the wall. But though she was so tired she was smiling at the men who were kneeling together on the hard floor, and she had the loveliest and most welcoming smile that David had ever seen.

And then he saw that the men she was smiling at were Eli, Jacob, and Tobias, kneeling with heads bent and hands clasped in the attitude of worship. And before them on the hard floor, just in front of the manger, they had laid their gifts; Eli's shepherd's crook that had been his father's, Jacob's cloak lined with the lamb's wool that he set such store by, and Tobias's little loaf of bread that he always ate all by himself in the middle of the night when he was guarding sheep, never giving a crumb to any one else no matter how hard they begged. And beside these humble men knelt the kings in their glory, and beside the simple gifts were the three rich fragrant caskets, just as though there were no barrier between rich people and poor people, and no difference in value between wood and bread and gold and jewels.

But what could be in that manger that they were all so intent upon it? David had another peep through his hole and saw to his astonishment that there was a Baby in it, a tiny new-born Baby wrapped in swaddling clothes. Normally David took no interest at all in babies but at the sight of this one he was smitten with such awe that he shut his eyes and ducked his head, just as though he had been blinded by the sight of a king with eyes like flame sitting upon a rainbow-encircled throne.

So this was the King, this tiny Baby lying in a rough stone manger in a stable. It struck David that of all the extraordinary places where he had encountered kings this night this was the most extraordinary of all. And then he gave a joyous exclamation. On the journey here he had cried because he had thought a barefoot dirty little boy would not be able to go to a king's birthday party, but surely even he could go to a birthday party in a stable. He leaped to his feet, dusted his knees, pulled down his rags, laid his hands on the latch of the door, and crept noiselessly in.

And then, standing by himself in the shadow by the door, he bethought him that he had no present to give. He had no possessions in the world at all, except his beloved shepherd's pipe, and it was out of the question that he should give that for he loved it as his own life. Noiseless as a mouse he turned to go out again but suddenly the mother in the blue cloak, who must have known all the time that he was there, raised her face and smiled at him, a radiant smile full of promise, and at the same time the man with the gray beard lowered the lantern a little so that it seemed as though the whole manger were enveloped with light, with that Baby at the heart of the light like the sun itself.

And suddenly David could not stay by himself in the shadows, any more than he could stay in a dark stuffy house when the sun was shining. No sacrifice was too great, not even the sacrifice of the little shepherd's pipe that was dear as life itself, if he could be in that light. He ran forward, pushing rudely between Balthasar and Tobias, and laid his shepherd's pipe joyously down before the manger, between Balthasar's jeweled casket and Tobias' humble loaf of bread. He was too little to realize as he knelt down and covered his face with his hands, that the birthday gifts lying there in a row were symbolic of all that a man could need for his life on earth—a cloak for shelter, a loaf of bread for food, a shepherd's crook for work, and a musical instrument to bring courage in the doing of it, and those other gifts of gold and jewels and spices that symbolized rich qualities of kingliness and priestliness and wisdom that were beyond human understanding. "Wise men from the desert with their mysteries," Balthasar had said. "Shepherds from the hills with their simplicities, and a little boy with the gift of music." But David, peeping through his fingers at the Baby in the manger, did not think at all, he only felt, and what his spirit experienced was exactly what his body felt when he danced about on the hills in the first hot sunshine of the year; warmth was poured into him, health and strength and life itself. He took his hands away from his face and gazed and gazed at the Baby, his whole being poured out in adoration.

IV

And then it was all over and he found himself outside Bethlehem, trailing along in the dust behind Eli, Jacob, and Tobias, footsore and weary and as cross as two sticks.

"Where's my camel?" he asked petulantly. "When I went to Bethlehem I was the leader of a caravan, and I had three great lords with me, and servants and torches."

"Well, you haven't got them now," said Eli. "The great lords are still at Bethlehem. When Jacob and Tobias and I saw you there in the stable we made haste to take you home to your mother, young truant that you are."

"I don't want mother," grumbled David. "I want my camel."

Eli glanced back over his shoulder at the disagreeable little urchin dawdling at his heels. Was this the same child who had knelt in the stable rapt in adoration? How quick can be the fall from ecstasy! "You keep your mouth shut, little son," he adjured him, "and quicken your heels; for I must get back to those sheep."

"Baa!" said David nastily, and purposely lagged behind.

So determinedly did he lag that by the time he had reached the well he found himself alone again. The well! The sight of it brought home to him his desperate plight. From his night's adventure he had gained nothing. Up there on the hill was the little house that held his sick father, his weeping mother, and his hungry little brothers and sisters, and he must go home to them no richer than he went. Poorer, in fact, for now he had lost his shepherd's pipe, thrown away his greatest treasure in what seemed to him now a moment of madness. Now he had nothing, nothing in all the world.

He flung himself down in the grass beside the well and he cried as though his heart were breaking. The utter deadness of the hour before dawn weighed on him like a pall and the cold of it numbed him from head to foot. He felt himself sinking lower and lower, dropping down to the bottom of some black sea of misery, and it was not until he reached the bottom that comfort came to him.

His sobs ceased and he was conscious again of the feel of the earth beneath the grass where he lay, hard and cold yet bearing him up with a strength that was reassuring. He thought of the terraces of olive trees above him and of the great bare hills beyond, and then

60

he thought of the voices he had heard singing in the wind up in the hills, and singing down below among the trees, and then suddenly he thought he heard voices in the grass, tiny voices that were like the voices of all growing things, corn and flowers and grasses. "They that sow in tears, shall reap in joy," they whispered. "He that goeth forth and weepeth, bearing precious seed, shall doubtless come again rejoicing, bringing his sheaves with him."

He got up, his courage restored, and stumbled over to the well, faintly silvered now with the first hint of dawn. He did not pray to be a rich man, he did not look in it for his heart's desire, he simply went to it to wash himself, for he did not intend to appear before his mother with dirty tear stains all over his face. If he could not arrive back home with bags full of gold and thousands of camels and tens of thousands of sheep he would at least arrive with a clean and cheerful face to comfort them.

Like all small boys David was a noisy washer and it must have been the sound of his splashings that prevented him hearing the feet of a trotting camel upon the road; nor could the surface of the well, much agitated by his ablutions, show him at first the reflection of the man standing behind him. It had to smooth itself out before he could see the swarthy face framed in the twinkling golden ornaments. When he did see it he blinked incredulously for a moment and then swung round with a cry of joy.

"So you thought I had forgotten you, did you, little son?" smiled Balthasar. "I would not forget so excellent a leader of a caravan. When you left the stable I followed after you as quickly as I could. See what I have for you."

He gave a bag to David and the little boy, opening it, saw by the first light of the dawn the shine of golden pieces. Lots of golden pieces, enough to buy medicines and healing salves for his father and food and warmth for all of them for a long time to come. He had no words to tell of his gratitude but the face that he tilted up to Balthasar, with eyes and mouth as round in wonder as the coins themselves, was in itself a paean of praise.

Balthasar laughed and patted his shoulder. "When I saw you give your shepherd's pipe to the little King," he said, "I vowed that you should not go home empty-handed. I think it was the little King Himself who put the thought into my head. Now I must go back to my country, and you to your home, but we will not forget each other. Fare you well, little son."

As he went up through the shadows of the olive trees David was no longer frightened of robbers, for he was far too happy. The trees were singing again, he thought, as the dawn wind rustled them. "Comfort ye, comfort ye, My people," they sang. And when he got out beyond the trees, and saw the great bare stretches of the hills flushed rose and lilac in the dawn, it seemed as though the hills themselves were shouting, "Glory to God!"

the christ-child lay on mary's lap

G.K.CHESTERTON

TRADITIONAL

the christ-child lay on mary's lap, his hair was like a light.

(O weary, weary were the world, but here is all a-right.)

the christ-child lay on mary's breast, his hair was like a star.

(O stern and cunning are the kings, but here the true hearts are.)

the christ-child lay on mary's lap,
his hair was like a light.
(O weary, weary were the world,
but here is all, aright.)

The christ-child lay on mary's breast,
his hair was like a star.
(O stern and cunning are the kings,
but here the true hearts are.)

The christ-child lay on mary's heart,
his hair was like a fire.
(O weary, weary is the world,
but here the world's desire.)

The christ-child stood at mary's knee,
his hair was like a crown
And all the flowers looked up at him
And all the stars looked down.

64

THE THREE GIFTS

by JANE T. CLEMENT

oseph woke sharply. He lay in the dark, staring, wide-eyed, out of the cave entrance to where in the night sky a shimmering seemed to fade and vanish among the stars; the thudding of his heart slowly quieted and the roaring in his ears died away. He listened. He could hear the slow breath of Mary and the little murmurs of the Child, on the pallet in the sheltered corner beyond the workbench. Then fear and the memory of this second visitation forced him to his knees on his own heap of straw, and to his feet, and he slipped quietly out into the yard. There by the door was the bench where Mary would sit with her Babe on her knees in the soft winter sun, and there he sank, and buried his face in his hands.

The Three Gifts

So now, here it was again, the hand of God, laid on
him, Joseph, poor carpenter, who, past his first youth,
had chosen a simple maid for wife, because the purity
and kindness of her face, the clearness of her eyes, had
spoken to his heart—and then had come task so great
he still had named it to no one. Not even to Mary had
he told the visitation of the Angel—nor the words so
awesome they filled his soul with terrible trembling. He
had only said to her, "When your son is born, His name
will be Jesus." And she had looked at him with gratitude but made no answer. So he had served her, protected her, yearned over her, feared for her. And now
the Child was here, so lovely and quiet, so filled with
life he feared to touch Him with his rough finger or
take Him on his arm.

Then had come the wonder of the bright star; the
golden voices in the dazzling night he would have
thought had been a dream if the shepherds had not
come seeking, and bringing little gifts, and smiling at
the Baby with tears on their dusty cheeks, full of holy
joy at the Child so new, so unspotted and fresh from
God.

And near the khan in this peaceful cave he had decided they would stay, where he had made things more
comfortable, and had begun to make a foothold as carpenter in this, David's city. He had hired out by the
day, brought home work to do, while Mary regained

strength and the Child grew, and the day of Purification drew near. So they had gone up to Jerusalem.

Then there had come another wonder, for among all the multitude in the Temple court there had been one, an old rabbi trembling and frail, who had started up with joy when they drew near, and with a light about his face had stretched out his arms for the Child, uttering praise and blessings, while the Child smiled into his eyes. And the old man had spoken words he, Joseph, could not comprehend: "a light to the Gentiles", "the salvation of God", "this Child is set for the rising and falling of many in Israel." And Mary, white-faced, stood listening with her hands on her heart, until the old man gave her back the Child and blessed them. And at that instant came the aged woman, who also sprang forward with a cry, as if she knew all, and the longing of her heart was now answered. And she, too, blessed them in a loud voice, and uttered praise, and declared to all that redemption had come. Then they had gone wordlessly home.

And then this third wonder, just this past night, the coming of the Three. Never, never would he forget the sight—how at the stir in the yard he had gone to the cave door, and there had seen, in the glimmering starlight, three great white shapes folding themselves down on their haunches, three camels, three attendants at their heads, and three robed figures stepping down and standing, hesitant, before the door. And then the tallest had come forward and had spoken. "We have come to worship Him, who was born King over Israel. We have followed His star and surely He lies within." Then Joseph had moved aside and the three had entered. Mary rested by the low stone manger where the Child lay. Above her a tiny oil lamp stood in a niche in the wall, throwing a flickering light upon their faces, but there was a golden shimmer in the room, and a sweet fragrance. Their donkey tipped his big ears forward as the three came in, and the light caught their jewels. The rustle of their garments as they knelt was like the rustle of a great wind; their dark eyes were filled with wonder and with joy, though weariness lay upon their faces.

And then the first had laid a small bronze coffer on the earthen floor before the manger. "Myrrh, in praise to the one God of Gods." And then the second had set beside it a small faience vial, sea-blue and scarlet, with a golden stopper. "Frankincense, in praise of God most high." And the third, the tallest, stooped and laid beside the other gifts the last one, a bag of golden mesh, through which gleamed golden coins. "Gold, in praise of the Lord of Hosts." Then Mary, tears on her face, bent over the manger and lifted the Child; she set Him on her lap, where all could see, and He slept untroubled while the three gazed and gazed, even as had the simple

69

shepherds. Then at last they had roused and raised themselves and bowed, and with a last look had turned and left. And out in the courtyard they had mounted, and the three great shapes heaved themselves up, and with stately tread went away into the night.

And Joseph had gone inside. Mary was busy with the Child, but he had stared for a long time at the glittering gifts before he dared to touch them. Then he had placed them one by one in the leather sack where he kept his tools, wrapping them first carefully in strips of old leather. And then he had pinched out the lamp, and he had at length drifted into fitful sleep.

And then the dream—clearer than waking, clearer than the brightest day. The voice, not of this earth, speaking to him, to Joseph, and to none other. "Rise, take the Child and His mother, and flee to Egypt, and there remain until I tell you; for Herod is about to search for the Child, to destroy Him."

At last Joseph in the dark before the cave leapt to his feet. What God had declared to him, that he must do. What the end would be—that was hidden, not for his eyes. He could only do this next thing, weak as he was. And they must go now, before the dawn, before the khan awoke and the courtyard was astir. Even now he feared a faint lightening in the east. He went inside swiftly, and in the starlight stooped over Mary. At his touch upon her shoulder she instantly awoke. With few words he told her what they must do, and unquestioning she rose to gather together the things they might need, and to prepare the Babe. Joseph fed the donkey and led him out before the door; over his back he strapped the pallet and hung the saddlebag. He helped Mary to mount and laid the Child in her arms. Last, at his own side he hung his leather sack. She looked at it and asked, "Is it not too heavy?" "The gifts. And I need my tools." A faint smile came over her face. "Our trust must be in God, not in gold. We are in His Hand," she said.

Then they moved off before the coming dawn.

II

Joseph had chosen the ancient road to Hebron of his forefathers, then into the more level desert of Beersheba. The swifter and more traveled highway near the coast he had feared, feeling Herod's men would hunt there first. Once across the desert he went up to the sea road, for he would be out of Herod's realm by then, beyond the reach of his men.

Now, on the twelfth day, they came into Raphia as evening drew on. From the blazing sun and the cheerless sand they had glimpsed from afar the ancient palms and the white roofs of the town, and in the westering light a cool wind had come from the distant sea. Mary's face had lifted; she had thrown back her head-covering and uncovered the Child's face. The donkey's steps quickened. Joseph's breath had come more easily, and the little knot of fear about his heart slowly eased as they passed into the town. The strange faces, the strange streets did not trouble him. Not many glances fell on them, as travelers were a common sight. On through the town they went, until at length the huddled houses thinned a bit, the winding street widened, and they came to the last well. It lay in a grove of palms, and near it sat an old man leaning against a tree. For utter weariness Joseph stood still, and the donkey with a great sigh stopped, and Mary slid from his back. The breeze had freshened, and the shadows were falling. Joseph went forward to the well, carrying their water jar. He paused near the old man, who turned his head to Joseph. Then Joseph saw he was quite blind, his old eyes filmed over. But his face smiled.

"Peace, father," said Joseph. "We are travelers, and seek water here, and rest for the night." He watched the old man to see if he could hear and understand. The old face smiled still more, the wrinkled hands gestured in the air.

"Welcome, my son. The water is the Lord's and He gives it to all men." He kept his face turned to them then, as Joseph leaned on the stone well rim and let down the skin bucket and hauled it up, first filling the stone trough for the tired and thirsty beast, and then

73

filling their jar and holding it for Mary. The water was cool and sweet. At the sound of the bucket dropping into the well a second time the old man spoke again.

"Where do you journey?"

Joseph did not answer, but stood wordless, pondering. And while he waited, wondering what to say, the Child began to cry, a small, clear little cry. Then the old man turned his face to Mary, and slowly over it came a glow as if the sinking sun shone on it, and he held out his hands.

"You journey down to Egypt, surely," he said softly. "And on this night my poor house is blessed to shelter you. I am a swineherd and my house is shunned by many. But God has been merciful to me." And trembling in his ancient haste, he dragged himself up and seized his staff.

"Yonder—" he pointed his staff through the trees, "and my son will welcome you, who brings home a wife in two days' time—a fair and pure little maiden—and he has made the house ready." He went on as he hobbled before them through the trees. "And the neighbors, the kind-hearted ones, brought anise cake and wine, melons and dates—"

After one look at Mary, Joseph unquestioning led the donkey after the old man, who still talked on, breathless and full of joy. They came to the edge of the tall palms and found the house, white and low, with a small court

74

and a bake oven near the door. The old man thumped
his staff on the ground as he hurried on and a young
man leapt to the door. He had a thin brown face and
dark anxious eyes. He came out at once at his father's
call.

"Wayfarers, my son, who seek the night's lodging
with us."

Then the young swineherd turned to Joseph and said
with dignity, "You are welcome to all we have, such as
it is." He turned to Mary. "And you will find no other
womenfolk here—not for two days' time. But then,"
and a little smile lit his somber face for an instant,
"then a woman will again tend the hearth my mother
loved. Come, go ye in. And we will care for the beast
and prepare supper while you rest yourself."

So Mary passed through the door into the cool, bare
room. She stood and looked around. Her eyes took in
the neat pile of pallets in the corner, the kneading bowl,
scrubbed clean, on the ledge a few clay dishes, a cook-
ing pot; and in the corner a small carved chest. By it
leaned a corn broom. And in a niche in the wall there
was a clay lamp. Two water jars stood by the door. The
room was spotless, empty, expectant. She smiled, thinking of the hurry and bustle to come, the modest feasting,
the young bride so soon to bring the room to life, to
give joy to the days of the old swineherd and his son.
And then she busied herself with the Child. She heard

the old swineherd outside. "Bring melons and bread from the storeroom, my son. This night we are blessed of God." And she heard Joseph murmur, "Keep it for the wedding feast," and the young man firmly, "Nay, it will be richer for having fed the travelers in God. She who is my betrothed would joyfully welcome you. Share our feast now. The Lord has given it."

Then Joseph stood in the door. He looked at her and his eyes came at last to the Child. His tired face softened.

"Indeed God cares for us," he whispered.

In the early light the donkey stood before the door. The old swineherd leaned upon his staff, his face sad now that they would go. Joseph slung the pallet over the beast's back. He fastened the saddlebag, and made ready for Mary to mount. But she stood and looked into his face. Then she spoke, "Joseph, there is a wedding at this house. And we have left no gift."

He stared at her. Then, "Take thou the Child," she whispered, and laid the swaddled Babe in his arms. She stooped to the ground where there lay Joseph's leather sack, and the water jar. With quick fingers she undid the thongs, and her hands searched inside. She pulled out a small bundle. Swiftly she unwrapped it, and in the early sunlight there glowed between her hands the vial of frankincense. A fragrance rose, faint and sweet. Then she turned to the door and went inside. The

young swineherd was laying the last pallet away. He turned at her step and his eyes grew round with wonder. She set the vial on the ledge, where it gleamed blue and scarlet and gold in the shadows. Then she spoke to the young man,

"Frankincense, in praise of God—that in the holy joy of marriage we may glimpse the mystery of His Unity and His promise for all men."

77

And they rode out of Raphia, on the shoreward path. The white dunes rippled in the sun, and the sapphire sea glistened beyond. White gulls dipped and flew and circled around them, calling, and the wind was cool. There was purity everywhere. And the leather sack hung lighter at Joseph's side.

III

Tanis—alien city, yet strangely home. For had not these bricks, generations ago, perhaps the very bricks of this small house, been shaped and set by their forefathers—in bondage, enslaved, under false gods? Yet now here they sought asylum, here they were safe from the new tyrant, here they kept the promise sent from God, the little Flame that would light the whole world.

Here too they had found welcome, a hand held out to them, bread for their need, and the voices of friends —nay, more than friends. When they had come into the city, those weeks ago, and had stood in the crowded market, amid the strange smells, the foreign cries, the strange wares—for the very fruits were new—a tall, dark man with skull cap and forelocks came up to them quietly and greeted them with the accents of home. In the name of the Lord he had asked them if they would accept his shelter, and had led them out of the noise and hustle, through narrow ways, to the tiny, ancient Jewish quarter.

The Three Gifts

There, in Simon the Potter's house, they were given a small room off the court, and there Joseph went out to his trade, finding work now and then—not much, but enough to bring a bit home to pay for their bread. Simon had a slim, dark-eyed wife, Rachel, and one small pale child, little Benjamin, with eyes like brown stars and long lashes. Benjamin loved Mary, but most of all he loved the Child. He would sit by His cot hour after hour, waiting for Him to stir and wake, and stand entranced, scarcely breathing, when the Child woke and clutched Benjamin's slender finger in His tiny fist. Rachel would pause in the doorway to gaze at her own child, her small face careworn yet aglow with love. Or she would stop her work at the handmill to watch the Child kicking on a pallet in the cool courtyard, while Benjamin dangled a small green bough above Him, laughing. Then she would say to Mary, "What life He brings us, and what joy. Blessed the day Simon brought you home." Or she would say, "Benjamin has been too much alone. That is why he thrives so slowly." But her face would shadow and grow pinched.

Sometimes in the evening, when the whir of Simon's wheel was still and the shutters of the shop were closed, they would all sit in the courtyard and watch the faint stars grow closer, brighter, until they seemed just above the rooftops to be plucked. And they would talk, not much nor many words from Joseph. But heart spoke to heart. And Mary, with the Babe on her lap, would speak with longing of the land that they had left, the land of her childhood.

"When we return, I will show Him the Sea of Tiberias all asparkle in the sun—and let Him watch the shining fishes in the nets the fishermen draw up upon the shore—and show Him the heron wading in the shallows. And I shall pick Him scarlet anemones—all His hands can hold." And Rachel would droop her head over her frail little son who lay asleep on her knees, listening to his shallow breathing, and her fingers would stroke his hot little brow, and the tears would glisten on her cheeks. Joseph, sitting in the deep shadows, would watch and listen. He was waiting for he knew not what, a sign from God, a word that would come.

So the days passed, and the weeks. As the Baby throve and grew strong, so little Benjamin faded. Fever glowed upon his cheeks, and his breath came short. He went now only from his own small cot to lie with his small face propped upon his hands beside the Child's pallet, his eyes shining with joy as he gazed and gazed at the small one, who smiled and smiled upon him in return. And Mary, a helpless aching in her heart, felt a wordless mystery between the two. She watched in awe. Joseph, coming home, would stand in the door, watching also, silent, his eyes shadowed and sad, yet a strange joy within him, as at a secret promise soon to be revealed.

The Three Gifts

Then there came a day when Benjamin lay flushed upon his cot and could not rise. His lashes lay dark upon his cheeks. His little hands were still but his heart beat like a small wild bird. Rachel was past tears. Upon her knees she bathed and tended him but her face was like a mask, nor could she speak. Mary, at her side, gave all the aid she could, and as night fell, together the two women watched as the little life flickered on.

Joseph, in their room off the courtyard, slept fitfully. The night was very still, the stars hanging low and brilliant. Before the dawn there came a faint stirring of the wind, a fragrance carried on the air, a golden shimmering—and Joseph woke, his heart pounding. Again the voice—again the summons not to be withstood. "Rise, take the Child, and go to the Land of Israel. For those who sought the Child's life are dead." He waited until his heart slowed, then obediently he rose and stood in the dimness, his mind already busy with what they must do. He heard the quiet breathing of the Babe—and then a small, stifled outcry from the farther room. Ah—Benjamin! why must they leave now. He went with haste across the court and stood on the threshold of the farther room. As he paused, his hands gripping the door frame, he saw in the flickering lamplight the two figures of Mary and the mother, bending over the small face bathed in sweat and deathly pale—and as he looked the great eyes opened for the last time, the white lips smiled, and the watchers heard faint but clear and joyful the one word "Jesus." Then the eyes closed and the last breath faded, and a stillness lay upon them all.

At noon the donkey stood tethered beyond the courtyard, by the house door in the narrow street. Mary, within, with tear-stained face, packed their last belongings. Beyond, beside the small bier in the farther room, could be heard the lamentations of the women. Joseph took down his leather sack from a peg upon the wall and began to gather up his tools. His heart felt numb. He only knew he was in the grip of something so great he must only stand before it helpless and unquestioning, taking the next step, laying his hand to the next task.

Then Mary's small hand lay upon his own, as he began to fasten the leather thong upon the sack, and she looked at him. "The myrrh." she whispered, "Fetch me out the gift of myrrh." He stared at her a moment. The frankincense and now the myrrh! But at the look upon her face he did not hesitate. His hands undid the sack again, and his fingers sought the small square bundle. He laid it on the floor and unwrapped it carefully. The dull rich gleam of copper met their eyes; the small coffer was embossed with a row of little fishes leaping around the rim, and the latch was shaped like a star. Mary took it gently in both hands, then turned and went swiftly from the room, across the court, and into the room of mourning, where a silence fell at her step.

The lamentations ceased, all heads were lifted, and, behind her in the doorway, Joseph heard her speak.

"Rachel, beloved sister, I give thee this gift for the anointing of thy child. For know that this day he truly lives. For a promise is now given us from God that death can rule no more but must go down to everlasting defeat, and the day of the Lord shall dawn upon the earth, even as it has already dawned in Heaven. Then shall we all truly live, and all sorrowing shall pass away."

Then she knelt and laid the coffer in the trembling hands of the mother, and kissed her once upon the brow. Turning, she went past Joseph with resolute face, and gathered up the Child where He slept. Without words they laid the last things upon the donkey, and Joseph helped her mount. Then they made their way through the narrow lanes and at last set their feet upon the road to El Quantara, the crossing that would take them to the highway leading them back to Israel. And in Joseph's sack were now only his tools, besides the mesh bag of golden coins.

IV

Along the dusty highway, in the morning light, went many travelers, some from Esh Shan, from Aleppo in the far north, come down the sea road to trade in slaves, to carry spice and amber down into Egypt, to barter purple dye for ivory and peacock plumes. Some traveled from the south, with gems and gold, with cotton spun like gossamer. Some went in chains, whipped if they stumbled. Others went in litters borne on the shoulders of enormous bondsmen richly clad. A wagon rumbled by, laden with wineskins. And weary donkeys trod the dust, heads down, ears forward, eyes half-closed. Out of Gaza, lying just behind, or into Gaza, lying just ahead, unending lines of wayfarers met and passed. The ancient ruined temple beside the road gave scant shade, as the sun already blazed with a foretaste of noon. Going north, to the right lay the desert brown and parched; to the left dunes and a hint of sea beyond—somehow a stir in the air, a sparkle, half mirage, half reality.

Joseph walked beside the donkey's head. His face was brown from the sun, like an old leaf, lined with care. Mary's veil was drawn close, and the Child well covered from the dust. He slept untroubled and in peace. So they came to the city gates and passed within, where the clamor hit them like a blow, and the alien air swept over them so strong that Joseph's hand tightened on the donkey's lead; the little group stopped, and with in-drawn breath Joseph waited, watched, and at length drew off to the left, where a narrow street seemed more quiet. There was no friendly face, no Simon to come up to them and ask them home. Tall, harsh-featured men brushed by; there was a stench of old fish, sweat, rotted vegetables, uncleanliness. Joseph led them on till the way widened, small shops appeared, and an old, neglected khan stood at a corner, its courtyard emptied of the night's trade, but still unswept. A half-grown boy shoveled at the piles of dung, and an old woman stood beside the wall feebly shaking the straw and dust from a worn pallet. Joseph stopped, and Mary pushed aside her shawl. The woman ceased her shaking, and let the pallet slip from her old hands. She looked at them.

"We seek a place to rest from the noon's heat," said Joseph quietly. "Then we journey on."

She jerked her head over her shoulder toward the court. "All's fit to lie in is that first hole in the wall. You can rest there if you want, and have five coppers to pay for it."

"Water?" said Joseph. "Our jar is nearly empty."

"Slave market, next street. There you'll find a well. If you can stand the stink."

Out of the tail of his eye he saw Mary clutch the Child closer, and heard her sigh. His hand tightened on the halter, and he led the donkey in. The little room was dark and bare, but passably clean, and was sheltered from the noise and heat. He laid his cloak over the straw in the corner, then went out to take the Child from Mary's arms and help her down. She drooped from weariness and he was glad to see her stretch herself

86

upon the straw and close her eyes, the Baby quiet at her side. He stood gazing down at them, his eyes dark with care, his mind heavy with dread and the question whether they yet were safe. Herod was dead. That much was sure. All men spoke of it, but also of Herod's son—and with the same fear and foreboding. Like father, like son, they muttered, and shook their heads darkly. Would this new ruler, Archelaus, not also seek out the Child, to slay Him? So they had slipped through Raphia, not daring to stop where they had stopped before, and spent the night at Yunis; and there again this past night the voice had come, warning that they must not return to Bethlehem, but must journey farther on.

So now Joseph stood and gazed at Mary and the sleeping Babe, and the worry gnawed at him again. They could return to Nazareth, he told himself. There they were not strangers, and there he could set up his shop. His mind eased a bit, and already he felt hungry for a sight of the Galilean hills, the peaceful valleys green and cool. He was weary to the bone. There he could rest. And he still had the gold. With that he could without trouble even build a little house, and buy more tools and wood and start his trade in comfort and in peace. He sighed, and passed his hand across his brow. It would not be so hard after all, to start afresh.

Outside the door the patient donkey snuffled in the

heat and stamped his hoof. Joseph remembered that they must have water, so he turned and slipped out, into the court, and then beyond, into the street. In the noonday dazzle he stopped, to get his bearings. The boy now sat upon the wall, and watched him idly. Joseph asked, "Which way to the well?" and the boy motioned with his scrubby finger to the left. With his empty water jar and his leather sack over his shoulder, Joseph went. It was not far, and then he came to a turning, and there the narrow way opened into a small square, in its center a large stone block, and beside it a well, with worn stone rim. The square was fairly empty, two or three tattered tents set up where clusters of humanity sprawled in the shade; an urchin or two loitered at the well rim, and a mongrel dozed beside the block. The stink of human filth and degradation hit him like a wave, and he stopped in his tracks. Even as he stood, wondering if he would have courage to draw from that well, from the dark street opposite emerged the figures of two men, one tall and dark and straight, the other short and fat, between them a laden donkey. They came slowly across the square to the well rim. Then Joseph saw the tall man, dark of skin, was chained at the wrists and at the ankles, so his steps were slow. The fat man, who wore a well-woven cloak bordered in blue and a loose head covering of white linen, untied a skin bucket

88

from the donkey and leaned over the well, lowering it quickly and hauling it up slowly with grunts and curses. He held the bucket under the nose of the beast, who slobbered and drank in great gulps. Then the fat man drew the bucket away and said loudly, with a sneer, to the slave, "Parched? Dying of thirst? Take that!" and he flung the dregs into the man's face. But the man stood unmoved, his eyes closed, while the drops of dirty water slid one by one down into his beard. Then he opened his eyes, and across the soiled cobbles and the shimmering heat his gaze met that of Joseph.

Their eyes met and held, and to Joseph, time seemed to stop. What he wrestled with he could not have said —but he fought and struggled in his heart, the blood thundered in his head, and for what seemed eternity he stood, rooted to the spot, a tempest in his breast. Then at last the tall Negro turned his face away and gazed into the dust; and Joseph came to himself and found his hand gripped tight upon his leather sack as if he could never loosen it, and underneath his fingers he could feel the gold. But he knew, as if the voice had spoken, what he must do.

He watched while the fat man led the donkey and the slave off beside the little huddle of tents, and began to drag out a shelter of sorts, to keep himself, at least, from the blazing sun and the night's chill, until market opened on the morrow. Then Joseph walked slowly across and stood there before the fat man, who stopped his puttering and looked up.

"How much?" said Joseph, quietly, nodding toward the slave.

"How much?" The fat man's voice was half amazed, half mocking. "Why should the likes of you ask?"

"Perhaps I have the command of a great lord laid upon me to purchase a slave. How much?" said Joseph.

"This is no mere slave. A king's ransom alone will purchase him," jeered the man.

"How much?" persisted Joseph.

"I take him down into Egypt, to sell to the Pharaoh perhaps. He came from a slave ship out of the dark lands, where he was king. I got him in Tyre, with a fortune. Now who is your master, that he can purchase him?"

"How much?" said Joseph. "Tell me how much and I go to fetch the scribe."

"Fetch the scribe, fool," sneered the man. "Twenty gold denares alone will purchase him."

Joseph turned and went swiftly across the square to where the scribe's booth huddled against an ancient wall. Inside, a wizened little man dozed, pens and scrolls beside him. Joseph nudged him gently with his foot and he roused at once and looked up sleepily.

"Will you write a bill of sale for a slave, now, on the instant?"

The man shuffled to his feet and gathered up his gear. He followed at Joseph's heels, blinking in the sun, across the square, to where the fat man waited, dumbstruck. The slave still stood motionless and straight beside the donkey. The scribe squatted in the shade and arranged his little desk. He set out his ink horn, and then looked up, his stylus poised.

"Let me see your gold," hissed the fat man.

"Not till it is writ fair and clear, then you give me the man as I give you the gold."

Greed, doubt, bewilderment, all played across the face of the trader. But at last, "What's to lose!" he muttered, and began to dictate to the scribe, who wrote with care and flourishes, and at last held up two documents, and his pen, and pointed here, and here for them both to make their scrawl. Then, and only then, did Joseph with trembling fingers undo the thong of the leather sack, and fumble inside for the mesh bag. This he drew out slowly and held it for an instant in his cupped fingers. Again the faraway night came back to him, the dim stable in the starlight, the great kings kneeling, the wonder and the awe, and the lovely Child sleeping while they gazed. Then he reached out for the document of purchase with one hand, and with the other he

held out the gold. The breath hissed in the fat man's throat. His eyes bulged and his jaw fell.

"But—but—it is too much even," he stammered.

"It is to free the slaves of all the world," whispered Joseph. "Take it!"

For an instant a look of terror swept over the man; he trembled and went pale. Then he grabbed the gold.

"Go, go!" he muttered. "Take him. Go! Out of my sight!"

"The key," said Joseph.

The man fumbled wildly in his wallet and pulled out a copper key. Joseph seized it and knelt at the Negro's feet, unlocking his chains. Then he stood and unlocked the chains about his wrists. He flung key and chains into the dust.

"Come," he said to the freedman, laying his hand on his shoulder, and turning him toward the well. The man's unshackled feet moved slowly, then more freely, as Joseph guided him across the cobbles. At the well he lowered the bucket quickly, hauled it up, and poured the water into their water jar. This he held to the man's lips and his hands trembled a bit as the man drank deeply. Then he touched the man's shoulder again, and together they went across the square, into the narrow street. Joseph led him swiftly, not stopping at the khan where Mary lay, on to the gate of the city, out to the highway. There he stopped. He turned and faced the dark man.

"This road leads down to Egypt and beyond to your own lands, perhaps. In Raphia, stop at the swineherd's house on the far side. There you will find shelter in the Lord's name. In Tanis ask for Simon the Potter, in the Jewish quarter, and tell him Joseph ben Jacob sent you. He will give you aid. Here are tools, so you may earn your way." He undid his leather sack. "And my tunic." He undid his outer garment. He held out both to the man, whose eyes glistened with tears. Only then did Joseph wonder . . . were his very words not strange, in a foreign tongue? But the man then suddenly clasped Joseph's outstretched hands, and spoke, truly in an alien tongue and yet Joseph knew them as if they were in his own,

"Blessed be His Name forever."

And Joseph answered, "It is spoken by God."

Then the man turned quickly and went southward on the highway. And Joseph stood half-naked, empty-handed, in the road, watching him. But such a joy flooded him he thought his heart would burst.

And Joseph cried out, "For one who serves the Word of God, what need has he of gold or tools?"

And the travelers streamed by him eyeing him as if he were crazed. But he cared not. And finally he turned to go back to Mary and the Child and to journey on to Nazareth.

POVERTY CAROL

ALL POOR MEN AND HUMB-LE, ALL LAME MEN WHO
FOR JESUS OUR TREASURE, WITH LOVE PAST ALL

STUMBLE, COME HASTE YE, NOR FEEL YE A- FRAID;
MEASURE, IN LOW-LY POOR MAN-GER WAS LAID.

2nd and 3rd verses:
THOUGH WISE MEN WHO FOUND HIM LAID RICH GIFTS A-

ROUND HIM, YET OX- EN THEY GAVE HIM THEIR HAY:

AND JES- US IN BEAU-TY AC- CEPT-ED THEIR

DU-TY; CON- TENT-ED IN MAN- GER HE LAY.

ALL POOR MEN AND HUMBLE,
ALL LAME MEN WHO STUMBLE,
COME HASTE YE, NOR FEEL YE AFRAID;
FOR JESUS, OUR TREASURE,
WITH LOVE PAST ALL MEASURE,
IN LOWLY POOR MANGER WAS LAID.

THOUGH WISE MEN WHO FOUND HIM   THEN HASTE WE TO SHOW HIM
LAID RICH GIFTS AROUND HIM,   THE PRAISES WE OWE HIM;
YET OXEN THEY GAVE HIM THEIR HAY: OUR SERVICE HE NE'ER CAN DESPISE:
AND JESUS IN BEAUTY   WHOSE LOVE STILL IS ABLE
ACCEPTED THEIR DUTY;   TO SHOW US THAT STABLE
CONTENTED IN MANGER HE LAY.   WHERE SOFTLY IN MANGER HE LIES.

A FREE TRANSLATION OF THE WELSH CAROL, "O DEUED POB CRISTION."

96

THE CHILDREN'S CRUSADE

by ERNST WIECHERT

eter Hamborn, erstwhile miner, now soldier without rank in one of the nameless infantry regiments at the end of the great war, stood before the locked gate of his father's property, forced and ready to turn his dust-covered feet to the highway. The pale autumn sun was just sinking behind the gray rooftop of the barn. He turned his eyes away from the frowning face of the farmer leaning on the fence opposite him, and lifted them to the parting light which laid borders of gold around the straw and the beams.

On his gray forehead one could read the heavy thoughts into which the sunlight shone confusingly. As he glanced once again over yard and garden, his look was clearly recognizable as that of a man in those lost years who tightened his pack, shortened the strap of his helmet, and now awaited the quiet command, while looking back from this dark threshold to an earth which had borne him, be it for days or hours, like his mother's earth.

"They are hungry, Father," he said softly, looking just past the farmer's face into the evening clouds. "It's been three years now, and the smallest is only five."

The farmer leaned on the gate from inside with both arms.

"Who ordered you," he asked, "to run away from my service and marry that woman? As the furrow, so is the fruit."

"They don't even remember what milk and butter taste like," said the other again, following the stately progress of the clouds.

"Salt and bread make cheeks red."

"Their eyes are old, and this time Jürgen did not laugh any more..."

"Every day ten like that come to my door."

"See!" said the man outside, raising his hand toward the sky, where a fleet of gold-rimmed clouds rode into the evening. "In three days perhaps we will be like that."

But the farmer only shrugged his shoulders.

For a while the soldier still held the gesture of his last words, watching the clouds earnestly, almost anxiously, as if they were a squadron of enemy planes. Then from

98

thoughtless habit he took hold of the straps of his empty rucksack, turned around shortly and strode toward the nearby highway. The dust rose in gray clouds under the heavy tread of his hobnailed boots. The patched and worn clothing of his occupation seemed oddly poor and joyless as he slipped past the bright mountain ash berries along the hedge-lined lane. And when on the nearby rise he again walked into the last rays of the sun and turned with bowed shoulders, he looked more like a beggar and an outcast than a hardened comrade of death about to return from an interlude of joy back to the smoldering arena of bloody action.

In those weeks whose early declining days gave warning of the coming winter, many such gray wanderers were seen making their way over the German land. They all had the heavy step of columns that had left whole countries behind them as once they had left villages and market places; they all had the same clothing plastered with sweat and earth; all had the same stamp on their faces as of men who looked in loneliness out of deep windows onto a strange world. Like leisurely walkers they stood by fences and at the borders of fields, hands in their pockets, and looked with seeming indifference at the fruits of the field which the earth gave to those who had stayed at home. Or they set foot on farms whose peace and well-being shook them up to the depths of their being. And then they went on, lips pressed together; and only at the bottom of their timid eyes could the misery and hate that filled them be sensed.

The eyes of the infantryman Peter Hamborn, however, veiled even this depth of misery, and with the same alienation they lifted, above the "Yes" or "No" of the farmers, towards the first easterly stars. Since his life had sunk from the steaming field to go down under the earth where there was neither wind nor sun nor bird cry, he had become a silent man, and it was his way to tread quietly, on the roads of peace as well as on the fields of battle.

Yet, when the curve of the Milky Way was already growing bright out of distant space, his rucksack was filled, and in his purse remained only the small amount of his return fare to his family. He realized from the stars—for he no longer possessed a watch—that he could not catch the train before the last, and that the time until midnight was his own. So he turned into the longer road through the fields which led through thinly planted woods, along the great moor, uphill and downhill to the station, away from the paved road; and walked along silent and bowed.

On the last hill he sat down for half an hour on the ridge between the fields, laid his rucksack beside him, folded his hands over his knees and looked motionless across fields that dropped away into the valley through which the railroad was later to take him. His eyes,

accustomed to the dark, gradually recognized the larger lines of the sleeping earth, field and wood, and the islands of resting farmhouses. Lights went out, as if covering themselves up to sleep peacefully, and others blossomed forth out of empty darkness, filling his heart with gentle sadness because of the circle of peace which they warmed. A slight breeze moved through the night, and here and there the sound of migrating flocks of birds, like the interrupted noise of a flapping sail, fell from the darkened sky.

Peter Hamborn's eyes saw all this, not so much with the sharpness of the soldier whose heart had cut up a thousand such nights into endless minutes, but with the prophetic spirituality of the one who looked upon the

Promised Land from Mount Nebo. At times the horizon's lines were veiled from him in a blaze of flame, though, and from changing lights he read signals of brazen brevity and force; then he smiled shyly and stared downwards again, as if the closed gate were again rising up before his feet, and as if it were a dream that God's hand was spreading out before him down there, and one dare not touch it with the tip of one finger without making it crumble to pieces in fog and dust.

Then he stood at the station for half an hour, away from the lantern's circle of light, hands in his pockets and coat collar turned up, since no superior officer was to be seen. He was half glad and half bitter that no eye of sympathy found and surrounded him, that he was nothing but one of millions, nameless, one who came and went, and that from his brow under the rim of his gray cap, nobody could read the extreme shock that had touched it, today or during the three years.

The cold dawn was already wearily groping through the soot and fog of the bleak town when he climbed up to his apartment. A small fire flickered in the stove where his wife sat over the sewing machine. He saw her glance at his face and the rucksack, and only shook his head mutely.

While he drank the hot coffee, and the meager peace of the little room surrounded him with kindness after the dark distress of the night, his thoughts ran along a narrow railway track, through day and evening, across a broad river to the edge of the earth, and he leaned his head against the whitewashed wall behind him and looked with fixed eyes over the damp roofs into the drizzling morning fog.

"There are still two days, Peter," she said softly.

He looked at her strangely. "Yes...two days," he repeated awakening.

Then Jürgen came. He stood between his father's knees and pushed his fingers between the buttons of his tunic, as he used to do. "I heard you," he said seriously, "but I couldn't wait...was it nice?"

Peter Hamborn nodded and tried to smile. But then he drew the slender boy in the patched gray nightshirt to him and hid his face behind the boy's warm shoulder.

"You're cold," he said unnecessarily loudly. "Come, I'll bring everything to your bed."

He bent over Andres and Eva, who lay nestled close together below the striped eiderdown, and sat down next to Jürgen, the opened rucksack before him on the floor. One thing after another, he built up on the wooden footstool what his hard journey under the evening clouds had allotted him, the butter and the two sides of bacon on top of it all.

"Such a farm!" whispered Jürgen. "You come like a king! But tell us now, and everything in the right order!"

Peter Hamborn drew the curtains of his feeling closer
together again and supported his head in both hands.
"Yes, Jürgen...it looked just as it always used to. The
hedge-lined lane with the mountain ashes, and the two
poplar trees at the gate. The boy was cutting straw, and
the geese were in the orchard."

"Weren't they plowing?"

"Yes, old Klaus was plowing the fallow field. It
smelled good, like at the baker's. They made a great
fuss when I came, and took me to my father right
away."

"Is he still ill?"

"Well, sometimes he gets up, and the doctor thinks
that it is gradually getting better, but it doesn't really
seem to be right. I had to sit down by him and of
course tell him about everything, about the war and
about my captain...and about you."

"Did...did he ask about me too?"

"Of course, Jürgen. About you most of all. And when
he is well again you are to go and visit him at last
and stay there a whole year. Riding and plowing and
breaking-in and everything. And you are the one who
is to have the greatest share of all this, because you are
the oldest and the best behaved. Things could be better
on the farm, you know, and he would have given me
more, but of course he is ill, and that's just how it
is..."

Jürgen lay motionless, his big, serious eyes directed at the window and his hands clasped tightly around his father's hand.

"I think, Father," he finally said softly, "Eva should have the most. She coughs, and in the morning she tells us she always dreams of a big roast hanging above her bed, but she can't lift up her hands, and that's why she moans so in her sleep. The rest of us, we'll manage all right."

Peter nodded in silence.

"Isn't it nice to go to the farm like that, Father," began the child after a while. "I imagine the birds singing everywhere and all the houses white in the sun and the people beaming all over when one says good morning to them. Quite different from here, quite different—just the way it was when the Saviour was on the earth.... You know, Father, sometimes when you're away I build it all up with sand and rocks and grass—that's how well I know the farm already. Maybe, Father, the next time you go there I'll already be confirmed, then perhaps I can come too, do you think I can?"

"I really think you can, Jürgen," said Peter confidently, running his free hand through his hair. "And it won't be such a long time now, either."

"Listen, Mother's winding the thread," whispered Jürgen. "How nice and soft it sounds...and today we'll have all we want to eat...." He closed his eyes, and the early lines in his forehead became smoother with every breath.

Peter Hamborn sat motionless until Jürgen had fallen asleep. Then he stood up quietly and went to the window. The daily life of the narrow street was growing out of the darkness and poverty, into the pale light. Lanterns went out, doors were opened, and the gray-faced beaten generation plunged into the morning's vaporous stream.

Through the half-light, Peter saw the two poplar trees at the farm gate, and behind them the evening clouds rimmed with light, and in the farthest distance, stretching away into colorless space, the torn-up earth with the splintered stumps of barked trees.

Two days later he went back to the front.

During the autumn that followed his departure, the days were shorter than the nights for the children in the lightless cities and throughout the German land. Of course, the days were filled with school, with collecting, and with slow-moving hours of waiting for food and clothing for the body, with hunger, and crouching by cold stoves. But through the nights the dreams marched in long, gliding processions. The darkness did not roll over the sinking souls like one single dark wave that joined morning to evening almost without a break. No, it dragged the stupefied senses from gloom to fantastic illusions so cruelly clear that their eyes opened in sudden wakefulness, and then closed again because their hands were held up to emptiness and the tormented souls plunged with a choked cry into the abyss of realization.

It was not like other times, flourishing times of peace when the fabled beings of fairyland walked radiant through magic gardens. The hidden longing of the day did not rise up in the night and take bright and happy forms which brought an afterglow to waking hours such as a star gives to the day. Sober, stripped of all brightness, the dream-angel passed over the hundreds of thousands of beds and cribs from sunrise to sunset. No flowers with glowing colors burst from his arms, no poetic image, no smile from God. And from the earthen vessel from which he lifted the lid no magic serpent lifted its hissing head crowned with gold, but only the food of the poor, heaped up in mountains. Dreams rose up from the depths of the body, and souls lay dead in the coils of greed.

On a free corner of the stove around which they sat from early twilight on, Jürgen had built up the farm he had never seen. The poplars stood by the gate, and the meager light from the lamp shone over the little roofs and made them look real. He could sit in front of it for hours, his narrow face supported in his cold hands and his deep eyes filled with a brightness that might have been on the faces of the shepherds when they knelt before the manger.

"The farmer is a king, our teacher said, Mother," he whispered, raising his eyes. "Is that true?"

"Yes, it's true," she said; but he did not understand the bitterness of her words.

He only nodded, and ran timid fingers over the sand of the fields. And continued the dreams that helped him through the need of the days and nights.

Yet two things came together in a marvelous way which moved and shook his soul deeply, which thrust him from dark suffering onto a path where new, unheard-of life was brought forth out of the depths of ruin.

They had gathered around the stove at the usual hour when little Eva, putting her doll tenderly to bed, began to sing softly, as she did every evening. And though the others usually paid little attention to her childish tunes, this time it happened that all of them together stopped what they were doing and listened to the plaintive tones; because the first words gripped them involuntarily, or because the child's unselfish motherliness, full of a dark eternity, bridged the stream that rippled unheeded between their cares and her play.

"Oh, Mother, Mother, give me bread," she sang in a high, solemn voice, rocking the doll gently from side to

side. "Or of hunger I'll be dead."

They held their breath and kept their eyes fixed on the child, forgetting one another and giving themselves up to the song, as if the painful death were taking place under their folded hands. And when the sound died away and the mother lowered her face over the sewing machine, hiding it, and broke out weeping, Jürgen's hand crushed the house of his dream earth in unconscious horror and he ran blindly out to the street, driven by a pale light which broke cruelly into his crumbling dreams.

A couple of days later, as he sat shivering with a slight fever in the confirmation class, the pastor was telling them about the Children's Crusades in the Middle Ages. And because his compassionate soul faced the true portrayal of misery, he found warm words that filled

even those long ago and far-away times with a living
light, so that they all hung on his words as he told them
about the passionate beginning of the crusade, its failing
strength and its wretched ending.

A deep sigh filled the quiet room when he was finished. It was only when he asked, in the over-anxiety
of the shepherd of souls, about the Promised Land,
where it was and what they knew about it, that they
gradually found the way back to their own dark lives.
Still, nobody laughed when Jürgen, called back from a
far distance by the friendly challenge, answered, "At
Grandfather's, where there are six cows in the barn."

The pastor looked at him, wordless, deeply touched
by the unexpected reply. Then he said softly, "It wasn't
like that in those days, Jürgen." And he did not ask
any more questions.

In the afternoon Jürgen had to go to bed, as his fever
was getting worse; and three days later when he got
up again his face showed that his soul, which had
walked at God's feet from childhood on, had wandered
over land and sea.

He no longer had to struggle with dark doubts, and
the strange—yes, impossible—showed him a peaceful
face, since the voice had called to him across centuries,
from the strains of a song and the afterglow of a wild
and sad event. There was nothing for him to do but to
arise like a second prophet, only not in the pulpits and

market places, but in secret, and to call to the journey whoever was in need of or worthy of the call.

In accordance with the incorruptible laws of boyish friendship and loyalty, he was sure of his choice without wavering, and certain of every detail of departure, journey and return. The compulsion that ruled his action, as well as the dreamlike clarity with which he saw his task, was shown by what he left behind for his mother. He wrote, "Dear Mother, I am going to Grandfather with Eva and Andres. Some others who need it too, are going with us. There will be twelve of us. We have wagons along for the little ones. We will fetch bread, and it will be like the Holy Land there. Since Eva sang as she did, you will know that I have to do this. We will probably be gone for two weeks. You must not worry, for there is One who watches over us. The key is behind the salt box. When we come back you won't need to cry any more. Jürgen."

Everything was got ready for the day when their mother went to the house of strangers to do sewing early in the morning and did not return until it was dark. They gathered at the other side of the suburb, where a miserable wood caught a tired shimmer of late autumn in its tree tops. Jürgen and Andres pulled the wagon in which Eva, doll on her arm, rode towards a bright fairyland. The others followed them in three groups, with similar wagons similarly armed, fitted out

with sticks and rucksacks, the youngest ones with wooden swords hanging threateningly at their sides.

There was little difference of race and blood amongst the twelve, such as there had been in former times. Then the town families, though bowed by the same drudgery, sought heaven and earth with eyes of their own; and the reflection of separate ways shaped the foreheads of the fathers, echoing faintly in the faces of their children. But war, reaching out afar over the circle of blood and into the most distant huts, had passed a leveling, gray hand over the clothing of their souls, making them uniform. And the determined eyes that now turned toward the future with an earnest awareness of all care and responsibility, quietly reflected the gray figures behind barricade and sewing machine that stared into the stony face of ultimate decisions.

There was Dietrich, son of the coppersmith, with his brother and sister; his father lay under Belgian earth for a year, and his mother now stood at the wash-tub day after day; yet they never had enough bread. Like his ancestors in the time of the great migration of the Germanic tribes, Dietrich stood at the shaft quietly and firmly directing his unflinching glance to the distant horizon.

There was Klaus, son of a miner, mocked and pushed around in school and at play because of the heaviness of his body and mind; he read secretly in the Bible, and every week he inquired of Jürgen whether God could still be living when there was so much hunger, so much blood.

And there was Hinrich, the child of the streetcar conductor, with white hair and steel-gray eyes, whose father was in Russia and whose mother was leading a bad life, obsessed with men and intoxication. His face quivered at every rough word, and he was entangled in a world of hatred and torment; out of this world he raised his hand against mother, school and God.

They nodded to one another, and silently began the journey to the Redeemer.

The last rays of the October sun clung to hill and field, warming them, and lifted the horizon into the painful blue of widened spaces; the sun's rays made the streets appear strangely clear and harsh, as if home and peace lay far beyond the distant gates which they cut in the space of heaven. Thin smoke lay over farms, which seemed hard, almost hostile in the landscape, divested of their protective greenery; and every sound from the fields where people were digging out the last potatoes, rose far above the earth as if over forsaken waters.

They who wandered on the roads below the gentle wind did not notice the sun very much, or the last colorful jewels that were scattered over hedge and ridge. It was as if the eyes of all were turned toward an inward vision and as if the features of all were uniformly shaped by the image they saw. Here and there a lowered glance perhaps saw the strange procession of children and followed it with understanding and silent sadness. But what would have seemed surprising, even mysterious in times of peace, had become commonplace in a destiny that had turned children into beggars for their lives.

So they traveled on unmolested, slightly bewildered by the unaccustomed existence, by the unconcealed appearing of the hours, overflowing with freedom, expanse, and light. Laughter and gay shouting of the little ones hovered like a twittering of birds over the group, and a quiet radiance passed over even the worrying faces of the leaders.

Not until the warming time of mid-day did a weary silence fall on their dusty road; and Jürgen, who walked mute and serious in the lead, exchanged a knowing look with the three others and pointed wordlessly to the hill ahead, where a little oak wood sent its flaming color to heaven, and the smoke of mid-day meals rose above a few scattered farms.

At the edge of the wood they pushed the wagons together to take advantage of the shade. While the younger ones lay down in the warm grass, the others talked briefly about what they had to do and where to go, and straight away went their separate ways to the farms. From these they returned after some time, some more and some less blessed by the compassion of those who had been witnesses of their strange arrival.

They ate and drank, awakened to new joyfulness by the comfort of the meal and the sunny spaciousness around them, from which the outlines of their home had already disappeared, encompassed by curiosity and sympathy, the expression of which lent them a slight feeling of pride and sadness.

Afterwards they rested while the shadows grew imperceptibly shorter, and when the remains of the food and drink had been put safely away, they fell into the same order as before and went down the slope, trying to sing softly, as they had heard the gray columns do.

Thus the crusaders, now in flashes of gaiety, now in gradually increasing despondency, went on towards their goal beneath the high autumn sky and the sinking sun. The picture that the youngest ones saw on the other side of the blue woods shone like a house in a fairy tale, or stretched out like a kingdom. Enormous dogs crouched at the gateways, guardsmen in armor raised their spears; but further on there was a Canaan, the land where milk and honey flowed. Their feet hurt, the strange land grew like a rising sea up to the edge of the road, the call of crows died away weirdly in the empty wood. But the leaders strode on unbowed, ahead of their hearts, and the beams of the setting sun grew like God's pillars of fire out of the western valleys.

Early mists were rising above a low meadow where a brook ran, when the first weeping burst out of a trembling heart, and wailed for what was lost. With a harsh word Hinrich reproached the weeping child, but Jürgen raised his hand and simply said, "Do you think that six hundred years ago they didn't cry? Let's go and ask for a place to sleep."

They found a shed filled with hay, and for the first time they saw the eyes of a human being overflow because of their suffering. The farmer stood before them, gloomy though not refusing; but his wife held a kerchief to her eyes and raised her hand to the first stars with a passionate gesture. With calm firmness Jürgen refused to tell their names and where they came from. He only said, "We are going to Grandfather. He has six cows in his barn, and my sister sang, 'Oh, Mother, Mother, give me bread...or of hunger I'll be dead.' So then we went."

Their hunger was satisfied and they were warmed, and then they stumbled dead tired into the shed. Jürgen stood for a little while below the dark roof and looked beyond the mist to the dim road they had to travel the next day. The stars rose with increasing brilliance out of the evening vapor, a stronger wind blew, full of

strange life, in the nearby forest, and queer noises unknown on paved roads came and went through the terrifying world.

He breathed heavily, trembling at the new existence and knowing that behind him was the sleep he had to guard. Then he closed the door carefully and felt for his place near his brother and sister. He stretched out between them as they stammered softly in unconscious sleep, drew them close to the warmth of his body and so crossed over into the other land, gripped by the consciousness that far from father and mother he was doing the same that they would have done.

The second day rose and set over unknown roads. Its

hours rolled more harshly over the hearts of the travelers, and at its end a forest, heavy with darkness and terror, pushed itself across their way. They stood at its edge, secretly troubled, having just been rejected with words of abuse at the door of the last farm. The sun had set suddenly in a flickering abyss, and tremendous thunderheads shot up to the sky in threatening white from the clustered treetops.

"Why are we stopping?" said Dietrich with hard determination. "It is the last night, and the forest is better than a house."

They plunged with a sudden run, eyes almost closed, into the towering darkness, pulling the swaying wagons behind them, covered with the falling last leaves as with a shower. The heavy odor of autumn flowed from the rustling roof, filling the children with a queer oppression, so that from the strangers in the sanctuary, as if from the breast of a lost creature, a single cry rose up in sharp lament among the silent tree trunks and died away under the stars.

But Dietrich, breaking into the thicket with brow gloomily furrowed, took up the last sound as it died away, broadened it to inarticulate, ecstatic melody, which guarded his fear like a spear, shattering the darkness before him, and so carried the hesitating souls through the echoing forest until the warmth and security of a spruce-roofed clearing received them like a hut.

The Children's Crusade

While the little ones lay in the moss like mown flowers, gliding from the world of terror into dreams of the coming day, the watch fire burned at their feet, its flickering light moving over green walls and lighting up the faces of the leaders, who stared into the dark distance, old, serious, composed.

High up, the wind was increasing, blowing as if through unknown houses, swelling in choirs whose organ tones lay threateningly over the listening souls, strange to the forest, and the sound of a nocturnal animal, rising from a distant thicket, passed shudderingly over their bent foreheads.

"We must watch...one hour each," said Jürgen softly, without taking his eyes off the comforting fire.

The others nodded wordlessly. Not until the noise of the animal once again glided to them among the tree trunks and seemed to bury itself in the moss at their feet did Klaus whisper, "Shouldn't we...two at a time...in case there isn't enough wood..."

"Afraid?" asked Hinrich sharply and scornfully.

They all looked sadly at the heavy, drooping body of the miner's son, until he, with a tormented smile, raised his eyes. But when he could not prevent two tears from rolling slowly down his pale cheeks, they bent over the fire without speaking and aimlessly stirred the meager cinders with their sticks, so that a soft drizzle of sparks was scattered over the clearing.

"Tomorrow we'll be there," said Jürgen after a while.

It seemed to them as if the wind blew harder with every heartbeat and as if the roaring of the tree crowns filled the whole dark earth. Now and then one of the branches that hung down into the clearing swayed gently back and forth; and the mysterious movement that rose from invisible treetops into their encircled depths, filled the flowing seconds with the tension of a cloud before it releases its load.

And it was only an action by them all, when Dietrich seized his wooden spear which he had picked up from the edge of the road that evening, and stepped to the boundary of the lighted area, where the wall of dark forest rose up out of the earth. Here he remained motionless, leaning on his weapon, urged by the same compulsion as the knee of one who prays, bending before the infinite.

When they were lying in their blankets already, with eyes still open and turned toward the watchman, Hinrich lifted his head softly, looked over the little camp and then whispered, as he stretched out on the ground again, "Will we ever get home again?...The world is so big...."

He received no answer, and then only the treetops were heard rustling above the shaking trunks.

Late in the afternoon they reached the road along which Jürgen's father had walked with heavy boots a couple of weeks earlier, and tree and hedge grew out of Jürgen's dream world into the clarity of first experience. He went at the head of the band, borne on wings of the storm, intoxicated with the fragrance of the dark earth. And when a herd of young horses in an enclosure near by neighed in aimless play and flew over the brown grassy earth with their glossy dark bodies stretched out, mane and tail streaming behind, he raised his arms above his head and his wild cry burst over them as if he lay on their necks and was peering over their out-stretched heads at the earth which was his own.

He stopped at the same spot where his father had raised his arm to the evening clouds in mute dialogue. Before him lay the farm. The poplars were leaning in the storm, and dark blue clouds rolled like tumbling mountains across the twilit land. Over the gray beams the roofs hung heavy, sheltering the harvest, and the odor of the fields filled the space between sky and earth.

Bent forward, hands supported on his staff, the child stood and stared into the countenance of his Promised Land. And did not know that his eyes were widened by the very fear of the dreamer who sees something unheard-of and hears the warning whisper of a soft voice from vanished life, saying that the next heartbeat will cause to disappear what rose up from the depths of bliss into fleeting brightness.

Only when the others crowded around him and

gazed, silent like him, down upon the promise, did he look around and, with his face almost distorted, grasp the shaft of his wagon in a hard grip and stride with painful knees, almost stumbling, down toward the gate.

It was locked, and at that same moment, while the little group still stood hesitating in front of it, the farmer came out of the door of the low house, hands in his pockets, without astonishment, as if he had already been standing at the window a long time and examining them critically, knowing in advance where they came from and why.

When he had reached the gate, he leaned over the gray fence with both arms and looked at them in silence, first with dull curiosity, then with increasing and unconcealed contempt. "Vagabonds!" he hissed.

Then there was a deathly silence on both sides of the gate, and above only the blustering of the poplar branches, like lashing whips.

And then Eva began to cry unexpectedly, with a wild hopelessness, as if her tears were bursting from all the eyes that stared and stood before the barred gates of Paradise.

"You are..." whispered Jürgen with white, smiling lips, "you are...well again?"

The farmer smiled too. "Vagabonds!" he said once again, louder than before.

"My father said...," began Jürgen.

The farmer raised his eyebrows as if the kindness of his heart were urging him to strained attention; but then he suddenly began to laugh, almost inaudibly, while his cold eyes scanned the crowded faces of the children, as if he were touching with a red-hot iron the trembling bodies of young animals crouching before him in the corner of a cage.

"What did he say?" he asked, leaning comfortably over the gate.

But Jürgen was silent.

Now when the farmer had come out of his house door, at the same time a man had stepped from the shed near the gate, with a rucksack on his back and a stick in his hand; during the whole exchange he had stood there silent and his eyes had traveled in gloomy watchfulness from one side of the gate to the other. One could tell that he was young in years, but the soiled gray of his war uniform gave something timeless to his appearance, and the empty coat-sleeve at his left side, fluttering up and down in the storm, moved like a flickering gap through his mournful image.

And at last, like a delayed answer to the farmer's question, Jürgen said, looking at the stranger, "Maybe...he'll have to come home like that too...and then it's not just his arm that will be missing...."

The farmer drew a crumpled letter out of his coat

pocket and threw it over the fence. "Give that back to your mother."

And the boy, his eyes still clinging to the strange man, smoothed the soiled sheet of paper and in the waning daylight slowly and attentively read his mother's letter.

He tucked it carefully into the breast pocket of his thin coat and raised his eyes to the evening clouds, as his father had done. Then he turned the shaft of his cart around and got ready to go back the same way they had come.

But Hinrich, the spear in his trembling fist, got hold of him with a hard grip. "Where do you want to go?" he shouted hysterically.

"Back...turn back...it's all not true...there's no Promised Land."

Coming out of suspended motion, the spear lifted with a sudden swing toward the gate. "You!" shouted Hinrich. "You farmer you! They're lying in the mud out there...and you? Do you know that our feet are bleeding, you dog?"

The shaft, missing its goal, shot against the gate with a crash, quivered with the force of the impact for the space of a moment and then fell powerless into the dust of the road.

The farmer had turned pale and raised his hands uselessly in front of his face; with a curse, he bent down to find a weapon. But Jürgen, becoming tall and serious, laid his hand on Hinrich's arm and looked back once more at the gate without passion. "Six hundred years ago *they* didn't arrive either," he said quietly. "It must be somewhere else, Grandfather...somewhere else altogether."

And then the little handful of travelers again went up the hill as darkness fell, walking very slowly, while the storm tore dust from their wheels, and the child's crying went far out over the land.

While the farmer went through the barns, cursing and banging doors, the one-armed man remained standing by the gate with head bent, as if listening to the last words of the boy; then he slowly left the farm, followed by his dog, which jumped around him barking.

When he had caught up with the children, who were pushing away from the place of their rejection in stunned bewilderment, he strode at Jürgen's side along the dark road with them. Nothing was to be heard except the roaring of the storm which filled the whole space of earth, and the soft jolting of the wheels on the uneven road.

"Tell me," began the soldier at last, and took hold of the shaft handle with his right hand. "It's all right to tell me...I'm the shepherd here on the farm. The sheep are still out on the moor. Every week I come to get what I need...just start." And then Jürgen told his story.

Just as he began, they came to a crossroads where a hill with overgrowth gave them protection from the wind. Here the soldier stopped, as if that was where he would have to leave them, and remained bent over, his gloomy eyes fixed on Jürgen's lips, while the others sat in the dust of the road, arms on their knees, a beaten army with no goal and no banner.

"Well," he said when Jürgen had finished, and straightened up. "A crusade...well..." And he laughed bitterly, so that his dog looked questioningly at him. Then he bent over again close to Jürgen and looked closely into his eyes. "What did you mean?" he asked earnestly. "You said...it isn't only the arm...and what?"

Jürgen first had to think back. Then he understood. "A piece of the heart must be lost, too, that's how it seems to me," he said very considerately.

The shepherd stood there a while longer, as if he were thinking over what Jürgen had said. Then he gripped the shaft and turned in to the narrow path across the field.

"Come along," he called back to them. "You must sleep warm and well today."

And then they stumbled through the stormy night, following his shadow, not thinking of what was to come, and dead to what had been; nothing but each step as they took it was their destiny for that hour.

Yet, while their souls went along beneath the storm, the soul of the man walking ahead of them was filled with heavy thoughts of the experience of that hour. He had enlisted under the colors as a young and very serious person after having worked hard on that farm. He had gone hungry and cold, had fought, silently and doggedly, as his way was. He had seen many horrors; he had not known that there could be so much blood in the world. Finally they had taken his arm off, and here he was, a wretched man in a land where a man was measured by the strength of his arms; he was becoming gradually filled with the bitterness of the cripple towards the healthy and the satisfied. And since his inner powers were not sufficient to bring him to recognition and reconciliation, he now hurled the burning hatred that had simmered in him at all who came within his field of vision and seemed superior to him; from the farmer who reluctantly tossed half-wages to him, to the pastor who spoke to him about God's mercy.

And, just as the bitterness in his thinking dispelled every kindness, every obligation, that rose up beyond his daily work, so also all that had been, all that still contained a bright memory, fell away, leaving behind only the hatred of the outcast, who in turn cast out of his life everything except the dog, into whose eyes he could look without pain.

So a few hours earlier he had gone to the pastor who had confirmed him, and he had withdrawn from the fellowship of the church with hard words. He had returned through the empty landscape to the farm like a lost man, to pick up his provisions there and then go to tend the sheep for another week.

He could not have said what it was about this group of helpless children that had gripped him and moved him to take them with him into the dark house between forest and moor. Perhaps it was the child's crying, for he had not seen any children, nor even heard their weeping, for a very long time. Perhaps it was the hate of the boy who attacked the farmer with his wooden shaft. Or it was the way the grandson had glanced at his empty sleeve and the words he had said about it.

Not that he was trying, while walking along, to think of how he might give joy to these wretched ones; yet, even in the terrible feeling of loneliness that was his until now, his brow gradually brightened as he heard the tired rolling of the wheels behind him and the stumbling steps of the band as they followed him blindly, as only his dog would do.

The low-roofed stable lay tucked into a stormy part of the forest. Before it, the moor extended in the pale light of night. They saw nothing of it. It was not until the lantern on the ceiling beam swung over stove and table and hayloft, a weak reddish light, which was swallowed up by the bottomless depths of the stable, from which only the heads of the sheep emerged in the foreground—not until then did wonder enter their awakening eyes, and the rigidity of strangeness melt into warmth and security, blossoming into the first smile that this day had brought forth.

The shepherd stood below the lantern, awkward, his eyes still gloomy, dazzled by the radiance which the dim light kindled in so many young eyes. Nothing was to be heard except the occasional movement of many animals, rising up like a gentle wave at the wall in the back and dying away with a push at the threshold; and the chorus of treetops in the storm, whose harmonies flared up and broke on the roof over their heads.

Until little Eva stood up in her wagon and, moved by a childish recollection, sent out into the darkness of the stable the question, "Is that...the stable of Bethlehem?"

No answer came. The shepherd only raised his hand, as if wanting to lay it on her head. But he let it drop again.

"You can lie down in the hay," he said in a rough voice. "Then afterwards you can eat."

They obeyed, after shoving the wagons together. But they did not sleep. They listened to the sounds of

earth in the night, they looked around like children in a strange house, whispering together about the strange things they saw. In their eyes as well as in their voices there was still the echo of their rejection, their terror at being lost on the ocean of the unknown.

But when the fire in the hearth became brighter and warmer, when they saw the one-armed man going back and forth and busying himself with preparations as if for a meal, when the dog let himself be petted and rolled up cosily in the blankets; then the first deep sigh rose out of the abyss of their experience, and quiet laughter flew, like a bird in late autumn, across the softly illumined heads.

The one-armed man did not turn around. He only stopped working stealthily, and bitter thoughts spread their reflection over his furrowed brow. They would be out in the night otherwise, he thought. And the night is not good....

Then Jürgen went up to him and asked to be allowed to help him. "It's not easy with one arm," he added quietly.

"What will your father say when you write that to him?" asked the shepherd.

"I won't write anything to him. Why should he have such worries there? When peace comes, he'll know about everything."

"Peace?" asked the shepherd with a bitter laugh.

"There will never be peace ... it's the same as with your Promised Land."

But Jürgen was very serious. "What is this here?" he asked urgently. "We were wrong. It wasn't there by the gate. Didn't you hear what my little sister said?"

"She talks the way children talk," said the shepherd, dismissing it.

"In those days too it was children who set out," said Jürgen, lost in thought.

"God has died," whispered the shepherd. "Do you understand? They killed Him out there. And when I came back here, I didn't find Him any more. Now one just has to get along somehow."

Jürgen's eyes looked at him full of horror. "How can you say that God has died?" he asked in restrained reproof. "Didn't you bring us here and take us in?"

Then the other fell silent and stepped back, almost as if he himself were now frightened at the boy's words.

After a while, when he was putting the fall vegetables into the water, he asked, with a glance at the hayloft, how many of them there were.

"Twelve," said Jürgen, who had crouched down in front of the fire, head held in his hands just as when he sat at the stove at home in front of the model of the farm. "Twelve," he repeated, looking up. "Don't you know, that's how many we have to be?" And from the moist depths of his exhausted eyes, in which the hearth flames flickered, the light of an altar beamed out on the questioner.

And then he drew his mother's letter out of his pocket, and no longer paid attention to what the other was doing.

The one-armed man, however, felt while he worked as if his blood were pounding in heavy beats and rushing together across his heart. To escape his restlessness, he left the hut without purpose and stood outside in front of the doorstep, turning his bewildered eyes into the night.

The cloud mass was torn up, and he saw the constellations in their old places shining over the moor, just as the outlines of the forest, also unchanged and silent, swung away into the dark and were lost. The storm tugged at his empty coat-sleeve and forced him into cold awareness of the helplessness of his life; yet at the same time his eye saw the reddish rectangular shape made by the lantern inside as it cast the outline of the window into the night. He stepped to the clouded panes and looked in.

He could see straight into the hayloft where the figures of the children were only shadowy shapes as they rested or quietly moved. But where the brightness of their faces was struck by the light, it blossomed before the dark background like the soft radiance of a nativity play. It was as if the reddish light of a star were falling from above through a patched roof, lighting up the age-old story to which the longing of the devout had given its unchangeable form.

Not that the man watching motionless felt anything symbolic about himself and the events of the evening. Perhaps it was even only because the accustomed darkness and bleakness around him had come to life, that he was so unusually affected. Perhaps after the hard experiences of the war and of being cast out from society and the bond with the eternal, this brightening of his life shook him up, as if in one step he were crossing the terrible threshold between hate and tears. But he stood in the lighted square cut out of the night as if blessed, even though the storm made him shudder; and it seemed to him that all this would disappear forever before his eyes if he were to step out of the light into the gloom.

But finally he tore himself away and went back to the doorway. Before raising his hand to the door, however, he turned around and went, face bent downwards, to the little shed where he kept his wood and a few supplies. He ran his hand up the wall, lifted what he found with little trouble from its wooden peg and only then returned to his guests, while his narrow lips smiled, almost embarrassed.

"Meat!" called Andres from the darkness of his shelter. "Eva, there's meat!"

Then they all stood around the fire, hay in their

tumbled hair, blankets still in their hands, staring in silence at the miracle that had come to them out of the night.

"You must have something warm," said the shepherd, as if making excuse. "I had to slaughter it this morning...it's better if you eat it than if he sells it."

"It's a lamb," said Jürgen, raising his shining eyes to him. "Do you see now that He has not died?"

But one could not tell by the shepherd's face whether he had understood. He only seemed not to be able to wait until the meal was ready, because he saw all the children's eyes following his motions; and not until the big feed box had been pushed under the lantern to use for a table and he had hunted up a row of white lime-wood bowls left by the previous shepherd, did a shy smile steal to his mouth.

Then Jürgen roused suddenly and unexpectedly from his trance with the singular demand that after their crusade they must all first wash their feet before they could sit down to the blessed meal. And so insistent and full of deeper meaning did his words sound that not a voice was raised against it. In fact there was even a general movement of joy to be felt, and each one pressed to be the first.

Still, it all took place quite joyfully, without argument or disturbance, as they followed Jürgen's earnest, almost solemn directions. Not until the others were already sitting in the hay again and dressing, and it was his sister's turn, did he raise his eyes unexpectedly to the shepherd, who was looking at Eva's head, lost in thought, and said very quietly, "She is our dearest one....Look at her feet...."

After that they sat down at the table, and the light of the lantern fell on the shining heads as they bent over the happiness of the food as if this was an action of devout piety. Nothing was to be heard but the soft sound of the spoons against the wood, the warning whimpering of the dog and the unseen crowding of animal bodies in the depths of the dark barn.

In this hour the gloomy face of the shepherd was

illuminated by an inward light; and as he let his eyes pass over the children's heads, he felt darkly and with a heavy spirit that the years of war could not have been the highest crest of the wave to which his life had risen; and that even the rustling of the earth under a shining plowshare must have a poorer sound than the blissful breathing of these hungry ones for whom he had prepared a meal.

With this feeling of wonderful transformation he put his arm around Eva, who sat at his right and who, satisfied and tired, had now leaned her head against his shoulder; he stayed like this, gazing with eyes closed into the depths of life which had risen up overnight out of a gray sea before him.

Then, when he had shown each of the children his place in the hay, he quietly stacked the dishes by the fire, laid a few big logs on the dying flames, took the lantern to see about his flock, having put feed before them, and went once more to the door, where he remained standing outside the threshold as before the meal, looking towards the stars which had risen in the east above the forest.

After a while the door near him opened and closed again, and he felt a figure next to him, though in the blackness of the night he could not recognize it.

He was just going to ask the child why he was not sleeping like the others, when he felt a restraining motion of the child's hand on his arm.

He fell silent, knowing that it was the grandchild, whose strange words still filled him.

Now nothing could be perceived but the great course of the storm across the forest and across the moor, under the high stars, and their own soft breathing, which was like a breeze against the black shield that sprang up before their feet and went up to the lights of the sky.

Then the quiet, faraway voice of the boy sounded through the great roaring, and since his face and his figure remained unseen, the words seemed to come from afar as if out of a deep forest or from a great body of water in a fog from which no sound of oars arose.

"And when the hour came," said the voice, "he sat down, and the twelve apostles with him.

"And he said to them: I have earnestly desired to eat of the Easter lamb with you, before I suffer.

"For I tell you that I shall not eat it until it is fulfilled in the kingdom of God.

"And then they held the Lord's Supper together."

After a while the same voice said, only still more quietly, "Do you know now that He has not died?"

But it did not wait for an answer, and only the sound of the door was heard as it opened and closed again.

Before the morning hour, when the constellation of the Big Dipper was already touching the treetops, and the breathing of the children went through the stillness as unchangeably as the rising and falling of an ocean at night, the shepherd got up, after sleepless listening, put his clothing in order in the dark and left the silent house, followed by his dog.

He did not give up until the pastor was awakened—for a cold half-light was just coming over the earth—and then he told about what had happened to him. Not with the manner or intention of spreading out his divine experience before the other, but only with the request that the pastor inform Jürgen's mother in order to spare her anxiety. He also asked the pastor to consider how money might be obtained for the children's return journey by train, and for something to fill their rucksacks and wagons, so that the Promised Land might not seem to them already in their childhood a fairy tale or even a lie. He himself wanted to keep them with him for about a week, unless the farmer should interfere.

The pastor, with moved words, promised to do this, without making the slightest mention of their conversation of yesterday. And the shepherd, already standing on the doorstep, merely said as he started to turn away that in regard to his leaving the church, he would like to think it over some more, if the pastor was not in a hurry about it.

After this the crusaders were in the Promised Land for eight days, and when this time had passed, it no longer seemed strange to them that at home they had been taught about the Redeemer and that He had taken the form of a servant and had borne all sin.

And when they looked out of the windows of the train, back toward the station where the one-armed man stood, only his empty coat-sleeve moving in the wind, they cried as if he might vanish from them, as on the walk to Emmaus, and as if they might never see him in the stony days of their lives.

Yet it suited their childlike souls that every turn of the wheels tore them away from what they had experienced and brought them nearer to the accustomed world of their previous existence. And they used big words to picture to one another how they would return home to their mothers and comrades as travelers afar and victors, and what astonishment there would be about themselves and the wagons of booty with which they would make their entry as if after a great harvest.

And when the unaltered breath of the stony city surrounded them after they had left the train; when the great stillness of the moor was drowned in the noise of wheels, and they parted at a street corner as if after an excursion with parents or teachers, a sobering drop fell into the bowl of brightness which they had carried through the days and nights for so long with solicitous hands. Without their knowing it, the gray light gradually came to their brows, the grayness that lay over the

German land in those days whenever two people at whose hearts destiny had struck looked at each other.

And though Jürgen's brow did not remain free of the shadow of the new earth which again surrounded him, yet he was the only one who returned as a leader the same way he had left: with head held high and filled with a light that could never lose its glow.

And when they again stood at the stove in their home, when their mother hugged them between laughter and

tears, and raised Jürgen's face to her still fearful eyes, he said very seriously, raising his hand to her lips, "Quiet, Mother, you mustn't say anything...we found it, and my eyes have seen the Saviour...."

And then he went quietly to the stove and passed a

careful hand over the model of the farm that still stood there as he had built it, until nothing was to be seen but a level heap of sand on a smooth sheet of iron.

About the author: *In 1938 Wiechert was interned in the Buchenwald concentration camp for five months, an experience which was reflected in his subsequent work.*

ONE STAR ABOVE ALL STARS

ONE STAR A—BOVE ALL STARS SHONE DOWN FROM HEAV'N A——FAR,

IT SHONE IN-TO OUR NIGHT, IT SHONE IN — TO OUR NIGHT.

THE SUN MUST YIELD BE—FORE IT, THE MOON IS DIM AND PAL-LID,

BE—FORE SUCH RA-DIANT LIGHT, BE-FORE SUCH RA-DIANT LIGHT.

ONE STAR ABOVE ALL STARS
SHONE DOWN FROM HEAVEN AFAR,
:IT SHONE INTO OUR NIGHT:
THE SUN MUST YIELD BEFORE IT,
THE MOON IS DIM AND PALLID
:BEFORE SUCH RADIANT LIGHT:

AND WHEN THE NATIONS HAD SEEN
THIS STAR IN HEAVEN RISEN
: SO WONDROUS BRIGHT AND CLEAR:
AS NONE THE SKIES CONTAINÈD,
THEIR HEARTS WITH WONDER TREMBLED
:IN AWE OF THINGS TO COME:

TO BE A CHILD OF MAN
DOWN TO THE EARTH GOD CAME,
:TO MAKE ANEW THE LIFE:
AND DEATH HE CAME TO CONQUER—
FOR THIS SANG ALL CREATION,
:AND EARTH AND HEAVEN REJOICED:

THEN IN ALL LANDS ARE LOOSENED
THE CHAINS AND BONDS OF EVIL,
:THEN BREAKETH EVERY SPELL:
LIGHT COMETH INTO DARKNESS,
THE OLD RULE THEN IS SHATTERED.
: IN GLORY COMES HIS KINGDOM:

THIS IS BELIEVED TO BE THE OLDEST CHRISTMAS SONG FOUND.   MUSIC ADAPTED FROM A TUNE BY JOHANN SEBASTIAN BACH

THE POOR CHILDREN'S CHRISTMAS

by ERNST WIECHERT

There were once two poor children who were brother and sister and had no parents any more. And since they had no relatives living, they had been given to a charcoal burner and his wife who lived deep in the woods, and there they had to help with the charcoal kiln and in the house.

The charcoal burner was a taciturn and gloomy man, but he had a good heart, and now and then he would give them something extra, a basketful of berries or a piece of rye bread with a slice of bacon. But he only did this secretly, for he was afraid of his wife, who was very angry by nature and would have liked best to see the wolf get the two children. For no matter how good they were or how hard they worked, she scolded them from morning to night, saying that they would eat her straw mattress away from under her and that the cat could carry away the work they did.

So the children had a joyless life; they were often hungry, and even more often they were beaten, so that the boy sometimes said that it would be better if they ran away secretly, out into the wide world. But one time when they tried to do this, a big, gray wolf had stood before them in the woods, staring at them out of bloodshot eyes and making circles around them and forcing them in this way closer and closer back to the charcoal burner's hut, like a snake drawing itself more and more tightly together. On the threshold, however, the wolf had disappeared, and there stood the charcoal burner's wife in his place, and the boy saw her quickly wipe blood away from her eyes.

Then they knew that this woman was a witch, and they never tried again to get away from her.

So they went on living in silence and fear and grief, and only in the night they would be of joyful heart for a while. Then they would lie nestled close to each other in the little shed where the cow stood, dig themselves into the warm hay and listen to the cow comfortably chewing her cud and occasionally rattling her iron chain. In the woods the foxes barked, the ice roared in the faraway lake, and a mouse rustled softly in the straw. Then the girl would lay her head on the boy's breast, hear his heartbeat and listen to the stories he told her. In them he always talked about a good fairy and how she gave him a magic sword; and how the two of them then took leave of the frightened charcoal burner and traveled through the woods to a far-off castle, where page boys and servants waited to look after them.

Then the girl smiled gently on the boy's breast, thanked him for the nice story and fell asleep comforted; but her brother still lay awake for a long time, his arm around his little sister, and the figure of the fairy moved further and further away until it disappeared in the darkness of the shed, and his tired eyes closed.

Once, at the time of the winter solstice, winter had fallen even more heavily and severely over the big woods than usual. All the young spruce trees were buried in the snow, the tops of the old trees were bent over, and in the nights the frost split the trees with crackling noises. Then the children shivered where they slept in the night, although the charcoal burner had secretly placed a rough blanket in the hay for them. Their breath froze in front of their mouths, and in the morning the girl's last two tears had stiffened to ice on her cheeks.

Then the brother would clench his fists and vow that the old woman should pay for this before the holy nights of Christmas were over. The girl, however, pacified him and reminded him with loving words of their mother, who would never have lifted her hand to do a wrong.

149

Before the hour of twilight, the charcoal burner signed to them to come to his side and whispered to them that in this night the animals could speak, because it was the Holy Night, and that they should really listen to them, and perhaps some comfort would be told to them through the mouths of these innocent creatures.

They decided to wait up the whole night so as not to miss anything when the cow or the mouse or the old porcupine told about the secrets of the future.

As twilight fell, the boy came out of the woods with a little spruce tree under his arm, and brought it into the kitchen, "because tonight is the Holy Night," he said to the charcoal burner's wife.

The Poor Children's Christmas

She merely took the axe from the wood block without speaking, chopped the green boughs off the little tree and threw them, along with the little tree trunk, into the fire on the hearth. "And because tonight is the Holy Night," she said mockingly, "put on your caps, go into the woods and bring home enough dry wood for all the holy nights. And if what you bring isn't enough you will have to kneel out in the yard until you yourselves are frozen to wood!"

The children were very frightened, for the first stars were already showing above the woods and the snow lay many feet deep above the dry twigs, and it was freezing so hard that the pine tree trunks in the woods split apart with loud cracking.

Then the boy, wild-eyed, went stealthily to the wood block and took the axe in his hand; but his sister held his hands firmly and looked at him imploringly, so that his strength wilted.

"Then let's die together in the snow," he said gloomily, took his sister by the hand and went out of the hut.

They first went and stood a while in the stall and listened in case one of the animals might speak to them. But when everything remained silent and only the field mouse rustled in the straw, he tied on his sister's snowshoes and his own, which he had woven of willow branches, took her by the hand, and then they went slowly into the darkness of the tall firs.

151

The stars trembled above them like thousands of candles, and it was so cold that they shuddered with the frost and saw their breath in front of them like a silver fog. The moon stood white and icy above the black treetops, and when the snow dropped down from the deeply bent boughs it looked as if invisible hands were throwing silver dust over the woods.

The girl cried softly, but the boy comforted her. "Let us go as far as the clearing where the charcoal burner feeds the deer," said the boy. "There we can dig ourselves a deep bed in the snow and imagine that we are lying in a white bed and that the fairy is strewing apples and nuts on our blanket. And then we'll go to sleep together and never go back to the bad woman again."

But before they came to the clearing, a little squirrel slid down the trunk of an ancient fir tree, so that it was cloaked in a silver cloud, sat on the lowest branch, looked at them with its intelligent eyes and said, "Look at the evening star over the clearing. It is the brightest star in the firmament and shines very white without flickering. That is the one you must keep following."

The children were quite amazed, for they had never heard a squirrel talk. But they remembered the words of the charcoal burner and they also saw the bright star above the woods. And after the boy had rubbed the girl's face with snow so that her cheeks would not freeze, they got up with new hope and went on.

152

When they came to the clearing, a deer was standing there tugging at the bundle of hay which the charcoal burner had left there for the hungry animals. It did not run away as usual, but looked quietly at them with moist eyes and said, "Be sure not to lose sight of the star, and be courageous, no matter what comes your way!"

They thanked the deer and then they came to an oak wood where it was quite light and the star hung clear and radiant before them in the leafless branches.

But when they had gone a little further and the girl was staggering from tiredness and cold, suddenly a gray animal stood before them, looking at them out of glowing eyes; and they saw that it was a wolf.

The girl began to cry; but the boy held her firmly by the hand and went fearlessly toward the animal, which stood without moving and cast no shadow. "Do you see the star?" he said loudly, "the holy star that shines on all poor people and invites them to the banquet?"

And he did not know how it came that just these words passed his lips.

But when he had said them, the wolf uttered a dull cry and crept, close to the ground, back into the thicket, as if an unseen bullet had paralyzed its back.

"Do you see now," said the boy, "that it is our star and that its power is greater than that of the wicked woman?"

And just as they were leaving the oak wood and were about to walk in among the black fir trees again, an owl came flying noiselessly over them, so that its black shadow frightened them; it sat on a low branch and looked at them with its fiery eyes.

"Are you going to say something to us too?" asked the boy. "See, my sister can't go on any longer now, and the star is still far away."

The owl leaned over on its branch and said,

"For the poor, for the poor
Cares the holy child's own hand."

Then the boy lifted his sister up onto his shoulders, because she could not move her feet any more, and while he painfully toiled onward through the deep snow he rubbed her hands to keep them warm. He protected her feet with his coat, next to his heart.

The owl flew along above them for a little distance, and noiselessly stretching out its soft wings called down to them,

"It shall heal all, it shall heal all,
The holy child's own hand."

But the star always remained just as bright and just as far away above the woods, and the boy's heart sank as he thought that perhaps he would still have to wander like this through the deep snow for half the night.

But just as he began to reel and thought that the best thing would be to let himself and his sister fall down into the snow, she called out softly and said, "A light! A light! I see a light."

Then the boy also saw before him below the fir trees a reddish glimmer burning quietly and comfortingly through the night; it was like a square coming out of a little window.

He went forward with new strength, and when his knees were about to give way, the girl laid her stiffened hands about his cheeks and said, "Dearest brother, only a few steps more! I see the holy child's own hand."

And there was the hut before them, and they had never seen it before. The roof hung low over the little window and was so deeply covered with snow that it seemed bent. But the light shone out from under it with wonderful quietness, and when they came quite close they saw that in front of it many deer and rabbits and badgers and birds were gathered, and before them they had the kinds of food they liked best. The animals looked trustingly at them and said, "Now the bitterest night has ended; now the fire is burning to warm your tired feet."

The boy knocked softly on the door, but hardly had his hand touched the cool wood when he sank on his knees because his feet would no longer carry him. And when the door opened and the man with the gray beard stood between the doorposts, he had to stretch out his arms to stop the brother and sister from falling at his

156

feet. He carried them in one at a time and laid them in the hay that filled one corner of the hut; and in the hay peacefully stood a gray donkey, who began to lick their benumbed fingers with his tongue.

They lay there quite still now until the snow and ice melted from their eyes; and since it still seemed to them as if they were dreaming, they kept their arms just as closely around each other as they used to do at home in their cold shed. The girl nestled her head against the brother's breast and listened to his heart beating fast and heavily.

Later, when they were able to open their eyes, they could hardly believe what they saw, for never had they seen anything of the kind, not even in their most beautiful dreams.

The hut was probably no bigger than the charcoal burner's hut at home, but in the stove a bright fire was burning that strewed its sparks out onto the floor boards and filled the whole room with a wonderful, reddish light. In this light gleamed the black beams that supported the roof, and the golden apples and nuts that hung from a little fir tree standing on an oak block next to the stove.

Before the fire sat the man with the gray beard, smoking a short pipe and carving at a child's toy that looked small and fragile in his rough hands. In a corner by the wall sat a young woman in front of a cradle,

and the woman's hair was as if spun of gold, so that the glow from the fire stood around her brow like a band of light.

But most beautiful of all was the child that lay in the cradle. It wore no dress or shirt, and its big eyes were turned toward the ceiling. It was quite small, but it seemed to the brother and sister as if all the light in the hut was gathered about the tiny figure and as if all else was there in order to gather this light and to lay it in the little hands. Never yet had they seen anything so beautiful, and they raised themselves with their painful and stiffened limbs so as to see the child better.

Then the woman said, without moving her eyes away from the child, "Now you can bring them to me."

The man laid his pipe and the toy on the edge of the hearth, went smiling to the children, took one after the other in his strong arms and carried them to the cradle, where he laid them carefully on the ground. And when he had taken off their mittens and shoes and stockings, the children saw with fear that their hands and feet were frozen all white and lifeless.

They began to cry, got up on their knees and raised their folded hands to the woman. She only smiled, however, and when she turned her eyes to the children, all the pain disappeared from their limbs.

Then she took the girl up into her lap and laid the tiny hands of the child in the cradle first on the girl's frozen hands and then on her feet. Scarcely had she done this when the blood returned to her numbed limbs, and with the blood the life came back, and she stood on her feet again as before.

Then the girl knelt down before the woman, laid her face in her lap and said, "Now help my brother too, for he carried me and warmed my feet with his heart."

The woman looked at the boy for a while and said, "Your hands and your feet and your heart have done what is good; but wasn't it only a short time ago that you wanted to take the axe to kill?"

The boy reddened and confessed it; but he also told about how much they had suffered and that he had not known of any other way out but this.

"We do not know," said the woman, "whether a way out of our need is not already prepared; and so long as we do not know, our hands must do no wrong. If you had killed, all this would have disappeared, the hut and we and the child. Only the love you bore to your sister held up this roof, and for the sake of this love you will be healed."

And she took the child's hands and laid them on the boy's hands, and slowly the life returned to them, but much more slowly than it had to his sister. And it was the same way with his feet.

Then the boy said, still kneeling before her, "Who are you, and who is the child, that it can heal dead limbs? And why is this hut standing here that I have never seen before, though I have often been in this place in the woods?"

The woman stroked the damp hair away from his forehead and said smiling, "This hut always stands wherever a loving child looks out for another. And if you had not protected your sister's feet next to your heart, you would not have seen the hut. But we three bear no name. We are love, and that is all."

But when she had said this they heard the animals outside running away over the hard snow, and they saw the bolt on the door moving. And even before the old man could take the pipe out of his mouth and stand up, the door opened and the gray wolf stepped over the threshold.

The girl cried out and fled to the woman's lap; but the latter stayed where she was and looked smiling toward the wild animal. And when it came nearer and directed its bloodshot eyes toward the girl's head, the woman took the child's tiny hand and laid it on the wolf's head. "This shall be the end of you for all time," she said.

And the animal's body trembled, so that all its gray hairs stood on end, and before the time of a heartbeat had passed it collapsed, and in its place there stood an oak block such as people use for chopping wood. The man took this and carried it in front of the fire, laid dry wood on it, took an axe in his hand and split the wood. And although the block shook with each blow, it remained where it had been placed and did not move.

"Don't you want to do it for me?" asked the man of the boy.

But the boy shook his head. "Even if she is dead," he said softly, "I still wouldn't like to do it."

Then the woman once again stroked his hair from his forehead and said, "That is good; now you two can stay with us and serve us."

When the fire in the stove was burning brightly, the man set a pan with milk on the fire and out of a little bag he shook into it something that was unknown to them, something with a fragrance that penetrated the whole hut. And the woman filled a big bowl with apples and nuts and cookies, and the donkey came out of his corner and looked at the man over his shoulder as if he quite belonged to the household. And the porcupine came out of its corner and drank from the bowl of milk that the old man set in front of it. The two children quietly held hands and did not know whether they were waking or dreaming.

When they had had something to eat and drink, and the golden shining nuts were gleaming, the boy gave a deep sigh and asked when they would have to go back home.

The old man smiled and said, "The first thing

163

tomorrow morning we will journey on; and wherever we journey to, there will be your home."

"I shall never forget this night," said the boy, "for it has been the most beautiful in my whole life." And he went to the door once more and looked up at the stars that twinkled in the icy space of heaven. And he saw the tracks of his snowshoes that led to the hut; they were pressed deep into the snow, and he shuddered when he thought of his wandering.

The man made them a place to sleep in the hay, and the donkey lay down beside them and warmed them. The fire slowly went out in the stove, and only the golden nuts on the little fir tree glinted now and then as if a warm wind were stroking them.

Yet when it had become completely dark, something still gleamed brightly about the cradle and the child, as if a light were behind them or as if the bright star were shining through the snow-covered roof down on the little life below.

The girl put her arms around her brother as she used to do and whispered into his ear, "So the good fairy came after all and freed us from all our suffering, even if she didn't bring you a sword."

"But she brought something else," answered the boy just as softly, "and that was only because you held onto my hands when they wanted to take hold of the axe."

"And I know what the child's name is, too," whispered the girl after a while.

"What is it then?"

"Its name is Peace."

"That is a wonderful name," said the boy after a while. Then they happily fell asleep. The last one was the porcupine, which rolled itself up in front of the hearth, and its quills shone softly when the ashes fell apart and the glowing coals gleamed from the little door of the stove.

COME, OH COME, DEAR CHILDREN ALL

GOTTLIEBIN DITTUS   JOHANN CHRISTOPH BLUMHARDT

COME, OH COME, DEAR CHILDREN ALL;
COME TOGETHER, GREAT AND SMALL;
CHRIST OUR LORD COMES TO YOUR DOOR,
CHRIST WHO LOVES YOU MORE AND MORE.

YOU HAVE SURELY PLANNED THE WAY
YOU WILL WELCOME IN CHRIST'S DAY;
YET CONSIDER IT ANEW,
IF YOUR WAY BE RIGHT AND TRUE.

CHRISTMAS IS NOT OUTWARD SHOW,
EVEN WHEN THE CANDLES GLOW —
WHEN THE GIFTS AND CHRISTMAS TREE
FILL OUR HEARTS AND ROOMS WITH GLEE.

IF TO TRUE JOY YOU WOULD COME,
MAKE YOUR LITTLE HEART MY HOME.
LET IT BE A CRADLE SMALL
WHERE MAY LIVE THE LORD OF ALL.

166

WHEN YOUR HEART IS PROUD AND VAIN,
OUTWARD SHOW WILL CAUSE ME PAIN;
IS YOUR HEART A STABLE LOW?
THEREIN I SHALL FEEL THE GLOW.

GLADLY WOULD I ENTER THERE,
OX AND ASS'S STABLE SHARE;
IS A PALACE IN YOUR BREAST?
THERE I'D FIND NO PEACE NOR REST.

SO DESTROY YOUR PRIDEFUL HEART,
IN ITS SIN I'LL HAVE NO PART;
MAKE OF IT A STABLE POOR,
THEN I'LL ENTER AT YOUR DOOR.

NOW CAN CHRISTMAS DAY BEGIN,
PERFECT JOY FILLS ALL WITHIN;
WHEN I COME TO BE YOUR GUEST
RICH ARE YOU, AND RICHLY BLEST.

WHEN THROUGH YOU A LIVING LIGHT
BREAKS AWAY FROM EARTH'S DARK NIGHT,
THEN CHRIST'S DAY WE SOON MAY SING;
JOY THROUGH ALL THE EARTH WILL RING.

O HOW BRIGHT THAT DAY WILL DAWN,
WHEN THE WORLD GREETS CHRISTMAS MORN,
AND GOD'S SHINING COUNTENANCE
FILLS ALL HEARTS WITH RADIANCE.

SONGS SHALL TURN TO JOYFUL CRIES
WHEN WE SEE BEFORE OUR EYES
HOW CHRIST'S DAY HAS BEEN PREPARED,
JOY WITH ALL CREATION SHARED.

AMEN, YES, SO LET IT BE.
SAVIOUR, WE BELONG TO THEE,
COME INTO OUR STALL TONIGHT;
FILL IT WITH THY LIVING LIGHT.

THE ANGEL'S SONG

told by MARIE ONNEN

nce upon a time on Christmas Day the angel Gabriel called a little angel to him and asked him to gather all the holy angels together.

The little angel flew over the heavens blowing his trumpet, and every angel who heard it hastened to respond to his call.

And the angel Gabriel said: "Today we are all going to the earth. I hope you remember that when our Lord Jesus Christ was born on earth to live and to die to save sinners, we the angels, taught the people a beautiful song. Many of them sing the song about God's peace and his goodwill which we taught them. Now Jesus wants us to listen to men's hearts. Every song that is sung today to the glory of God and for no other reason should be brought up to the throne of God."

168

Then all the holy angels sang a song to the glory of God and then flew down to the earth as Jesus had commanded.

And the heart of the little angel, who had gathered the holy angels together with his trumpet, beat loudly because he had been found worthy to go with them down to the earth. He saw that they scattered to the North, the South, the East and the West, and he hurried after them so as not to be late. Suddenly he felt the touch of a tender hand and he saw that the angel Gabriel was flying at his side. Gabriel said to him, "I see the desire to do what Jesus has commanded is shining in your eyes. You expect that everywhere on earth

169

you will hear songs to the glory of God and all you will have to do will just be to carry them up to God's throne. Don't you know that the earth is still dark and that the task we have received from Jesus is a very difficult one? You know, don't you, that the people killed Jesus when he was on earth and that even now they do not love the Son of God who taught us that we should love all men because we are all brothers and sisters, children of God our Father, our creator."

Then the little angel was very sad and said, "But the angel's song stayed on earth. You yourself said it was sung everywhere. Shall I not find any? Do you really think that I shall have to return to heaven with empty hands?"

"I do not wish to discourage you," Gabriel said, "only to warn you that the task will be difficult. You must be patient and you must listen very, very carefully." He had scarcely finished speaking when they reached the earth.

"Now you must continue your way without me," said Gabriel. "I must go where there is a lot of misery and that would be too sad for someone like you coming to the earth for the first time."

So the little angel went on his journey alone and came to a place that was very quiet and lonely. "I will look here," he thought, "maybe here, where all is quiet there will be some singing to the glory of God."

He flew to a town and saw a lot of people walking in the streets; feeble lights shone from many of the houses. When the little angel grew accustomed to the darkness of the earth, he saw that the lights came from the candles on the Christmas trees in the people's houses. His heart beat for joy because where Christmas trees were lit up people were sure to speak about Jesus and sing to the glory of God. The little angel flew hurriedly into one of the houses and listened. Yet he had hardly entered when all the lights seemed to grow dim and it seemed as if he had strayed into a dark night, like being in an oven. And in this gloom he heard the voices of children quarreling over their toys.

"Oh," he thought, "everything could be so nice and

happy here and yet there is neither light nor singing!"
and he went out of the house with a heavy heart.

He flew further on and came into a large room where
a huge Christmas tree was lit from top to bottom. "I
shall be sure to find the song here," thought the little angel and hovered hopefully above the heads of the people
in the room. But looking down he noticed that the candle
flames seemed to be growing smaller and smaller. He
heard the people laughing and talking and obviously
no one noticed that the room was getting dark. Suddenly there was the sound of music and singing, but it
was so out of tune that the little angel fled. There was
not one note here to the glory of God; one hardly dared
think of God here. His heart became sadder and sadder.
Was there no song on earth that he could take to heaven?

Slowly he flew on and suddenly he saw another light.
As he drew near he saw that it was coming from a church
and he heard the bells ringing so joyfully and hopefully
that he took courage again and began to look at the
people who were going to church—a long procession
of little black figures. The little angel knew at once
that they were orphan girls who were going to church.
The little angel was so certain that he would find what
he sought·that he decided to listen to what the children
were saying to one another. But he winced as he began
to listen, for the bigger girls at the end of the row were
saying, "We are going to sing in church tonight. *We* sing

better than the town choir; *we* have been chosen. You'll see how *we* shall be admired—perhaps we shall be given some nice presents...."

The little angel was so sad about all that he had heard. Grown-ups and children were singing for their own glory and their own pleasure and not thinking at all about Jesus and his great love. So he went into the church and sat in a seat right at the very back. He thought to himself, "Oh, dear, I shall have to go before the throne of God with empty hands because I cannot find a song sung to his glory anywhere," and he covered his face with his wings and wept. People sang. Yes, people sing on earth but only with their lips and not with their hearts. The service in the church was almost over and the little angel still hoped to hear a hymn sung to the glory of God.

Listen! Is that the organ playing the song of the angels? The organ pealed forth, and suddenly a pure clear voice is heard singing, "Glory to God in the highest."

The little angel leapt up for joy! But ah! As suddenly as the singing started it ceased and the little angel knew that it was one of the orphan girls. He noticed the little bent head between the other girls and thought he would listen at that heart. He hurried up to the pews near the organ. But then he saw the children were splitting their sides with laughter, and one of them whispered to a smaller child, "You are sure to be sent to bed for being

173

so stupid."

The small child blushed and looked round terrified. The angel listened hard but he heard nothing more, so he bent nearer and the little heart said, "Now they are all laughing at me and it is all my fault." And the angel saw that the little girl was ashamed and dared not raise her eyes any more, and again he was very sad. "There is no one on earth who can sing the angel's song," he thought; and he fled from the church.

He hurried to the outskirts of the town and no longer wished to meet anyone or listen to the voice of a child.

He flew into the country and came to an open field. Looking up into the sky at the stars shining so peacefully he was filled with such a longing to be back there that he found it almost impossible to stay on the earth any longer. But, looking at his empty hands, he had not the courage to appear like that before God. So he wandered about in the darkness for a long time not knowing what to do. At last he came to a dark wood and there he sat down on the trunk of a tree and wept quietly.... While he was crying, a light drew softly nearer and nearer, but the sad little angel did not notice it until it was close to him. Then a gentle voice said, "What are you doing here? Have you been sent to this place?"

The little angel hung his head and said, "I looked and listened everywhere, but I could not find a song sung to the glory of God anywhere. The earth is dark; I am afraid to stay here and yet I am afraid to go back to heaven. Look at my hands, they are empty and I have nothing to lay before the throne of God."

"Have you found absolutely nothing?" asked Gabriel. "Nothing, except one note from a little girl who sang alone in a big church. I trembled with joy because the voice was pure and came straight from the heart, but when I drew near the child so as to catch the song and take it up to heaven, her voice was silent and her heart was only thinking about earthly things. Her heart was ashamed of the pure, simple sound she had sung. Oh, it is so sad." The little angel buried his head in his hands and wept because of the wickedness of men.

The angel Gabriel, who is God's chief servant and who had already been to the earth many times before, put his hand on the bent little head and asked, "Why are you so discouraged? Did I not tell you beforehand that it was a difficult task? Have you forgotten that he who is chosen to bring up to heaven the angel's song sung by someone on earth has to listen carefully, yes,

very carefully? Because you did not immediately find what you were looking for you fled, instead of staying and believing with your whole heart that you would find the angel's song in men's homes. Come back with me and I will show you how to listen." Then the two angels flew back to the town. And the angel Gabriel said, "Now, I will take you with me back *into the past:* all you see and hear you must keep in your heart,— then you will certainly find a song sung to the glory of God."

He passed his hand lightly over the little angel's eyes and he found himself in a house. Everything was simple but well cared for. A cheery fire burned in the grate and flowers in red pots on the window-sill gave a cheerful look to the whole room. It was wonderfully quiet. As the little angel looked more carefully, he saw a cradle standing in a corner with a little baby girl lying in it, looking round with large and wondering eyes. Two people were bent over the cradle. They looked at the child, and then at one another, and smiled. The man spoke and said, "This is our child's first Christmas. Let us sing the Christmas song! She is still very tiny, but it is never too early to learn about Jesus."

Then the parents sang the angel's song and it sounded so joyful and pure that the little angel wept and thought, "They sing from thankful hearts to the glory of God." He wanted to take the song with him but he suddenly realized that he was only seeing a vision of the past and that he was really still flying beside Gabriel above the big town.

"Oh!" he exclaimed, "it was only a dream! I thought I had found the song, but now it is nothing!" Gabriel did not answer. Again he passed his hand lightly over the eyes of the little angel so that again he saw a vision of the past. He thought he was on the earth again, but this time in a dark street. There were crowds of people about and a lot of noise. His eyes were drawn irresistibly to one spot where, just in front of a shop window, a young woman was standing, holding a little girl by the hand. They stood there quietly for some time as though not noticing the noise going on around them. The little angel made up his mind to follow them. They went into the shop, bought some things, and then went out on their way up the dark street. At last they stopped in front of a house which they entered. The woman carried the child up the steep staircase and put her down in front of one of the many doors. Then she opened the door and, entering, lit the lamp and stirred the fire. With surprise the little angel recognized the woman. She was the one he had seen bending over the cradle. Now he saw that she was dressed as neatly as ever. He recognized the furniture, but there were no flowers. The room was even simpler and poorer than before; the woman was pale, her eyes were sad, and her dress was drab and poor.

Once in the room, the little girl began to trot about on her fat little legs. "Mummy," she asked, "when is it Christmas Eve?" Taking the little one in her arms, the young woman went to the wall and stood before the picture of a young man. "Look, my child," she said, "look at your father! Tomorrow he will be singing the Christmas song in heaven to the glory of God and we will sing it on earth." The little angel heard the sound of a sob but in it he perceived a rare, pure tone. He bent his head with reverence and whispered, "A grieved heart that sings to the glory of God."

Scarcely had he thought this when, looking up, he saw that he was still flying by the side of Gabriel above the town. He was so disappointed that he could not speak. He had only been looking into the past and so he could not take the song up to God. But Gabriel looked at him so kindly and reassuringly that he did not feel so disappointed. Instead he felt a great longing to know what happened to the woman and her child.

Again, Gabriel passed his hand over the little angel's eyes and again he thought he was on the earth. This time he was in the room of a patient in hospital. The talking and noise of the large ward penetrated into the quiet room where a young woman lay. Her eyes were closed and her features drawn with pain. A nurse was sitting by the side of the bed with a child on her knee and the child seemed to be very anxious as she looked at the sick woman. The angel of death also stood by the bedside but the nurse and the child did not see him although the sick woman felt his presence. She opened her eyes and looked at the child. "Dearie," she whispered, "tomorrow your Mummy will sing the angel's song in heaven and you—you must sing it on earth. Promise me, dear, that you will only sing it to the glory of God."

The child stroked her mother's hand. Perhaps she did not hear what her mother said or perhaps she did not understand, but she answered, "Mummy, I know the song so well, I can sing it now." And without waiting for an answer, she sang it right through, and the angel realized that the child was not singing alone—the heart of the woman sang with her—and then, the vision vanished.

The angel Gabriel, who was still beside the little angel, said, "Look down at this large house beneath us. You must go in there and stay there until you have found a song that you can take up to the throne of God."

So the little angel flew down and was soon in one of the large rooms of an orphanage. There was a beautiful Christmas tree in the middle of the room. Little boys and girls were sitting round it, laughing and chattering. Some were reading, others playing or talking about Christmas. People came and went, giving cakes and sweets to the children. The little angel thought to himself, "I wonder why I have been sent here. I can't hear anything. No one is thinking about the birth of Christ. But still I will have patience. I'll stay and wait." He sat down in a corner of the room and looked around. It seemed as if he were waiting a very, very long time, and when he found himself doubting whether he would find a song, he thought that the orphan house must surely be larger than just this one room. So he flew through all the rooms and corridors and at last came to one of the dormitories where rows of white beds were

standing along the walls. A little girl was lying in one of them and, drawing nearer, he saw that she was grieving. Moved by pity he bent over her, but of course she did not know he was there. She stared into the darkness with her great sad eyes.

At that moment the door of the dormitory opened and an elderly woman entered. She walked up to the bed and spoke. "Why are you not downstairs in the hall where the Christmas tree is so beautiful and where everybody is so happy with our presents? Come now, jump out of bed and come with me." But the little girl shook her head vehemently and would not get up. "Are you afraid of being laughed at for what happened tonight in church?" "No, it is not that," whispered the child. "Can't you tell me then? What is the matter?" But a sob was the only answer. "My child, now that your own mother has gone to heaven, God has brought you here. It is he who has put me in the place of your own mother. Can't you trust me a little?"

The little figure sat up. She leaned her head against the woman's shoulder and said, "Was it he who brought me here? Does he want me to be your child?"

"Yes, I really believe so."

Again there was silence. Then the child began to speak. "My own Mummy died on Christmas Eve. I still remember it very well. It happened in a hospital. I sat on the nurse's knee and had to sing the angel's song. Mummy said something about it that I did not quite understand but still I remembered it. Now I understand it all very well. Mummy said that it should only be sung to the glory of God. Since she died, I have often sung it and I always meant just to think about Jesus and sing it to the glory of God, but really I sang it to be honored by people. All I thought about was how to sing well and be praised, and yet I always wanted something else, although I did not know what."

The little angel kept quite still and listened and a lively hope filled his heart. The little girl continued, "As we were going to church we all said that the whole congregation would listen to us, and I was so proud that we could sing so well. I only thought of men, not God. The church service was almost over when suddenly the organ began to play the angel's song, and at the same time I thought of Mummy and her last words. I remembered that she was singing to the glory of God in heaven and that I should do the same on earth. I clean forgot that I was in church and I just sang with the organ. But as soon as I had sung one phrase I realized where I was. Everybody looked at me and all the children laughed. So I stopped singing. Now Christmas is almost over and I still haven't kept my promise."

When the little girl had finished speaking, the mother gave her a hug and kissed her. "Christmas is not yet over and there is still time to put right what we have done wrong. Oh my child, we all have to feel ashamed of thinking more of men than of God." And the mother of the orphanage folded her hands and prayed with the child.

"Now," she said, "come along and we will sing as we should—you and I and all the others."

Trembling for joy, the little angel followed them into the hall. Everybody was quiet as they entered, for they both had such earnest yet joyous faces that you couldn't help looking at them.

Then the mother told the little girl's story, and she also told about the love of God and the birth of Jesus. Last of all she told them about the angel's song and how men sang it. She did this in such a way that all the children wanted to sing the song to the glory of God, just like the angels.

The father of the orphanage began to play on the organ, and with everyone standing there quietly and reverently, the little girl sang the song and this time she sang it wholeheartedly to the glory of God.

It seemed to the little angel as if the hall were growing lighter every minute and as if it were filled with pure and lovely music. When the song was ended, he hovered over the heads of the children and then, with a cry of joy, rose up to the throne of God.

Here all the angels were assembled once more. With thankful hearts they laid at God's feet the songs they had brought from the earth. There were hymns sung in

the field, sung in narrow streets, and sung by poor
people, and there were also those sung by rich and
eminent men. It was a brilliant and varied array.

The last to arrive before God's throne was the little

angel. He bowed reverently and laid the child's song at
God's feet as a pearl of great price.

heaven's gate has opened

ENGLISH by
INGE PEINLICH

SHEPHERDS' CHRISTMAS SONG
OBERINN VALLEY, AUSTRIA

NOW HEAVEN'S GATE IS O-PENED; WE HEAR THE JOYOUS SHOUT;

SEE AN-GEL BOYS AND AN-GEL GIRLS A-ROLL-ING IN AND OUT!

FOR EV-'RY BOY AND EV-'RY GIRL IS SOM-ER-SAULT-ING IN A WHIRL,,

FIRST UP AND THEN DOWN AND NOW HERE AND NOW THERE, SO GRACEFULLY

AND JOY-OUS-LY THEY'RE TURN-ING EV-'RY-WHERE, WHERE. HAL-LE-LU-JA, HAL-

LE - LU - JA, HAL - LE - LU - JA, HAL - LE - LU - JA.

NOW HEAVEN'S GATE HAS OPENED;
WE HEAR THE JOYOUS SHOUT;
SEE ANGEL BOYS AND ANGEL GIRLS
A-ROLLING IN AND OUT!
FOR EV'RY BOY AND EV'RY GIRL
IS SOMERSAULTING IN A WHIRL
FIRST UP AND THEN DOWN
AND NOW HERE AND NOW THERE-
SO GRACEFULLY AND JOYOUSLY
THEY'RE TURNING EVERYWHERE.

NOW, FRIENDS, LET'S GET TOGETHER
TO BE THE FIRST OF ALL
TO FIND AND SEE THE HOLY CHILD
A-LYING IN THE STALL:
'SAY, LITTLE BOY, SO GAY & SWEET,
DO YOU WANT ANYTHING TO EAT?
SOME APPLES OR PEARS
OR SOME NUTS OR SOME CHEESE,
OR PORRIDGE FULL OF PLUMS
& ANY OTHER FRUIT YOU PLEASE?'

187

HALLELU-NEIN

by MARIA BERG

*The story of the Naughty Little Angel who Sang
Hallelu-Nein instead of Hallelu-ja*

n a wonderful summer evening, in the middle of the seventh heaven, it happened that God the Father lifted his head and knitted his brow. He had been sitting the whole day long on his shining throne, smiling quietly to himself, and under his eyes a clear Sunday had gone by, giving joy to all good people. Now the angels were outdoing themselves in singing Hallelu-ja. The big and powerful angels, these shining princes and mighty ones of heaven, had voices like booming organs and resounding trombones. The little angels, these tots with their little wing-buds, sang like violins and pipes, twittering and brisk as a flight of finches.

188

Hallelu-nein

Now, as evening descended and the stars flamed upwards to God's feet, the little angels knew it was bedtime. But before that they had climbed up, many hundreds of them, on the Hallelu-ja steps, which are Jacob's ladder, those Biblical steps made of marble clouds with golden edges, which lead from the first to the seventh heaven and reach even higher.

The big angels never sleep. They have many tasks and errands and often go up and down the ladder, their robes sweeping over the steps and their golden armor clashing. The smallest angels fringe both sides of the steps every evening. They sit there like rows of organ pipes, little arms around their knees, and watch how gently the sun goes down and the moon-ship rises, and they sing their evening song, their Hallelu-ja. Sometimes, when the sky is pearly pink at sunset-time, their singing can be heard on the earth.

But that evening something was not in order—there was unrest through all the seven heavens, and no one knew why. Weren't the little angels singing as usual? Of course they were, they were singing beautifully. Yet as the big angels listened more and more sharply, a misgiving came into their beautiful earnest eyes. Michael, the mighty angel in the blazing armor, shook his head and whispered to his nearest companion, "Do you hear? There is some discord in the little ones' singing. One little angel is singing out of tune."

"Out of tune? I don't think so. But something is wrong with the beat." The big angels continued to wonder. They would gladly have stopped the trouble before it could disturb the heavenly Father—but it was too late. God had already raised his head from his hands, and the blue lightning of his eyes shot up and down the

Hallelu-ja steps. His lips opened: "There is a little angel sitting down there who keeps singing Hallelu-nein instead of Hallelu-ja. Bring me the rascal!" Thus spoke God and he hid a smile. He even tried to deepen his frown to add severity to his goodness. The trembling of his brow made the heavens shake—thousands of wings began to roar and Michael's sword came out of its sheath with a flash. Hallelu-nein? Yes, now you could hear it clearly. Hundreds of little angels were singing Hallelu-ja diligently and well, like good children who have learned their lesson, but one little voice, ever so high and sharp, squeaked up to the heights: "Hallelu-nein, Hallelu-u-ui-nein."

How cheeky it sounded! How defiant and self-willed! The big angels froze with horror. Was this not a declaration of war on the great traditional Hallelu-ja that had rung out through eternity? This wicked, rebellious Hallelu-nein, where did it come from? Had it crept in from the earth where, alas, men only too often say "nein" when God would so much rather hear an obedient "ja"?

Indignantly the angels hastened to look for the little sinner. Cherubim and seraphim fluttered up and down excitedly, and the Hallelu-ja ladder shook under their step. And sure enough, there on the lowest step crouched a little angel, a tiny mite with wild, bristly ginger hair forming a stubborn tuft on his head. All the other small angels had soft, silky curls, but this one looked like a hedgehog, he was so prickly. The little rascal looked calmly up into the faces of the tall angels. "Hallelu-nein," he squeaked energetically. The angels looked at each other and shook their heads, stunned at such impertinence. But then they grew impatient. Michael, stretching out his shining arm in its golden armor, grasped the little angel by his belt. "Nein," he screamed, kicking his little legs. "Hallelu-nein!"

What a crosspatch! Michael's face became red and hot with indignation. "Wait, you little scoundrel!" With one movement of his wings, Michael flew up through all the seven heavens and stood before God's countenance. He put the little angel down. Oh, how small and miserable he looked in the sight of God's glory, trembling in his thin garment as if touched by the cold of the universe! And yet he shouted again, "Hallelui-ui-ui-nein!"

The angels' flaming faces went pale with fright. Had they ever experienced such cheek? Certainly, once, many billions of light-years ago, there had been a great revolution in heaven. At that time thousands and thousands of magnificent, powerful angels had changed their Hallelu-ja into Hallelu-nein, and Lucifer, the light-bearer, had been their leader. Ever since that hour there had come into the world that evil, hateful destructive "nein." And now this little angel, this unfortunate imp, had become infected with it. How dreadful!

Wrathful and yet weeping, the angels looked at their little brother. Many covered their eyes with their wings in order not to see this tiny, wicked creature hurled into the abyss with one wave of God's hand. But the heavenly Father's voice suddenly resounded, like a very deep, resonant bell.

"What has come over you, little one? Who taught you this bad word?"

The little angel swallowed a little, and then said bravely, "No one—it has been in my heart for a long time."

"Really? So you belong to that sort, do you?" God the Father looked down thoughtfully at the tousled little head and was silent for a time. A smile was waiting behind his eyes, but no one saw it. "Try once more," he said in a fatherly way, "it is quite easy. Hallelui-ja. Hallelui-ui-ui-ja!"

"No," sobbed the little angel. "I can't—it always turns into Hallelu-ui-ui-nein. It just comes out by itself."

" That is bad." God the Father shook his head. "Then we will have to think of other ways for you to learn it again, your own Hallelu-ja."

Then Michael stepped forward, flaming in holy wrath. "God our Father!" he said. "Great King of all realms! Why do you not crush this evil little serpent? Why do you tolerate his presence in your heaven? He does not deserve one further word from you! Leave him to me. I shall soon teach him a right and proper Hallelu-ja!"

But God the Father lifted a restraining hand. "Michael," he said reprovingly. "What do you think? Do you imagine I want a host of slaves in my heavens who only sing Hallelu-ja because they fear you and the edge of your sword? No. I want to be honored and served in freedom and love, right down to the smallest angel. And if it pleases me, the hour will also come when I shall change the last Hallelu-nein into a Hallelu-ja." Michael thrust the point of his sword into the ground, fell on his knees beside it, and was greatly ashamed.

Then God called Raphael, the protecting angel of the wanderer, and guardian of all who are searching and have gone astray. Raphael is always gentle and serene. To him God said, "Go, and take with you this little angel who cannot sing Hallelu-ja but only Hallelu-nein. Guide him and show him all the glories of heaven and earth. When at last he can sing Hallelu-ja, bring him back to me, not before."

That is how it came about that the angel Raphael and the little angel who could not sing Hallelu-ja passed together through the gates of heaven and wandered out silently into the starry night. The sun had set a long time ago and the little angel, who usually by this time was lying asleep in his heavenly trundle-bed, looked around curiously. He was not the least bit sorry over his banishment—on the contrary, it seemed a wonderful adventure. He had been given a warm fur-lined cloak, for the night was cold. He looked almost like a little prince now, except for his perky nose and his undignified-looking shock of hair. Raphael couldn't help looking at him secretly again and again. He was amazed that the little fellow was so happy.

"Who could have put this cuckoo's egg into heaven?" thought the big wise angel and smiled. But when the little fellow started cheerfully singing to himself and twittering his "Hallelu-nein," his anger rose. "Stop that, you little scamp," Raphael said severely. "You don't deserve all this fuss. I think Michael was quite right after all. A good whipping would have been the best thing for you."

194

The little fellow made a face and looked at Raphael reproachfully. "You are all so horrid to me, you big angels," he said, and his voice trembled. "What have I done to you? Just because you're big and I'm little, do you think you can do what you like? I'm somebody, too. Or don't you think so?" His blue eyes suddenly filled with tears. The little fellow tried quickly to wipe them away, but Raphael had seen them and his big warm heart was filled with pity.

"I didn't mean it like that," he said, trying to speak comfortingly. "Come here. You mustn't cry. Give me your hand."

The little one put a fat, trusting little hand into the big angel's warm fingers and felt quite safe and secure. And so they wandered together as friends over a silver cloud meadow that led to the Milky Way, Raphael suiting his steps to the little one's short legs.

"What is your name?" Raphael asked after a while.

"Me? I'm Purzel!" answered the little one importantly, looking up eagerly at Raphael as if expecting an admiring "Ah." When Raphael only nodded kindly, Purzel was bitterly disappointed.

"It seems you don't know me. Think just a minute. Haven't you ever heard of Purzel?"

"No, my little one. How could I? There are thousands of little angels like you, and besides I find the name Purzel a little odd for an angel, almost unbecoming."

"Do you?" With a jerk the little fellow pulled his hand out of
Raphael's and stood up straight,
setting his little arms akimbo
indignantly. "Now I'll tell you
something. Do you know why I'm
called Purzel? It means 'somersault', and I've purzeled twenty-
seven times from the top of the
highest apple tree in Paradise.
Twenty-seven times!"

Raphael laughed out loud—he
couldn't help it. "Good heavens! You're the funniest
little chap I've ever come across. Twenty-seven times!
Oh, Purzel!"

Raphael couldn't stop laughing, but the little fellow
felt deeply injured. "You mustn't laugh at me! You
mustn't!" Purzel stamped his foot. "You grown-ups are
horrid—you either laugh at us or scold us, one or the
other!"

Still laughing, Raphael picked up the little one and
kissed him on both cheeks and his sulky little mouth.
Purzel grew quiet. He hugged the big angel tight.

"You're good," he said. "I like you."

And so there was peace between the big and famous
angel Raphael, whose name is recorded in the Book
for ever, and little foolish Purzel who was stubborn and

196

would not sing Hallelu-ja. Again they walked hand in hand, but Purzel was lively now and started to talk, not taking his eyes off Raphael's smiling face. He told a string of stories, pranks and adventures he had experienced in his short life, rather like the mischievous life story of a little rascal on earth.

"Strange," Raphael thought, "strange how one forgets one's own childhood. How soon we grow up! What a pity, a real pity!" He pressed the little one's hand tenderly and promised himself to take good care of this foolish little Purzel whose short legs stumbled so often, in keeping with his name.

Meanwhile Raphael and Purzel had gone higher and higher. The stupendous vault of night stretched over their heads, its dome strewn with stars. A narrow bridle path, woven with moonbeams, led toward the heights; right and left, however, yawned the tremendous abyss of the universe. "Be careful," warned Raphael, "if you turn somersaults and fall down there, that will be the end of you. I should never find you again."

"You wouldn't, but the heavenly Father would!" said Purzel confidently. "He would stretch out his hand and catch me."

Raphael smiled. The little one's trust pleased him. But he wanted to test him further. "I don't know, Purzel, whether God would do that. Do you believe he is

197

so much concerned with you? Such a foolish, naughty little angel, who cannot even sing Hallelu-ja?" Purzel was silent and hung his head. He sucked his left thumb thoughtfully. Then, peering up into Raphael's face, he noticed the twinkle in the archangel's eyes.

"You're just teasing," he said, greatly relieved. "God the Father looks after me always, just because I am so little. But you wait! When I am big, very big and clever like you, and when at last I can sing Hallelu-ja, then you'll find out something. I'll sing it more beautifully than you, even."

"God grant it be so!" nodded Raphael earnestly. "But now be quiet for a while, for you are going to see something wonderful, something so beautiful and glorious, something so great and mysterious, that all the angels in heaven who have seen it so far have burst into a jubilant Hallelu-ja. Perhaps you will learn here, too, how to sing Hallelu-ja."

At this Purzel felt quite solemn. A rushing murmur had arisen all around, growing stronger with every step. Silvery star-dust whirled everywhere, catching in Raphael's hair and tickling Purzel's nose. "Achoo!" he sneezed. Purzel was out of breath. They were drawing near the zenith, near a surging stream of radiant white light. And now a powerful storm caught in their garments. Raphael's wings flapped powerfully of their own accord, and the terrified little Purzel clutched Raphael's knees and called out, "Help me! I'm so frightened. Oh, I'm so frightened!" Raphael stooped down, picked up the little one and held him securely against his bosom.

With one clasping movement of his mighty wings he swung away from the path of light right into tremendous thundering space. Purzel kept his eyes closed, covering them tight with his fists. He trembled all over. But Raphael's voice sounded in his ear, "Look and behold!" That was a command that even self-willed Purzel had to obey; he timidly opened his eyes, which grew bigger and bigger as he looked, and his little mouth gaped with awe.

They were both hovering in the midst of a most wonderful dance of the stars. Gigantic balls and spheres of shining light were dancing through a mild blue light, sliding past each other and greeting each other with music and the sound of bells. They were rolling along carefully and watchfully, guided by an unseen hand, leaving behind them glistening paths and sparkling trails of light in the velvety darkness, and each movement was music. Now and then long-tailed comets rushed through the whirl, disintegrating rocket-like in a fiery rain of golden sparks. Soft moons sought some cloud island to rest on, or a quiet dream-lake wherein they could be reflected. "Here is the axis of the world," explained

Raphael. "God makes the gigantic work run by his little finger. Is this not wonderful? Can you sing Hallelu-ja now, Purzel?"

The little fellow cleared his throat and tried—and tried again two or three times. But the small voice would not obey. "Just try," Raphael said encouragingly. "Just try a bit harder."

"No," said Purzel. "It won't work. Alas, it won't work. I was too frightened just now." He put his little hand to his heart, which was still beating hard, and just then a shooting star shot past the tip of his nose with a hissing sound. He felt most uncomfortable. He clutched Raphael's neck and begged, "Take me away. I want to go home!" But Raphael shook his head sadly.

"I may not do that, Purzel. You can't go back to heaven before you have learned to sing 'Hallelu-ja.' "

All at once Purzel realized what had happened to him. He felt the weight of his banishment, and wept with homesickness. Raphael was silent. He knew how impossible it is to comfort a banished angel. Instead he gathered a few little clouds with his breath, and shook them vigorously and made a cozy little bed. "You are tired, Purzel. You must sleep," he said, and he rocked him with his arm the whole night through.

Next morning Raphael took the sleeping Purzel out of his feather-cloud bed and carried him down to earth.

There he flew through a lovely meadow valley toward a shady beech wood and laid him down beside a little brook. "Good morning," he said as Purzel opened his eyes and looked wonderingly around him.

"Where am I?" asked the little one. "Where is my trundle-bed, and what country is this?"

"It is the earth. The beautiful sunny earth. But now be quick and get washed. There is plenty of water here."

"Washed?" yawned Purzel. "Why should I? It's only in heaven one has to be clean. It doesn't matter on earth."

This made Raphael really angry. "You should be ashamed of yourself. Whatever next? Are you forgetting your lesson so soon? You can't imagine what you look like; you cried half the night and you wiped away your tears with your grubby little hands. You are a mudlark, that's what you are. You aren't a little angel any more!"

In spite of his resistance Raphael took off Purzel's little garment, then his shoes and dipped him into the stream up to his neck. But when Purzel continued howling, Raphael gave him a few good duckings and Purzel came up sputtering indignantly. Gradually, though, he took a liking to the cool clear water in which quick little silver fish were playing. He tried to catch them, he dabbled, shouted and splashed. He squirted water on the smiling Raphael, and couldn't contain himself.

"Out you come," commanded Raphael. "We have a

long way to go and you haven't had your breakfast yet."

But nothing was further from Purzel's mind than obeying. He was so happy in the water now! It was the most glorious thing. He swam and dived like a little duckling. After a while Raphael called again and Purzel cried at him defiantly, "You go alone then! I want to stay here. I want to stay in the water all day long!"

Raphael's clear forehead darkened with displeasure. He said nothing but turned his back on the ungrateful Purzel. With long silent steps he walked away through the beech wood. Thousands of sunlight sparks danced where his feet had touched the ground.

Purzel was alone. For a little while he shrieked and made a big noise, full of exaggerated merriment, convincing himself that he was extraordinarily happy. But the silence and the solitude began to weigh heavily on his heart. He stood in the stream up to his little stomach and looked around. A menacing whirl of wind blew through the treetops, a cloud hid the rays of the sun, and Purzel began to shiver. A huge bumblebee buzzed around him fiercely, and he tried to beat it off, afraid. And as if there was not enough to frighten him, suddenly a big water rat darted from under the overhanging bank, a fat scruffy creature. It bared its sharp teeth and bit Purzel in the leg. Oh, how he yelled! He made a great leap out of the water, snatched up his little shirt, and fled.

"Raphael," he shouted through the forest. "Can't you hear me? Raphael!"

But there was no answer. There was no sign of him anywhere. Purzel's little heart beat so loud that he could hear it, deserted as he was. Here he was all alone in a strange wood, with unknown dangers round every corner—like that wicked, beady-eyed water rat.

"Oh," moaned Purzel to himself, "if only I wasn't so terribly hungry!"

He began to run, and little drops of sweat trickled down his face. He had put his little shirt on behind a bush, but his feet were bare and he could feel every sharp stone. Purzel was limping badly. At last the woods began to open. There was a cottage in a cluster of fruit trees and Purzel could see the first ripe fruit gleaming in the branches.

Purzel slipped into the garden. Under a tree stood a basket full of juicy dark blue plums. They smelled delicious. Purzel's mouth watered. He sat in the long grass.

He ate and ate, he stuffed and stuffed as much as he could, and spat out the stones with gusto. His little mouth and chin were red with juice and his fingers were sticky, but he licked them clean.

However, this grand feast had a sudden end—Nero the watchdog came bounding through the garden. He had been making his round of the house and had seen the little thief. Purzel began to run, and how! But Nero was faster. He got hold of the little fellow's shirt and began to tug and tear and ripped off a big piece with his teeth. In that desperate moment Purzel remembered his wings. They were still rather small and clumsy but they could lift him a little.

Purzel fluttered like a little fledgling and just managed to get over the fence. He landed with a thump in the grass. There he sat rubbing his seat. He began, "Oh, you bad earth! Oh, you wicked, horrid world! Raphael, where are you?" Just at that moment he saw a tall slim figure walking through the waves of golden wheat. It was Raphael, the good angel, letting his fingers glide

205

caressingly through the ears of grain as he walked along. How beautiful he is, thought Purzel, and his heart leapt toward him in love and remorse.

"There you are!" Raphael said when he saw Purzel. He looked into his eyes searchingly and what he read there seemed to please him.

"Are you still angry with me?" asked Purzel timidly.

Raphael shook his head. His face was shining from within. "Look, Purzel," he cried, pointing at the beautiful earth with a movement of his hand, "all this comes from God and through God. Those golden waves are a wheat field and mean bread for the people. This land is blessed and therefore holy. Don't you feel it so? Can you still not sing Hallelu-ja?"

The little one was about to open his lips—but he suddenly turned pale. He felt terribly ill.

"No," he groaned, holding his little stomach. "I can't. I'm sorry I can't. I've eaten much too many plums..."

Every day Raphael had some sort of trouble with Purzel. He had only to let him out of his sight for a moment and something had happened to him. Once he fell on his nose and had a nosebleed for hours. Another time he stubbed his big toe on a stone, because he had no shoes. Or a wasp stung his little finger. One morning he woke up with a toothache and his cheek swelled.

Hallelu-nein

That with all this nobody mentioned singing "Halleluja" is quite understandable.

"Poor little fellow," Raphael often thought. "You have to endure so much of the world's trouble yourself now. If only you could sing Hallelu-ja, foolish little Purzel!"

But Purzel became quieter and sadder, and you need a joyful heart to sing Hallelu-ja. Purzel was homesick, and it got worse as the days went by. He became quite sick from it, and Raphael had to carry him on his arm more and more often because he was too tired to walk. In the evenings, however, he always became a little livelier. Then he would start begging Raphael until he gave in and carried Purzel far into the sunset sky, far, very, very far until one could see the shining gates of heaven in the distance.

Raphael did not like doing this, for Purzel never wanted to turn back. Purzel did not call out so loudly and rudely as he had at first, but he wept silently and bitterly, which was much worse.

Winter had come to the earth, the first snowflakes swirled, and the shop windows were decorated for Christmas. One evening Raphael and Purzel walked hand in hand through the twilit streets of a large town, right among the people. No one took any notice of them. Only a tiny, half-starved kitten crossing their path recognized the heavenly visitors, meowed piteously and rubbed its head against Purzel's leg.

"Let's take it along with us," said Purzel. "I'll share my milk with the kitten."

Raphael nodded kindly. Purzel was tired again, so Raphael picked him up, carrying him on his right arm and the kitten on his left. The great, good angel never complained, but some evenings his arms were quite stiff and lame because of the many times he had to carry weary Purzel.

The two of them lived together in a little snowed-in weekend cottage at the edge of the city. No one came near it in the winter. When they had found it, it was empty except for a broken deck chair which the people had left behind. Raphael had collected all the things that were necessary—a small table, a little bed, two chairs, a stove and a large red rubber ball for Purzel to play with. Their life was very humble and poor, for it was God's will that Purzel should know poverty.

And so this December evening they again wandered through the crowds of the large city, amid the noise of cars, the bells of the trolley buses, and the thundering rumble of the subways and elevated trains. Raphael peered into the many shop windows. He wanted to buy a pair of warm fur-lined boots for Purzel.

"I don't need boots!" Purzel protested. "I want to go back to heaven and I want to walk barefoot on the soft clouds. If I have to stay on earth much longer it will just be too much for me. Then I'll simply die, and be dead, and that will be the quickest way back to heaven for me."

But Raphael was firm. They entered a shoe store and waited patiently for someone to serve them. Raphael had taken on the appearance of a simply dressed woman and had tied a kerchief over his shining curls. Almost anxiously he counted the silver pieces in his old purse. And Purzel looked like any other little boy come to try on new shoes and getting a bit impatient.

"What a beautiful child!" said the cheerful lady behind the counter. "Are you looking forward to Christmas, little boy? What would you wish the Christ Child to bring you?"

Purzel looked up suddenly and his eyes were wide and wondering. His face was thin but it lit up with such a joyful smile that the lady couldn't take her eyes off him.

"Oh, I know what I'll wish for!" Purzel whispered. "But I won't say. Could it really happen?"

He looked at Raphael anxiously. Raphael, under his kerchief, nodded and smiled.

"Perhaps, Purzel, perhaps!"

After that day Purzel was more cheerful. He plodded through the snow in his new boots and no longer begged so often to be carried. He became more responsible and careful and no longer tripped over his own feet, and he obeyed at once. Raphael was well pleased with him and loved him more and more.

One day Raphael sat down and, with a golden pencil, wrote a long letter.

"What are you writing?" asked the little one. He was playing with his kitten close by.

"I'm writing your Christmas report, Purzel."

"Oh, my! That will be a report! Do you have to?"

"It has to be, Purzel."

"Can't you tell me a bit about what you have written? Read it to me, won't you?"

"I can't do that. You will know it at the right time."

Purzel fell silent and thoughtful, watching Raphael intently as he wrote, but Raphael's expression remained friendly and Purzel felt at ease. He only asked casually, "Are you writing down everything? Even about what happened at the brook? And about the plums I stole?"

But Raphael only laughed and Purzel was no wiser than before.

Then came Christmas Eve. The streets of the city were quiet but the windows of the houses were bright.

Christmas trees were lit behind the window panes, and children's voices were singing "Silent night, holy night."

Purzel and Raphael were sitting in the small cottage deep in snow, in front of a tiny Christmas tree with three red candles, an apple and a golden nut on it. On the little table lay a box of blocks, a tiny trumpet and a large heart-shaped cookie. Purzel had taken a bite out of it but he couldn't get it down, he found swallowing so hard, so he broke it into tiny crumbs and fed it to the purring kitten.

"Let's sing a Christmas song," Raphael suggested. "Don't you agree, Purzel?"

"No, please, no singing! I can't bear it, it hurts...."

Raphael was silent. He knew that the little one could think only about Christmas in heaven, the great hall with its streaming lights, the joy and the Hallelu-ja singing. In comparison, this little earthly Christmas Raphael had been able to prepare for Purzel seemed quite miserable.

"I'm sorry, Purzel," said Raphael softly. "I would gladly have bought you all the beautiful things in the shops, but we are poor. I haven't any money."

Purzel looked up. His expression was remarkably old and wise. "How can you think I care for things bought with money? I am no human child, I am an angel."

Raphael realized that little Purzel had grown a good deal, inwardly and outwardly, and that he would never forget his calling or lose himself in the dust of the earth, this banished angel of the kingdom of heaven.

The candles were burning low; they flickered and spluttered and threw mysterious shadows across the room. Purzel kept his eyes fixed on the door, as if he were waiting, waiting with his heart almost bursting. But no one came and it grew dark.

Raphael got up from his chair, picked up Purzel, and carried him to bed. When he kissed him good night Raphael noticed that his little face was wet with tears. And Raphael himself felt like weeping.

Perhaps an hour passed, but Purzel was still not asleep. He lay quietly in his bed and listened to the sounds of the night outside. Sometimes he heard a distant sound of bells or a whisper at the window. Once he even thought he saw a little light glinting through a crack in the door.

"Raphael," he whispered excitedly, "can you hear anything? There is someone outside."

"Purzel, go to sleep now. It's high time. You must be mistaken."

"Please, Raphael, won't you go see?"

Raphael rose and his garment glittered in the darkness. He opened the door, but nothing unusual was to be seen outside, only a few dark trees in the garden and above them the night sky full of brilliant stars.

"Leave the door open, please. I want to see the stars," Purzel begged.

"But you'll freeze."

"You've wrapped me up too well in my warm blankets."

Raphael sat down on the doorstep, his garment flowing over the steps like silver. Purzel could see the silhouette of his folded wings and his raised head, listening, leaning against the doorpost.

"He must have heard something, too," thought Purzel. "He is listening and waiting like me."

But everything was quiet and Purzel dropped asleep. How long he slept he never knew. He was suddenly wakened by a beam of light falling on his closed eyes.

"Is it daytime already? Must I get up?" he asked. A soft laugh was all the answer. Then he felt himself lifted up as Raphael peeled his blankets off him.

"Come, Purzel. We have a worthy guest. Don't you see who he is?" Purzel opened his eyes wide and his heart began to beat fast. Michael, in his shining armor,

stood before him in the doorway, filling the frame completely. The room was filled with the splendor of his
golden armor. Purzel trembled a little, between fear
and happiness.

Just then he heard a sound he knew well—the
jingling of silver sleigh bells! Purzel shouted for joy.
"Santa Claus and his sleigh! I knew it! I knew it!"
Struggling, Purzel jumped down from Raphael's arms,
raced through the room and, as Michael stepped aside in
the doorway with a smile, he shot out into the open.
Oh, how everything had changed! The quiet garden
swarmed with little angels sitting and fluttering every-

214

where, on the water tub, on the garden fence, the eaves of the roof and the tree tops. Santa Claus had stopped his glass sleigh, drawn by reindeer, by the garden gate.

Purzel was greeted with shouts of joy by all the little angels. But he was so dazed and almost blinded with joy that he missed the steps and tumbled head first into the snow. There he sat in the snow as if in a dream, rubbing his eyes. He still couldn't quite trust them. All around him the little angels were laughing merrily at the funny somersault, which had amused them tremendously.

Raphael picked him up. "Purzel!" he said laughing. "You're just the same old Purzel!" Michael smiled, too, but urged them to get into the sleigh.

"Santa Claus is waiting," he reminded them, and sure enough there was good old Santa Claus waving to them from the sleigh, and his white beard shone with good will. Purzel was quickly wrapped up in a fur blanket and packed into the sleigh. But he had hardly sat down between Santa Claus and Raphael when he jumped up again shouting, "Stop! I have to get out again! I've forgotten something!"

"What have you forgotten, Purzel?"

"My kitten. I promised him he should never go hungry again."

"But hurry!"

Purzel darted into the house. Raphael looked up with

215

a quiet smile at Michael, who was waiting on his white steed at the side of the sleigh.

"You do not know him as well as I do. Purzel has a good heart."

They drove through the winter forest, and it looked on the miracle sleigh, full of amazement. The silent snow-covered fir trees opened their eyes wide. Little wood folks and all the little wood spirits crept out of the bush—they become very restless on Christmas Eve. But no will-o'-the-wisp could lure away the heavenly sleigh, it knew its course.

Around the sleigh flew the little angels, Purzel's playmates. They teased him because he had to sit quiet and well-behaved in the sleigh.

"Flying is not the chief thing," Raphael comforted him. Then he went on: "The most important thing is to sing Hallelu-ja. If you don't learn it tonight you will never learn it."

Purzel looked at Raphael, startled. The angel had spoken with such a stern, solemn voice that Purzel began to tremble. Softly he tried to sing his first Hallelu-ja to himself.

"Ha—Halle—lu—u—ui," he tried. "Halle-lu-u-ui."

He could get no further. Again and again he got stuck. His heart was gripped with fear and his little hands went cold. But then something happened that

216

made Purzel forget all his cares and fears. From the depths of the dark forest a ray of light fell onto the snow and there, under ancient fir trees with their lichen beards was a little hut, a little stable surrounded by sheep. The roof was thatched with moss and the two windows were like eyes lit up from within, softly and glowingly. High above the stable there glistened a wonderfully bright star.

The sleigh stopped. And suddenly Purzel felt his heart drawn as by an invisible thread to the stable. How it pulled him and tugged him! He could hardly climb out of the sleigh fast enough. He almost stumbled over the kitten in his hurry. He ran and ran—pushing his way past a few kneeling shepherds—and stood by the crib in the stable.

"Purzel, is that you?" asked the little child lying on the hard straw. "Have you come at last, you foolish little Purzel? It's for your sake I am here in the manger again and have made myself poor and small. For you, just for you."

"For me?" asked Purzel, trembling all over, for he had recognized God the Father in the child's eyes.

"Yes, for you, and for all the foolish Purzels who cannot sing Hallelu-ja...."

Purzel drew a deep breath and gave a joyful shout: "But I can, now I *can* sing Hallelu-ja!" His tongue had

217

become loosened. Although a little shaky and out of tune, Purzel sang his first Hallelu-ja.

He knelt before the manger. Around him resounded a powerful song, carrying him up as if on clouds. His high, clear childlike voice rang out above all the other jubilant voices. Raphael and Michael looked at each other again and again for joy, their eyes shining.

"Can you hear?" whispered Raphael to Michael, between weeping and laughing. "Can you hear how well he can sing? I knew it. Only love could win Purzel, only the eternal love that overpowers angels and men."

Ever since, each evening at sundown, on the highest step of the Hallelu-ja ladder sits a merry little angel, with a kitten in his arms. His name is Purzel. We know him well. He is one of the happiest of all and sings his "Hallelu-ja" masterfully. He sings "Hallelu-ja, Hallelu-u-u-ja...."

And never again has a Hallelu-nein been heard in heaven.

MID-WINTER

IN THE BLEAK MID-WINTER
  FROSTY WIND MADE MOAN,
EARTH STOOD HARD AS IRON,
  WATER LIKE A STONE;
SNOW HAD FALLEN, SNOW ON SNOW,
  SNOW ON SNOW,
IN THE BLEAK MID-WINTER
  LONG AGO.

OUR GOD, HEAVEN CANNOT HOLD HIM
  NOR EARTH SUSTAIN;
HEAVEN AND EARTH SHALL FLEE AWAY
  WHEN HE COMES TO REIGN;
IN THE BLEAK MID-WINTER
  A STABLE-PLACE SUFFICED
THE LORD GOD ALMIGHTY
  JESUS CHRIST.

ANGELS AND ARCHANGELS
  MAY HAVE GATHERED THERE,
CHERUBIM AND SERAPHIM
  THRONGED THE AIR:
BUT ONLY HIS MOTHER
  IN HER MAIDEN BLISS
WORSHIPPED THE BELOVED
  WITH A KISS.

WHAT CAN I GIVE HIM,
  POOR AS I AM?
IF I WERE A SHEPHERD
  I WOULD BRING A LAMB;
IF I WERE A WISE MAN
  I WOULD DO MY PART;
YET WHAT I CAN I GIVE HIM —
  GIVE MY HEART.

CHRISTINA ROSETTI

BROTHER ROBBER

by HELENE CHRISTALLER

he hut hung like a swallow's nest on the southern slope of the Apennines. Built of the same stone as the rock on which it stood, it appeared a part of nature, not a work of man. A small window opening was stopped with straw to keep out the cold wind that blew over the mountains.

The inside looked wretched, even though Brother Angelo was trying to clean and decorate the hermitage for Christmas. His brown habit was tucked up to his knees, and he was sweeping together a big pile of rubbish with a homemade broom—pieces of wood and bark, ashes and brushwood. At last the dirty red of the rough brick floor became visible, and the young Franciscan put the broom in the corner. Satisfied, he looked around the bare, gloomy room. Through the half-open door came the faint light of day, together with a moist, chilly draft.

The monk broke a dry branch into pieces and threw them into the fire burning in a crooked brick stove. He hung a rusty kettle filled with water over the flame, and, shivering, closed the door. The flickering flame of the stove gave a dim light in the room.

"It ought to be warm when the brothers come home, and festive," he murmured. Proudly he examined the rough wooden cross on the wall, which he had decorated with fresh ivy. Two white candles were fastened to the beams of the cross. They were to burn for the Christmas Eve celebration.

The water began to boil, puffing out big clouds of steam. The fire flickered and crackled, showering the monk with sparks as he clumsily threw handfuls of meal into the pot for soup. The small room was warming up, except for the draft from the window, and for the north wind, blowing in through the chimney, filling the hut with smoke.

Brother Angelo sat down on the floor close to the fire, folded his delicate brown fingers across his thin knees, and listened for something outside. His soft, fair hair hung down to his shoulders. The well cut features with the aquiline nose and fine mouth were those of a young Knight of the Cross rather than of a brown-clad penitent monk.

223

Suddenly the door opened and a small, gaunt man came in, barefoot and carrying a coarse, half-filled sack on his back and a little pitcher of wine in his hand. Brother Angelo started up devotedly and relieved him of his burden.

"Come to the fire and warm yourself, Brother Francis," he said eagerly. "It is cold outside, but the soup is boiling already and the brothers will be here soon."

The dark-haired man with the emaciated face, in which great eyes shone, looked around the little hut. "You have been quite busy, Brother Angelo. The Holy Child may well visit our hut. Would that our hearts, too, might be well prepared!"

"Yes, Brother Francis." The youth's reply sounded slightly embarrassed. The older man raised his eyes in question.

The younger kept silence and bowed his head.

"You were alone this morning?"

"Not the whole time. I had a great fright. Three robbers from the mountains—they are known here, I think—came and asked me for food."

"And you?"

"I sent them away and scolded them well for their bad ways. I told them God would damn them eternally."

"You said that and sent them away?"

"Their hands were red with blood."

"They stretched them out for help and you left them unfilled?"

"They were robbers, Brother Francis."

"They were brothers, Brother Angelo."

"Brothers? The robbers?"

Francis looked at him severely and his great eyes blazed. "Yes, the robbers," he said emphatically.

The young man blushed and did not answer.

"They wander in cold and hunger," Francis continued, "and you make yourself comfortable in the warm house. Oh, Angelo, your heart is not so well prepared for Christmas as this hut is."

Tears sprang to the youth's eyes. "Be not angry with me, my brother, I will make good where I failed!"

A mild light began to glow in the monk's serious face. "If you want to make it good, take this sack with bread and the pitcher with wine and go out into the mountains to seek the robbers. Take the food to them and ask their forgiveness for your hardness. Then return, so that we may celebrate Christmas together with a pure heart."

"And if they kill me in anger?"

Francis smiled, serene and unworried, and remained silent.

Thereupon the young man bowed his head obediently, threw the sack over his shoulder, and walked out of the house without a word of contradiction.

A thin blanket of snow covered the mountains. Mighty old oak trees stood out boldly in dark masses from the dazzling white; here and there stood a gnarled olive tree rooted in the stony soil, still with a few ripe olives on it. Snow covered the branches, and when the wind blew on them, fell to the ground with a soft rustling.

Angelo kept his eyes turned to the ground looking for footprints. There were deer and fox tracks coming from the near-by forest. And there, that was a mule, with a driver who wore heavy wooden sandals. But here—these were naked feet; they went criss-cross in confusion rather as if several people had walked one behind the other. Blood in one of the footprints appeared again and again.

The monk followed these footprints. They were leading into the mountains. The sun was no longer high,— he must hurry if he wanted to find the robbers before nightfall! A snow flurry had started and whirled a few handfuls of white flakes into the monk's face. Soon gaps were torn in the clouds and the sun smiled through, only to be swallowed up again by gray monsters chased by the strong wind. His brown habit was whipped about him and his long fair hair tossed while he battled patiently against the wind, his eyes turned to the ground, all the time taking care not to spill the wine in the pitcher.

The landscape was growing wild and desolate. He

came across a ruined hut, but it was abandoned. Big boulders with caps of snow were scattered over the mountain slope. In the distant plain a dense sea of fog was swelling, hiding the church towers and pinnacles, the winding river and the houses. Not a sound penetrated to him, no ringing of bells, not a voice could be heard. Silence of death, stones, defiant rocks, ice, snow, howling storm. A flock of crows flew cawing over the wanderer's head towards the plain, disappearing in the billowing gray masses of fog.

The monk stood still. He wiped the sweat from his brow and looked back. How long had he been walking in this wintry silence, in dull obedience, towards an adventurous goal? Just in this way he had left wealth and family upon a word of the friar who was now sending him to the robbers. His face began to light up from within as he thought of Brother Francis. "No, not dully and lifelessly like a corpse," he cried aloud. "I go in joyful obedience on the way you send me, Brother Francis!"

With new zeal he climbed over the rocks. Here on the summit the wind had blown away the snow and blotted out the footprints. The fog was creeping up on him from the valley, dampening his fair hair and the hem of his robe so that it flapped heavily against his legs.

"You robbers, where are you?" he cried aloud in his perplexity. But only the echo answered and another flock of crows flew hurrying over him. Dark caves and clefts yawned in the rocks here, not a tree gave life to the wilderness, no water rushed over the stones. Everything was white and gray, the last blue patch had vanished from the sky, and the sun was hanging, pale like the disc of the moon, behind dark veils.

Suddenly a black, dishevelled head appeared behind a rock, staring at the approaching friar with sinister, burning eyes. The young man's step faltered. Horror gripped his heart. He turned pale.

"Ho there," the robber shouted, rising to his feet in anger. Slowly another figure rose and threatened the frightened monk with his hairy fist. A third was plucking a crow he was about to roast over a small, smouldering fire.

"It seems you want to share our Christmas treat, pious brother?" he mocked. "I can't promise you more than a leg."

"What do you want, monk?" the first one bellowed at him, making Angelo tremble. "To give us a penitential sermon as you did this morning? It's hard preaching to empty stomachs! Look out!"

"No," said Brother Angelo humbly, stepping close. He laid down the sack of bread and placed the pitcher of wine carefully on a ledge. Then he knelt down in the snow and said pleadingly, "Dear robbers, forgive me for sending you away from the threshold today with such hard words. I have come now to bring you some bread and wine and to ask your forgiveness for my sin." And he remained on his knees with head bowed. The wild men looked at the delicate, aristocratic figure, at the youthful, sensitive face. The oldest of the robbers turned pale, bit his stubborn lips and turned away. As for the second, the hot blood rose to the black tufts of hair above his brow. He covered his eyes with his hands like a child who feels ashamed. But the third, the youngest, laughed a little, embarrassed, and said, "We'll gladly forgive you, because you are a good man. We felt very hungry today...."

"Why don't you get up?" asked the pale one.

"Stay and eat with us," said the other.

Brother Angelo stood up and shook the snow from his habit. "I cannot stay and eat with you," he said timorously. "Brother Francis expects me for midnight mass down at the monastery. And I must hurry, for it will soon be night. But perhaps you can visit us in the monastery some time when you are in need of something."

"And Brother Francis? Will he not scold us?"

The face of the young man lit up. "He calls you brothers."

"Brothers!" said all three as with one voice, and then kept an uneasy silence.

"Farewell, brother robbers," said Angelo, extending

his delicate fingers to take the blood-stained hand. "Good-bye." Without answering a word, the three wild fellows stared after the young monk as he disappeared rapidly from their sight. Nor did any one of them reach for the wine or bread, and each avoided the glance of his companions. Now the fog had swallowed up the figure of the young man and the desolate countryside lay silent and white. Then clear notes could be heard in the distance, sounding now like the deep ringing of bells, now like the chanting of a priest at the altar, and then again like the jubilant song of a skylark. And so the old Christmas song was carried up to the three lost men:

> "Adeste fideles, laeti triumphantes,
> Venite, venite ad Bethlehem."

There is a legend that at a later time these same three robbers came down and joined the Brotherhood of Franciscans and led a blessed life until their peaceful end.

REJOICE ALL THE HEAVENS

1697
STRASSBURGER GESANGBUCH

RE-JOICE ALL THE HEAVENS, RE-JOICE ALL THE EARTH, RE-
RE-JOICE ALL THE HEAVENS RE-JOICE ALL THE

JOICE A-GAIN ALL THINGS WITH GLAD-NESS AND MIRTH! ON
EARTH, RE-JOICE A-GAIN ALL THINGS WITH GLADNESS & MIRTH!

EARTH HERE BE-NEATH US, IN HEAV-EN A-BOVE US, THE
ON EARTH HERE BE-NEATH US, IN HEA-VEN A-

CHILD IN THE MAN-GER PRAISE WE WITH GLADNESS!
BOVE US, THE CHILD IN THE MAN-GER PRAISE WE WITH GLAD-NESS!

REJOICE ALL THE HEAVENS,
REJOICE ALL THE EARTH,
REJOICE AGAIN ALL THINGS
WITH GLADNESS AND MIRTH!
ON EARTH HERE BENEATH US,
IN HEAVEN ABOVE US,
THE CHILD IN THE MANGER
PRAISE WE WITH GLADNESS!

EARTH, WATER, AIR, FIRE,
AND LIGHTNING FROM HEAVEN,
AND PEOPLE AND ANGELS
SING GLADLY TOGETHER!
ON EARTH HERE BENEATH US,
IN HEAVEN ABOVE US,
THE CHILD IN THE MANGER
PRAISE WE WITH GLADNESS!

232

THE LEGEND OF THE
CHRISTMAS ROSE

by SELMA LAGERLÖF

obber Mother, who lived in Robbers' Cave in Göinge forest, went down to the village one day on a begging tour. Robber Father, who was an outlawed man, did not dare to leave the forest, but had to content himself with lying in wait for the wayfarers who ventured within its borders. But at that time travellers were not very plentiful in Southern Skåne. If it so happened that the man had had a few weeks of ill luck with his hunt, his wife would take to the road. She took with her five youngsters, and each youngster wore a ragged leathern suit and birch-bark shoes and bore a sack on his back as long as himself. When Robber Mother stepped inside the door of a cabin, no one dared refuse to give her whatever she demanded; for she was not above coming back the following night and setting fire to the house if she had not

233

been well received. Robber Mother and her brood were worse than a pack of wolves, and many a man felt like running a spear through them; but it was never done, because they all knew that the man stayed up in the forest, and he would have known how to wreak vengeance if anything had happened to the children or the old woman.

Now that Robber Mother went from house to house and begged, she came one day to Övid, which at that time was a cloister. She rang the bell of the cloister gate and asked for food. The watchman let down a small wicket in the gate and handed her six round bread cakes —one for herself and one for each of the five children.

While the mother was standing quietly at the gate, her youngsters were running about. And now one of them came and pulled at her skirt, as a signal that he had discovered something which she ought to come and see, and Robber Mother followed him promptly.

The entire cloister was surrounded by a high and strong wall, but the youngster had managed to find a little back gate which stood ajar. When Robber Mother got there, she pushed the gate open and walked inside without asking leave, as it was her custom to do.

Övid Cloister was managed at that time by Abbot Hans, who knew all about herbs. Just within the cloister wall he had planted a little herb garden, and it was into this that the old woman had forced her way.

At first glance Robber Mother was so astonished that she paused at the gate. It was high summertide, and Abbot Hans' garden was so full of flowers that the eyes were fairly dazzled by the blues, reds, and yellows, as one looked into it. But presently an indulgent smile spread over her features, and she started to walk up a narrow path that lay between many flower-beds.

In the garden a lay brother walked about, pulling up weeds. It was he who had left the door in the wall open, that he might throw the weeds and tares on the rubbish heap outside.

When he saw Robber Mother coming in, with all five youngsters in tow, he ran toward her at once and ordered them away. But the beggar woman walked right on as before. She cast her eyes up and down, looking now at the stiff white lilies which spread near the ground, then on the ivy climbing high upon the cloister wall, and took no notice whatever of the lay brother.

He thought she had not understood him, and wanted to take her by the arm and turn her toward the gate. But when the robber woman saw his purpose, she gave him a look that sent him reeling backward. She had been walking with back bent under her beggar's pack, but now she straightened herself to her full height. "I am Robber Mother from Göinge forest; so touch me if

you dare!" And it was obvious that she was as certain she would be left in peace as if she had announced that she was the Queen of Denmark.

And yet the lay brother dared to oppose her, although now, when he knew who she was, he spoke reasonably to her, "You must know, Robber Mother, that this is a monks' cloister, and no woman in the land is allowed within these walls. If you do not go away, the monks will be angry with me because I forgot to close the gate, and perhaps they will drive me away from the cloister and the herb garden."

But such prayers were wasted on Robber Mother. She walked straight ahead among the little flower-beds and looked at the hyssop with its magenta blossoms, and at the honeysuckles, which were full of deep orange-colored flower clusters.

Then the lay brother knew of no other remedy than to run into the cloister and call for help.

He returned with two stalwart monks, and Robber Mother saw that now it meant business! With feet firmly planted she stood in the path and began shrieking in strident tones all the awful vengeance she would wreak on the cloister if she couldn't remain in the herb garden as long as she wished. But the monks did not see why they need fear her and thought only of driving her out. Then Robber Mother let out a perfect volley of shrieks, and, throwing herself upon the monks, clawed and bit at them; so did all the youngsters. The men soon learned that she could overpower them, and all they could do was to go back into the cloister for reinforcements.

As they ran through the passage-way which led to the cloister, they met Abbot Hans, who came rushing out to learn what all this noise was about.

Then they had to confess that Robber Mother from Göinge forest had come into the cloister and that they were unable to drive her out and must call for assistance.

But Abbot Hans upbraided them for using force and forbade their calling for help. He sent both monks back to their work, and although he was an old and fragile man, he took with him only the lay brother.

When Abbot Hans came out in the garden, Robber Mother was still wandering among the flower-beds. He regarded her with astonishment. He was certain that Robber Mother had never before seen an herb garden; yet she sauntered leisurely between all the small patches, each of which had been planted with its own species of rare flower, and looked at them as if they were old acquaintances. At some she smiled, at others she shook her head.

Abbot Hans loved his herb garden as much as it was possible for him to love anything earthly and perishable. Wild and terrible as the old woman looked, he couldn't help liking that she had fought with three monks for the privilege of viewing the garden in peace. He came

238

up to her and asked in a mild tone if the garden pleased her.

Robber Mother turned defiantly toward Abbot Hans, for she expected only to be trapped and overpowered. But when she noticed his white hair and bent form, she answered peaceably, "First, when I saw this, I thought I had never seen a prettier garden; but now I see that it can't be compared with one I know of."

Abbot Hans had certainly expected a different answer. When he heard that Robber Mother had seen a garden more beautiful than his, a faint flush spread over his withered cheek. The lay brother, who was standing close by, immediately began to censure the old woman. "This is Abbot Hans," said he, "who with much care and diligence has gathered the flowers from far and near for his herb garden. We all know that there is not a more beautiful garden to be found in all Skåne, and it is not befitting that you, who live in the wild forest all the year around, should find fault with his work."

"I don't wish to make myself the judge of either him or you," said Robber Mother. "I'm only saying that if you could see the garden of which I am thinking you would uproot all the flowers planted here and cast them away like weeds."

But the Abbot's assistant was hardly less proud of the flowers than the Abbot himself, and after hearing her remarks he laughed derisively. "I can understand that you only talk like this to tease us. It must be a pretty garden that you have made for yourself amongst the pines in Göinge forest! I'd be willing to wager my soul's salvation that you have never before been within the walls of an herb garden."

Robber Mother grew crimson with rage to think that her word was doubted, and she cried out: "It may be true that until today I had never been within the walls of an herb garden; but you monks, who are holy men, certainly must know that on every Christmas Eve the great Göinge forest is transformed into a beautiful garden, to commemorate the hour of our Lord's birth. We who live in the forest have seen this happen every year. And in that garden I have seen flowers so lovely that I dared not lift my hand to pluck them."

The lay brother wanted to continue the argument, but Abbot Hans gave him a sign to be silent. For, ever since his childhood, Abbot Hans had heard it said that on every Christmas Eve the forest was dressed in holiday glory. He had often longed to see it, but he had never had the good fortune. Eagerly he begged and implored Robber Mother that he might come up to the Robbers' Cave on Christmas Eve. If she would only send one of her children to show him the way, he could ride up there alone, and he would never betray them— on the contrary, he would reward them, in so far as it lay in his power.

Robber Mother said no at first, for she was thinking of Robber Father and of the peril which might befall him should she permit Abbot Hans to ride up to their cave. At the same time the desire to prove to the monk that the garden which she knew was more beautiful than his got the better of her, and she gave in.

"But more than one follower you cannot take with you," said she, "and you are not to waylay us or trap us, as sure as you are a holy man."

This Abbot Hans promised, and then Robber Mother went her way. Abbot Hans commanded the lay brother not to reveal to a soul that which had been agreed upon. He feared that the monks, should they learn of his purpose, would not allow a man of his years to go up to the Robbers' Cave.

Nor did he himself intend to reveal his project to a human being. And then it happened that Archbishop Absalon from Lund came to Övid and remained through the night. When Abbot Hans was showing him the herb garden, he got to thinking of Robber Mother's visit, and the lay brother, who was at work in the garden, heard Abbot Hans telling the Bishop about Robber Father, who these many years had lived as an outlaw in the forest, and asking him for a letter of ransom for the man, that he might lead an honest life among respectable folk. "As things are now," said Abbot Hans, "his children are growing up into worse malefactors than

241

himself, and you will soon have a whole gang of robbers to deal with up there in the forest."

But the Archbishop replied that he did not care to let the robber loose among honest folk in the villages. It would be best for all that he remain in the forest.

Then Abbot Hans grew zealous and told the Bishop all about Göinge forest, which, every year at Yuletide, clothed itself in summer bloom around the Robbers' Cave. "If these bandits are not so bad but that God's glories can be made manifest to them, surely we cannot be too wicked to experience the same blessing."

The Archbishop knew how to answer Abbot Hans. "This much I will promise you, Abbot Hans," he said, smiling, "that any day you send me a blossom from the garden in Göinge forest, I will give you letters of ransom for all the outlaws you may choose to plead for."

The lay brother apprehended that Bishop Absalon believed as little in this story of Robber Mother's as he himself; but Abbot Hans perceived nothing of the sort, but thanked Absalon for his good promise and said that he would surely send him the flower.

Abbot Hans had his way. And the following Christmas Eve he did not sit at home with his monks in Övid Cloister, but was on his way to Göinge forest. One of Robber Mother's wild youngsters ran ahead of him, and close behind him was the lay brother who had talked with Robber Mother in the herb garden.

The Legend of the Christmas Rose

Abbot Hans had been longing to make this journey, and he was very happy now that it had come to pass. But it was a different matter with the lay brother who accompanied him. Abbot Hans was very dear to him, and he would not willingly have allowed another to attend him and watch over him; but he didn't believe that he should see any Christmas Eve garden. He thought the whole thing a snare which Robber Mother had, with great cunning, laid for Abbot Hans, that he might fall into her husband's clutches.

While Abbot Hans was riding toward the forest, he saw that everywhere they were preparing to celebrate Christmas. In every peasant settlement fires were lighted in the bath-house to warm it for the afternoon bathing. Great hunks of meat and bread were being carried from the larders into the cabins, and from the barns came the men with big sheaves of straw to be strewn over the floors.

As he rode by the little country churches, he observed that each parson, with his sexton, was busily engaged in decorating his church; and when he came to the road which leads to Bösjö Cloister, he observed that all the poor of the parish were coming with armfuls of bread and long candles, which they had received at the cloister gate.

When Abbot Hans saw all these Christmas preparations, his haste increased. He was thinking of the festivities that awaited him, which were greater than any the others would be privileged to enjoy.

But the lay brother whined and fretted when he saw how they were preparing to celebrate Christmas in every humble cottage. He grew more and more anxious, and begged and implored Abbot Hans to turn back and not to throw himself deliberately into the robber's hands.

Abbot Hans went straight ahead, paying no heed to his lamentations. He left the plain behind him and came up into desolate and wild forest regions. Here the road was bad, almost like a stony and burr-strewn path, with neither bridge nor plank to help them over brooklet and rivulet. The farther they rode, the colder it grew, and after a while they came upon snow-covered ground.

It turned out to be a long and hazardous ride through the forest. They climbed steep and slippery side paths, crawled over swamp and marsh, and pushed through windfall and bramble. Just as daylight was waning, the robber boy guided them across a forest meadow, skirted by tall, naked leaf trees and green fir trees. Back of the meadow loomed a mountain wall, and in this wall they saw a door of thick boards. Now Abbot Hans understood that they had arrived, and dismounted. The child opened the heavy door for him, and he looked into a poor mountain grotto, with bare stone walls. Robber Mother was seated before a log fire that burned in the middle of the floor. Alongside the walls were beds of

virgin pine and moss, and on one of these beds lay
Robber Father asleep.

"Come in, you out there!" shouted Robber Mother
without rising, "and fetch the horses in with you, so
they won't be destroyed by the night cold."

Abbot Hans walked boldly into the cave, and the lay
brother followed. Here were wretchedness and poverty!
and nothing was done to celebrate Christmas. Robber
Mother had neither brewed nor baked; she had neither
washed nor scoured. The youngsters were lying on the
floor around a kettle, eating; but no better food was
provided for them than a watery gruel.

Robber Mother spoke in a tone as haughty and dic-
tatorial as any well-to-do peasant woman. "Sit down
by the fire and warm yourself, Abbot Hans," said she,
"and if you have food with you, eat, for the food which
we in the forest prepare you wouldn't care to taste. And
if you are tired after the long journey, you can lie down
on one of these beds to sleep. You needn't be afraid of
oversleeping, for I'm sitting here by the fire keeping
watch. I shall awaken you in time to see that which
you have come up here to see."

Abbot Hans obeyed Robber Mother and brought
forth his food sack; but he was so fatigued after the
journey he was hardly able to eat, and as soon as he
could stretch himself on the bed, he fell asleep.

The lay brother was also assigned a bed to rest upon,

but he didn't dare sleep, as he thought he had better keep his eye on Robber Father to prevent his getting up and capturing Abbot Hans. But gradually fatigue got the better of him, too, and he dropped into a doze.

When he woke up, he saw that Abbot Hans had left his bed and was sitting by the fire talking with Robber Mother. The outlawed robber sat also by the fire. He was a tall, raw-boned man with a dull, sluggish appearance. His back was turned to Abbot Hans, as though he would have it appear that he was not listening to the conversation.

Abbot Hans was telling Robber Mother all about the Christmas preparations he had seen on the journey, reminding her of Christmas feasts and games which she must have known in her youth, when she lived at peace with mankind. "I'm sorry for your children, who can never run on the village street in holiday dress or tumble in the Christmas straw," said he.

At first Robber Mother answered in short, gruff sentences, but by degrees she became more subdued and listened more intently. Suddenly Robber Father turned toward Abbot Hans and shook his clenched fist in his face. "You miserable monk! did you come here to coax from me my wife and children? Don't you know that I am an outlaw and may not leave the forest?"

Abbot Hans looked him fearlessly in the eyes. "It is

246

my purpose to get a letter of ransom for you from Archbishop Absalon," said he. He had hardly finished speaking when the robber and his wife burst out laughing.
They knew well enough the kind of mercy a forest robber
could expect from Bishop Absalon!

"Oh, if I get a letter of ransom from Absalon," said
Robber Father, "then I'll promise you that never again
will I steal so much as a goose."

The lay brother was annoyed with the robber folk
for daring to laugh at Abbot Hans, but on his own
account he was well pleased. He had seldom seen the
Abbot sitting more peaceful and meek with his monks
at Övid than he now sat with this wild robber folk.

Suddenly Robber Mother rose. "You sit here and
talk, Abbot Hans," she said, "so that we are forgetting
to look at the forest. Now I can hear, even in this cave,
how the Christmas bells are ringing."

The words were barely uttered when they all sprang
up and rushed out. But in the forest it was still dark
night and bleak winter. The only thing they marked
was a distant clang borne on a light south wind.

"How can this bell ringing ever awaken the dead
forest?" thought Abbot Hans. For now, as he stood out
in the winter darkness, he thought it far more impossible
that a summer garden could spring up here than it had
seemed to him before.

Behold That Star

When the bells had been ringing a few moments, a sudden illumination penetrated the forest; the next moment it was dark again, and then the light came back. It pushed its way forward between the stark trees, like a shimmering mist. This much it effected: The darkness merged into a faint daybreak. Then Abbot Hans saw that the snow had vanished from the ground, as if someone had removed a carpet, and the earth began to take on a green covering. Then the ferns shot up their fronds, rolled like a bishop's staff. The heather that grew on the stony hills and the bog-myrtle rooted in the ground moss dressed themselves quickly in new bloom. The moss-tufts thickened and raised themselves, and the spring blossoms shot upward their swelling buds, which already had a touch of color.

Abbot Hans' heart beat fast as he marked the first signs of the forest's awakening. "Old man that I am, shall I behold such a miracle?" thought he, and the tears wanted to spring to his eyes. Again it grew so hazy that he feared the darkness would once more cover the earth; but almost immediately there came a new wave of light. It brought with it the splash of rivulet and the rush of cataract. Then the leaves of the trees burst into bloom, as if a swarm of green butterflies came flying and clustered on the branches. It was not only trees and plants that awoke, but crossbeaks hopped from branch to branch, and the woodpeckers hammered on the limbs

248

until the splinters fairly flew around them. A flock of starlings from up country lighted in a fir top to rest. They were paradise starlings. The tips of each tiny feather shone in brilliant reds, and, as the birds moved, they glittered like so many jewels.

Again, all was dark for an instant, but soon there came a new light wave. A fresh, warm south wind blew and scattered over the forest meadow all the little seeds that had been brought from southern lands by birds and ships and winds, and which could not thrive elsewhere because of this country's cruel cold. These took root and sprang up the instant they touched the ground.

When the next warm wind came along, the blueberries and lignon ripened. Cranes and wild geese shrieked in the air, the bullfinches built nests, and the baby squirrels began playing on the branches of the trees.

Everything came so fast now that Abbot Hans could not stop to reflect on how immeasurably great was the miracle that was taking place. He had time only to use his eyes and ears. The next light wave that came rushing in brought with it the scent of newly ploughed acres, and far off in the distance the milkmaids were heard coaxing the cows—and the tinkle of the sheep's bells. Pine and spruce trees were so thickly clothed with red cones that they shone like crimson mantles. The juniper berries changed color every second, and forest flowers covered the ground till it was all red, blue, and yellow.

Abbot Hans bent down to the earth and broke off a wild strawberry blossom, and, as he straightened up, the berry ripened in his hand.

The mother fox came out of her lair with a big litter of black-legged young. She went up to Robber Mother and scratched at her skirt, and Robber Mother bent down to her and praised her young. The horned owl, who had just begun his night chase, was astonished at the light and went back to his ravine to perch for the night. The male cuckoo crowed, and his mate stole up to the nests of the little birds with her egg in her mouth.

Robber Mother's youngsters let out perfect shrieks of delight. They stuffed themselves with wild strawberries that hung on the bushes, large as pine cones. One of them played with a litter of young hares; another ran a race with some young crows, which had hopped from their nest before they were really ready; a third caught up an adder from the ground and wound it around his neck and arm.

Robber Father was standing out on a marsh eating raspberries. When he glanced up, a big black bear stood beside him. Robber Father broke off an osier twig and struck the bear on the nose. "Keep to your own ground, you!" he said; "this is my turf." Then the huge bear turned around and lumbered off in another direction.

New waves of warmth and light kept coming, and now they brought with them seeds from the star-flower.

Golden pollen from rye fields fairly flew in the air. Then came butterflies, so big that they looked like flying lilies. The bee-hive in a hollow oak was already so full of honey that it dripped down on the trunk of the tree. Then all the flowers whose seed had been brought from foreign lands began to blossom. The loveliest roses climbed up the mountain wall in a race with the blackberry vines, and from the forest meadow sprang flowers as large as human faces.

Abbot Hans thought of the flower he was to pluck for Bishop Absalon; but each new flower that appeared was more beautiful than the others, and he wanted to choose the most beautiful of all.

Wave upon wave kept coming until the air was so filled with light that it glittered. All the life and beauty and joy of summer smiled on Abbot Hans. He felt that earth could bring no greater happiness than that which welled up about him, and he said to himself, "I do not know what new beauties the next wave that comes can bring with it."

But the light kept streaming in, and now it seemed to Abbot Hans that it carried with it something from an infinite distance. He felt a celestial atmosphere enfolding him, and tremblingly he began to anticipate, now that earth's joys had come, that the glories of heaven were approaching.

Then Abbot Hans marked how all grew still; the

birds hushed their songs, the flowers ceased growing, and the young foxes played no more. The glory now nearing was such that the heart wanted to stop beating; the eyes wept without one's knowing it; the soul longed to soar away into the Eternal. From far in the distance faint harp tones were heard, and celestial song, like a soft murmur, reached him.

Abbot Hans clasped his hands and dropped to his knees. His face was radiant with bliss. Never had he dreamed that even in this life it should be granted him to taste the joys of heaven, and to hear angels sing Christmas carols!

But beside Abbot Hans stood the lay brother who had accompanied him. In his mind there were dark thoughts. "This cannot be a true miracle," he thought, "since it is revealed to malefactors. This does not come from God, but has its origin in witchcraft and is sent hither by Satan. It is the Evil One's power that is tempting us and compelling us to see that which has no real existence."

From afar were heard the sound of angel harps and the tones of a Miserere. But the lay brother thought it was the evil spirits of hell coming closer. "They would enchant and seduce us," sighed he, "and we shall be sold into perdition."

The angel throng was so near now that Abbot Hans saw their bright forms through the forest branches. The lay brother saw them, too; but back of all this wondrous beauty he saw only some dread evil. For him it was the devil who performed these wonders on the anniversary of our Saviour's birth. It was done simply for the purpose of more effectually deluding poor human beings.

All the while the birds had been circling around the head of Abbot Hans, and they let him take them in his hands. But all the animals were afraid of the lay brother; no bird perched on his shoulder, no snake played at his feet. Then there came a little forest dove. When she marked that the angels were nearing, she plucked up courage and flew down on the lay brother's shoulder and laid her head against his cheek.

Then it appeared to him as if sorcery were come right upon him, to tempt and corrupt him. He struck with his hand at the forest dove and cried in such a loud voice that it rang throughout the forest, "Go thou back to hell, whence thou art come!"

Just then the angels were so near that Abbot Hans felt the feathery touch of their great wings, and he bowed down to earth in reverent greeting.

But when the lay brother's words sounded, their song was hushed and the holy guests turned in flight. At the same time the light and the mild warmth vanished in unspeakable terror for the darkness and cold in a human heart. Darkness sank over the earth, like a coverlet; frost came, all the growths shrivelled up; the animals and birds hastened away; the rushing of streams was hushed; the leaves dropped from the trees, rustling like rain.

Abbot Hans felt how his heart, which had but lately swelled with bliss, was now contracting with insufferable agony. "I can never outlive this," thought he, "that the angels from heaven had been so close to me and were driven away; that they wanted to sing Christmas carols for me and were driven to flight."

Then he remembered the flower he had promised Bishop Absalon, and at the last moment he fumbled among the leaves and moss to try and find a blossom. But he sensed how the ground under his fingers froze and how the white snow came gliding over the ground. Then his heart caused him even greater anguish. He could not rise, but fell prostrate on the ground and lay there.

When the robber folk and the lay brother had groped their way back to the cave, they missed Abbot Hans. They took brands with them and went out to search for him. They found him dead upon the coverlet of snow.

Then the lay brother began weeping and lamenting, for he understood that it was he who had killed Abbot Hans because he had dashed from him the cup of happiness which he had been thirsting to drain to its last drop.

When Abbot Hans had been carried down to Övid,

those who took charge of the dead saw that he held his right hand locked tight around something which he must have grasped at the moment of death. When they finally got his hand opened, they found that the thing which he had held in such an iron grip was a pair of white root bulbs, which he had torn from among the moss and leaves.

When the lay brother who had accompanied Abbot Hans saw the bulbs, he took them and planted them in Abbot Hans' herb garden.

He guarded them the whole year to see if any flower would spring from them. But in vain he waited through the spring, the summer, and the autumn. Finally, when winter had set in and all the leaves and the flowers were dead, he ceased caring for them.

But when Christmas Eve came again, he was so strongly reminded of Abbot Hans that he wandered out into the garden to think of him. And look! as he came to the spot where he had planted the bare root bulbs, he saw that from them had sprung flourishing green stalks, which bore beautiful flowers with silver white leaves.

He called out all the monks at Övid, and when they saw that this plant bloomed on Christmas Eve, when all the other growths were as if dead, they understood that this flower had in truth been plucked by Abbot

Hans from the Christmas garden in Göinge forest. Then the lay brother asked the monks if he might take a few blossoms to Bishop Absalon.

And when he appeared before Bishop Absalon, he gave him the flowers and said: "Abbot Hans sends you these. They are the flowers he promised to pick for you from the garden in Göinge forest."

When Bishop Absalon beheld the flowers, which had sprung from the earth in darkest winter, and heard the words, he turned as pale as if he had met a ghost. He sat in silence a moment; thereupon he said, "Abbot Hans has faithfully kept his word and I shall also keep mine." And he ordered that a letter of ransom be drawn up for the wild robber who was outlawed and had been forced to live in the forest ever since his youth.

He handed the letter to the lay brother, who departed at once for the Robbers' Cave. When he stepped in there on Christmas Day, the robber came toward him with axe uplifted. "I'd like to hack you monks into bits, as many as you are!" said he. "It must be your fault that Göinge forest did not last night dress itself in Christmas bloom."

"The fault is mine alone," said the lay brother, "and I will gladly die for it; but first I must deliver a message from Abbot Hans." And he drew forth the Bishop's letter and told the man that he was free. "Hereafter

257

you and your children shall play in the Christmas straw and celebrate your Christmas among people, just as Abbot Hans wished to have it," said he.

Then Robber Father stood there pale and speechless, but Robber Mother said in his name, "Abbot Hans has indeed kept his word, and Robber Father will keep his."

When the robber and his wife left the cave, the lay brother moved in and lived all alone in the forest, in constant meditation and prayer that his hard-heartedness might be forgiven him.

But Göinge forest never again celebrated the hour of our Saviour's birth; and of all its glory, there lives today only the plant which Abbot Hans had plucked. It has been named CHRISTMAS ROSE. And each year at Christmastide she sends forth from the earth her green stalks and white blossoms, as if she never could forget that she had once grown in the great Christmas garden at Göinge forest.

Lo! A Light is in the East

OTTO SALOMON 1921

J.W. REIMANN 1747

Lo! A Light is in the east – open wide your hearts with haste.

In the east the shine we see, who will now our comfort be?

In the crib a little child. In the crib a little child.

Lo! A Light is in the east –
open wide your hearts with haste.
In the east the shine we see,
who will now our comfort be?
In the crib a little child.

Come, to seek him we will go.
Come, behold our Light of joy.
E'en though icy winds may blow
Let our joyful praises show
by the manger, for the child.

Yea, he comes, he is not far,
soon will come our morning star,
then our night will be aglow,
hail! the saviour of the world
makes his entrance in our midst.

Fire, Light, so shall it be
heralds of his glory, see!
Yea, it tells us of the time
when the world shall be his own.
Come to us, Lord Jesus Christ!

THE WORKER IN SANDALWOOD

by MARJORIE L. C. PICKTHALL

he good curé of Terminaison
says that this tale of Hyacinthe
is all a dream. But then Madame points triumphantly to the
little cabinet of sandalwood in
the corner of her room. It had
stood there for many years
now, and the dust has gathered in the fine lines of the
little birds' feathers, and softened the petals of the lilies
carved at the corners. And the wood has taken on a
golden gleam like the memory of a sunset.

"What of that, my friend?" says Madame, pointing
to the cabinet. And the old curé bows his head.

"It may be so. God is very good," he says gently. But
he is never quite sure what he may believe.

On that winter day long ago, Hyacinthe was quite
sure of one thing and that was that the workshop was

261

very cold. There was no fire in it, and only one little lamp when the early dark drew on. The tools were so cold they scorched his fingers, and his feet were so cold he danced clumsily in the shavings to warm them. He was a great clumsy boy of fourteen, dark-faced, dull-eyed, and uncared for. He was clumsy because it is impossible to be graceful when you are growing very fast and have not enough to eat. He was dull-eyed because all eyes met his unlovingly. He was uncared for because no one knew the beauty of his soul. But his heavy young hands could carve things like birds and flowers perfectly. On this winter evening he was just wondering if he might lay aside the tools, and creep home to the cold loft where he slept, when he heard Pierre L'Oreillard's voice shouting outside.

"Be quick, be quick, and open the door, thou *imbecile.* It is I, thy master."

"Oui, mon maitre," said Hyacinthe, and he shambled to the door and opened it.

"Slow-worm!" cried Pierre, and he cuffed Hyacinthe as he passed in. Hyacinthe rubbed his head and said nothing. He was used to blows. He wondered why his master was in the workshop at that time of day instead of drinking brandy at the Cinq Chateaux.

Pierre L'Oreillard had a small heavy bundle under his arm, wrapped in sacking, then in burlap, and then in fine soft cloths. He laid it on a pile of shavings, and

262

unfolded it carefully; and a dim sweetness filled the
dark shed and hung heavily in the thin winter sunbeams.

"It is a piece of wood," said Hyacinthe in slow surprise. He knew that such wood had never been seen in
Terminaison.

Pierre L'Oreillard rubbed the wood respectfully with
his knobby fingers.

"It is sandalwood," he explained to Hyacinthe, pride

263

of knowledge making him quite amiable, "a most precious wood that grows in warm countries, thou great goblin. Smell it, idiot. It is sweeter than cedar. It is to make a cabinet for the old Madame at the big house."

"*Oui, mon maitre,*" said the dull Hyacinthe.

"Thy great hands shall shape and smooth the wood, *nigaud,* and I will render it beautiful," said Pierre, puffing out his chest.

"Yes, Master," answered Hyacinthe humbly, "and when is it to be ready for Madame?"

"Madame will want it perhaps next week, for that is Christmas. It is to be finished and ready on the holy festival, great sluggard. Hearest thou?" and he cuffed Hyacinthe's ears again furiously.

Hyacinthe knew that the making of the cabinet would fall to him, as most of the other work did. When Pierre L'Oreillard was gone he touched the strange sweet wood and at last laid his cheek against it, while the fragrance caught his breath. "How it is beautiful!" said Hyacinthe, and for a moment his eyes glowed, and he was happy. Then the light passed and with bent head he shuffled back to his bench through a foam of white shavings curling almost to his knees.

"Madame will want the cabinet for Christmas," repeated Hyacinthe to himself, and fell to work harder than ever, though it was so cold in the shed that his breath hung in the air like a little silvery cloud. There was a tiny window on his right, through which, when it was clear of frost, one looked on Terminaison; and that was cheerful, and made him whistle. But to the left, through the chink of the ill-fitting door, there was nothing to be seen but the forest, and the road dying under the snow.

Brandy was good at the Cinq Chateaux and Pierre L'Oreillard gave Hyacinthe plenty of directions, but no further help with the cabinet.

"That is to be finished for Madame at the festival, sluggard," said he every day, cuffing Hyacinthe about the head, "finished, and with a prettiness about the corners, hearest thou, *ourson*?"

"Yes, Monsieur," said Hyacinthe in his slow way; "I will try to finish it. But if I hurry I shall spoil it."

Pierre's little eyes flickered. "See that it is done, and done properly. I suffer from a delicacy of the constitution and a little feebleness of the legs these days, so that I cannot handle the tools properly. I must leave this work to thee, *gaucheur*. And stand up and touch a hand to thy cap when I speak to thee, slow-worm."

"Yes, Monsieur," said Hyacinthe wearily.

It is hard to do all the work and to be beaten into the bargain. And fourteen is not very old. Hyacinthe worked on at the cabinet with his slow and exquisite skill. But on Christmas Eve he was still at work, and the cabinet unfinished.

"The master will beat me," thought Hyacinthe, and he trembled a little, for Pierre's beatings were cruel. "But if I hurry, I shall spoil the wood, and it is too beautiful to be spoiled."

But he trembled again when Pierre came into the workshop, and he stood up and touched his cap.

"Is the cabinet finished, *imbecile?*" asked Pierre. And Hyacinthe answered in a low voice, "No, it is not finished yet, Monsieur."

"Then work on it all night, and show it to me completed in the morning, or thy bones shall mourn thine idleness," said Pierre, with a wicked look in his little eyes. And he shut Hyacinthe into the shed with a smoky lamp, his tools, and the sandalwood cabinet.

It was nothing unusual. He had been often left before to finish a piece of work overnight while Pierre went off to his brandies. But this was Christmas Eve, and he was very tired. Even the scent of the sandalwood could not make him fancy he was warm. The world seemed to be a black place, full of suffering and despair.

"In all the world, I have no friend," said Hyacinthe, staring at the flame of the lamp. "In all the world, there is no one to care whether I live or die. In all the world, no place, no heart, no love. O kind God, is there a place, a love for me in another world?"

I hope you feel very sorry for Hyacinthe, lonely, and cold, and shut up in the workshop on the eve of Christ-

mas. He was but an overgrown, unhappy child. And I
think with old Madame that for unhappy children, at
this season no help seems too divine for faith.

"There is no one to care for me," said Hyacinthe.

And he even looked at the chisel in his hand, thinking
that by a touch of that he might lose it all, and be at
peace, somewhere, not far from God. Only it was for-
bidden. Then came the tears, and great sobs that shook
him, so that he scarcely heard the gentle rattling of the
latch.

He stumbled to the door, opening it on the still woods
and the frosty stars. And a lad who stood outside in the
snow said, "I see you are working late, comrade. May
I come in?"

Hyacinthe brushed his ragged sleeve across his eyes
and nodded "Yes." Those little villages strung along the
great river see strange wayfarers at times. And Hyacinthe said to himself that surely here was such a one.
Blinking into the stranger's eyes, he lost for a flash the
first impression of youth, and received one of incredible
age or sadness. But the wanderer's eyes were only quiet,
very quiet, like the little pools in the wood where the
wild doves went to drink. As he turned within the door,
smiling at Hyacinthe and shaking some snow from his
cap, he did not seem to be more than sixteen or so.

"It is very cold outside," he said. "There is a big oak
tree on the edge of the fields that had split in the frost

and frightened all the little squirrels asleep there. Next year it will make an even better home for them. And see what I found close by!" He opened his fingers and showed Hyacinthe a little sparrow lying unruffled in the palm.

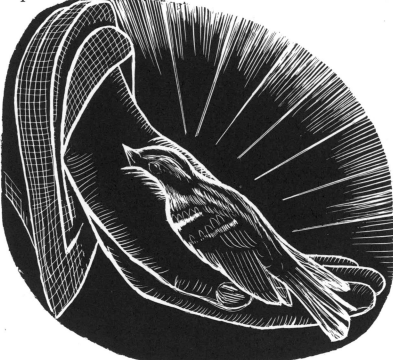

"*Pauvrette!*" said the dull Hyacinthe. "*Pauvrette! Is it then dead?*" He touched it with a gentle forefinger.

"No," answered the strange boy, "it is not dead. We will put it here among the shavings, not far from the lamp, and it will be well by the morning."

268

He smiled at Hyacinthe again, and the shambling lad felt dimly as if the scent of the sandalwood were sweeter, and the lamp-flame clearer. But the stranger's eyes were only quiet, quiet.

"Have you come far?" asked Hyacinthe. "It is a bad season for traveling, and the wolves are out."

"A long way," said the other. "A long, long way. I heard a child cry—"

"There is no child here," put in Hyacinthe. "Monsieur L'Oreillard says children cost too much money. But if you have come far, you must need food and fire, and I have neither. At the Cinq Chateaux you will find both."

The stranger looked at him again with those quiet eyes, and Hyacinthe fancied that his face was familiar. "I will stay here," he said; "you are late at work, and you are unhappy."

"Why as to that," answered Hyacinthe, rubbing his cheeks and ashamed of his tears, "most of us are sad at one time or another, the good God knows. Stay here and welcome if it pleases you; and you may take a share of my bed, though it is no more than a pile of balsam boughs and an old blanket in the loft. But I must work at this cabinet, for the drawers must be finished and the handles put on and the corners carved, all by the holy morning; or my wages will be paid with a stick."

"You have a hard master," put in the other, "if he

would pay you with blows upon the feast of Noel."

"He is hard enough," said Hyacinthe, "but once he gave me a dinner of sausages and white wine; and once, in the summer, melons. If my eyes will stay open, I will finish this by morning. Stay with me an hour or so, comrade, and talk to me of your travels, so that the time may pass more quickly."

And while Hyacinthe worked, he told,—of sunshine and dust, of the shadow of vine-leaves on the flat white walls of a house; of rosy doves on the roof; of the flowers that come out in the spring, anemones crimson and blue, and white cyclamen in the shadow of the rocks; of the olive, the myrtle, and the almond; until Hyacinthe's fingers ceased working, and his sleepy eyes blinked wonderingly.

"See what you have done, comrade," he said at last; "you have told me of such pretty things that I have done but little work for an hour. And now the cabinet will never be finished, and I shall be beaten."

"Let me help you," smiled the other. "I also was bred a carpenter."

At first Hyacinthe would not, fearing to trust the sweet wood out of his hands. But at length he allowed the stranger to fit one of the drawers. And so deftly was it done that Hyacinthe pounded his fists on the bench in admiration. "You have a pretty knack," he cried. "It seemed as if you did but hold the drawer in your hands a moment, and hey! it jumped into its place."

"Let me fit in the other little drawers while you rest awhile," said the stranger. So Hyacinthe curled up among the shavings, and the other boy fell to work upon the little cabinet of sandalwood.

Hyacinthe was very tired. He lay still among the shavings, and thought of all the boy had told him, of the hillside flowers, the laughing leaves, the golden bloom of the anise, and the golden sun upon the roads until he was warm. And all the time the boy with the quiet eyes was at work upon the cabinet, smoothing, fitting, polishing.

"You do better work than I," said Hyacinthe once, and the stranger answered, "I was lovingly taught." And again Hyacinthe said, "It is growing towards morning. In a little while I will get up and help you."

"Lie still and rest," said the other boy. And Hyacinthe lay still. His thoughts began to slide into dreams, and he woke with a little start, for there seemed to be music in the shed; though he could not tell whether it came from the strange boy's lips, or from the shabby tools as he used them, or from the stars.

"The stars are much paler," thought Hyacinthe. "Soon it will be morning, and the corners are not carved yet. I must get up and help this kind one in a little moment. Only the music and the sweetness seem to fold me close, so that I may not move."

Then behind the forest there shone a pale glow of dawn, and in Terminaison the church bells began to ring. "Day will soon be here," thought Hyacinthe, "and with day will come Monsieur L'Oreillard and his stick. I must get up and help for even yet the corners are not carved."

But the stranger looked at him, smiling as though he loved him, and laid his brown finger lightly on the four empty corners of the cabinet. And Hyacinthe saw the squares of reddish wood ripple and heave and break, as little clouds when the wind goes through the sky. And out of them thrust forth the little birds, and after them the lilies, for a moment living; but even as Hyacinthe looked, settling back into the sweet reddish-brown wood. Then the stranger smiled again, laid all the tools in order, and, opening the door, went away into the woods.

Hyacinthe crept slowly to the door. The winter sun, half risen, filled all the frosty air with splendid gold. Far down the road a figure seemed to move amid the glory but the splendor was such that Hyacinthe was blinded. His breath came sharply as the glow beat on the wretched shed, on the old shavings, on the cabinet with the little birds and the lilies carved at the corners.

He was too pure of heart to feel afraid. But "Blessed be the Lord," whispered Hyacinthe, clasping his slow hands, "for He hath visited and redeemed His people. But who will believe?"

Then the sun of Christ's day rose gloriously, and the little sparrow came from his nest among the shavings and shook his wings to the light.

AS 1 WAS WATCHING by MY SHEEP

AS 1 WAS WATCHING by MY SHEEP
ANGELS AWOKE ME FROM MY SLEEP.

    SAYING, "A CHILD IS BORN THIS NIGHT,
    UNDER A STAR THAT SHINES SO BRIGHT.

LOW IN A STABLE LIES HE THERE
THAT SHALL REDEEM THE EARTH'S DESPAIR."

    WHEN 1 HAVE FOUND THIS WONDROUS SIGHT,
    I'LL STAY AND WATCH by DAY AND NIGHT.

THIS LOVE I'LL GUARD FOR ALL TO SEE,
SO WILL MY HEART MOST JOYFUL BE.

COLOGNE, PETER VON BRACHEL, 1623

274

THE FOREST BEAR

by REIMMICHL

is real name was Blasius Peer, but he was known to every one as the Forest Bear. And this was because he had a gray straggly beard and gray straggly hair like a bear's. He wore the same suit year in and year out, coarse woollen trousers, waistcoat and jacket, which had once been black but now with age were of an indefinable brown hue, almost red. Furthermore he lived all by himself, up there in the Steiger Forest. The old bachelor's whole world consisted of a ramshackle little hovel, black with age, and a small plot of ground, barely enough to supply winter feed for two goats, or maybe half a cow, or, rather, a whole cow every second year. Around all this grew a dense wall of

275

straight-stemmed lofty fir trees, and above was a piece of blue sky, or gray, according to the weather.

By trade old Blasius was a carpenter, but he didn't grow fat on that. In the first place he only had the soft pinewood to work with, secondly he didn't know how to make more than one kind of chest and cupboard, and thirdly he had no idea of the value of money. He thought that forty groats a day was a fabulous sum to earn. Thus it came about that he still had not cleared the small mortgage on his little place during the past thirty years.

For himself Blasi needed very little or practically nothing. Meat he tasted only once or twice a year, and very little at that, wine he had never touched in all these years, and brandy maybe three or four sips each year—just enough to moisten his stone-hard crust of bread during winter whenever he went down to the little church of St. Nicholas to make confession, and the weather was cold. But in spite of this, Blasi was a spendthrift, and this is how it happened.

He possessed an enormous Christmas crib—which had become by far the biggest for miles around and which grew bigger from year to year. Blasi loved this manger scene with body and soul, with heart and mind. It was his joy and passion. Every groat that he could (and sometimes could not) spare went into the crib. Every year something new had to be added—a few figures or at least some decorations; he did not give up on this even if he had to go hungry for it. In the course of years he caused his manger scene to suffer from a veritable overcrowding. He had four hundred sheep (alas, all of wood!), a hundred and fifty shepherds in every imaginable posture, more than fifty angels, some two hundred townspeople pieces from the High Priest and mayor down to the chimney sweep and beadle, all kinds of artisan and business folk, the three holy kings with a retinue of one hundred and eighty, and camels and horses besides, not to mention the houses, huts and tents on the outskirts of the cities of Bethlehem and Jerusalem. Seven years before Blasi had treated himself to the biggest expense of his life when he returned from the fair in Halle with a small barrel organ that played twelve different tunes.

Every year when All Saints Day came around, Blasi

without fail would put away his carpenter's tools and accept no more orders, for now it was high time to see to his crib if he wanted to have it ready and in good shape for Christmas. First of all he constructed a huge mountain. On this he carefully placed all the beautifully gnarled root stocks, the fine crinkled mosses, the pretty pebbles and the clear transparent crystals that he had so painstakingly collected in the mountains during the year. Then he "planted" whole forests of delicate little trees, made paths and roads and covered them with shining silvery sand. He even put gleaming glaciers on the highest mountain peaks. And of course the little rushing brooklets and translucent lakes had to be there too. All this gave him plenty to do for at least three weeks. Then followed the cities and houses and the hundreds of figures, and there was so much in the way of small repairs, painting and gluing to be done that it easily filled out another four weeks. During the last week he had to work almost nonstop day and night, until the last little man and little lamb were exactly in their place in good time.

He went to great pains to give the whole work of art its proper surroundings. As if it were not enough that the ground around his own hut fairly bristled with trees, Blasius now brought in whole hampers full of young spruce seedlings and branches, made wreaths from yew

twigs, and placed dozens of young trees behind and beside the manger until in the end the whole room looked like a forest and there was hardly room for him to turn around, or even to open the door of his adjoining little bedroom. In order to make the woods in his room shining, he hung the many branches with tinsel and glass beads.

And then came Christmas Eve, and the real celebration at his crib. On the window sills he had lit twelve big wax candles, shielded by tin screens so that their light fell fully on the crib. Oh, how the crystals, the silvery sand and the glass beads glistened and sparkled, how the windows of the houses and temples flashed, and the whole mountain became a mass of shimmering, scintillating points of light! As the candle flames flickered, dancing shadows went across the landscape and made the tiny figures seem to come alive and bow to each other in greeting and move about in happy confusion. The lights seemed to be brightest where the Angel of the Annunciation hovered. You felt as though heaven itself were open and the angel just emerged from its sea of celestial light.

More than half an hour Blasi sat before his shining crib, completely still, hands folded, quiet as a mouse, his mouth wide open, gazing rapturously at its glory. Then he got out his barrel organ and ground out one tune after another. He could not sing, much less play any instrument, but some music for the Christ Child he must have, and here the organ served him excellently. It did not matter in the least that its whole repertoire consisted of waltzes and polkas, that some notes were rather out of tune and others terribly screechy—to the Forest Bear it sounded like the sweet music of angels, and after grinding out all twelve pieces he started all over again and played and laughed and cried. He lived so deeply in his joy in the crib that he finally forgot everything around him and felt himself to be one of the shepherds having just heard the glad tidings from the angel and wanting to go to the Christ Child now for worship and to make him really happy with his barrel organ music. So he played and gazed in wonder until it was high time to go down to the village for the midnight service.

That is how the Forest Bear celebrated Christmas.

Every year a great number of people came up to the little hut in the forest to admire the big, beautiful crib. Among others there came a certain Professor Hermann from Innsbruck. He used to roam the valleys of the Tyrol summer and winter, collecting proverbs and folk songs and inquiring about traditions and legends and studying the life of the mountain folk so that he could write books about them. Professor Hermann was always very pleased to find anything that was genuine tradition and original, and he liked the crib of the Forest Bear immensely. He was very keen to buy it, offering six hundred guilders for it, cash down.

A flicker of something like anger flashed over old Blasi's face. He straightened up his gnarled body, his old joints creaking, and said, No! This crib was not for sale, not for all the riches of the world. Rather would he sell his house—but no! not that either, for there could be no better place outside of heaven than his little wood hut and he would not exchange it even for the emperor's palace at Innsbruck. He estimated his crib to be of ten times more value than his hut, including its stone foundations. Blasi had never made such a long speech in his whole life. He hardly ever spoke more than three words at a time, although he liked to listen to others talking. There was only one thing that he could not bear to listen to for long, and that was whenever he heard of the need, suffering and misery of his fellow men. Then his heart, which was as soft as butter, welled up until his eyes overflowed, and he gave up the last coin in his pocket because he felt he could not possibly leave any cry for help unanswered or any need unheeded. So there you have it—the Forest Bear was a spendthrift.

Professor Hermann took an instant liking to the queer old bird from the forest, even more so than to his ingenious crib. He laughed and said that such odd fellows there must be, and that the world would be a hundred times more beautiful if there were more queer folk like him in it.

There was no more talk of the deal. But the following year old Blasi had new, grand ideas. He wanted to take out the partition dividing his little bedroom from the living room in order to enlarge the crib even more, right into his bedroom, as there was not enough space left in his living room. Alas, though, Blasi's soft heart played him a trick, and this is how it came about....

About a quarter of an hour's walk from his own hut at the edge of the forest, there lived a widow, Ladscheider by name, with her five small children. The little plot of land she lived on was heavily mortgaged, and one day, without warning, a hardhearted creditor suddenly called in a capital of six hundred guilders. The poor soul now faced complete ruin. As Blasi passed by the Ladscheider house one morning in October he found the widow sitting at her door weeping and lamenting brokenheartedly. She told him with many sobs that she could see no way out at all except to farm out her children all over the village and to hire herself out as a servant. She would willingly bear anything so long as she did not have to be separated from her children.

Blasi's heart was flowing out from both his eyes, yet he did not know how to comfort her because he was so clumsy of speech, and in any case he himself knew no way out. His head was drooping down, lower even than

the widow Ladscheider's, as he slowly and sadly turned home to his own hut. But as he went homewards with halting steps his heart grew more and more heavy and began to urge him: "Blasi, get an advance on your piece of land and give the money to the widow." But his head thought otherwise: "Money from my land? It is mortgaged anyhow and if I could pay this off there would hardly be four hundred guilders left over."..."Blasi, sell your crib. The professor will give you exactly six hundred guilders for it!"..."Sell my crib? That's an inhuman demand!"..."It's much more inhuman to leave your neighbor in such need!"..."Why, every man is his own nearest neighbor."..."That is just what the innkeepers said in Bethlehem when they turned Mary and Joseph away so roughly. Have you no pity on the little orphans?"..."Of course, of course. I have great pity for them, but it is not I that am driving them out of their home."..."Yes, but you let it happen and you are no better than the man who does it."

Thus his heart argued against his head, and his head against his heart, and nearly brought the Bear to despair. This hard struggle went on for several days, until in the end the head became too weak and the heart gained the upper hand. The sacrifice had to be made.

Old Blasius found it very hard to separate himself from his crib; it can hardly be more painful when body and soul have to leave each other. But what can a man do if his heart is as soft as butter? Old, inexperienced Blasi made it even harder for himself than necessary by having a solemn farewell with his treasure. He erected the crib during the following days, even though it was not yet Christmas by a long way. Late in the evening of All Saints Day he lit the twelve candles and took up the barrel organ. When the mountain began to sparkle and gleam his eyes began to burn like fire, and after he had played the first piece the tears flowed freely down his cheeks; with the second piece he started to howl out loud, shaking and twitching as if in convulsions. There was nothing else to do but blow out the candles and hide himself in his little bedroom.

Next morning he braced himself with all his might for what lay before him, put on his best clothes and set out for Innsbruck without once looking back at the crib scene. Having got there he inquired for the professor's home and stumbled in. "Herr Professor, I will sell my crib. You can have it for six hundred guilders!"

The professor looked almost cross. What could be the matter with the queer old bird from the forest? Had the money-devil grabbed him as well now? That looked bad for the world. But to Blasi he only said coolly, to put him to the test, "Six hundred guilders is too much for that old junk; I'll give you three hundred."

Blasi's eyes lit up for a moment, then clouded over again. "Six hundred guilders it will have to be. I won't do it for less," he replied, trembling.

"What if I give you seven hundred?"

"No, I don't need seven hundred—six hundred, neither more nor less. That is the bargain."

On saying this Blasi again was shaking from head to foot as with the ague. The professor began to realize that some matter of prime importance was behind all this, and he probed and questioned until finally he knew about the hard constraint and distress, the misery and suffering, of Blasius. Now it was the professor's turn —something seemed to sting in his eyes and he had to retire quickly into the back room. Only after quite a time did he come out again. He counted out six hundred-guilder bank notes on the table and said, "Here is the money. I will buy the crib, only just now I have nowhere to put it. So the manger will have to stay in your hut as long as you live. When you die, I will have it brought here."

The eyes of the Forest Bear opened as wide as saucers and his mouth gaped as wide as a stove door. He sank into a chair, sprang up again, and almost fell on the professor's neck. The latter now became businesslike and put a quick end to the scene. "Let us put it all down now in black and white and file it at the court registry.

As long as you live the crib is yours. When you die it becomes my property. Do you have any objections?"

Blasi, of course, had none; he was absolutely speechless. Two hours later, on his way home, he felt he simply *had* to sing today, and sing he did. It sounded more like a sort of gargling than actual singing, but to him it sounded beautiful, and he sang:

> As I was watching by my sheep
> Angels awoke me from my sleep.
> What joy I know,
> Joy I know,
> Oh, oh, oh!
> Oh, oh, oh!
> Benedicamus Domino,
> Benedicamus Domino.

The Forest Bear was crying, but the heart in his breast split its sides with laughing. His head was shaking itself, and in the end all three swam in purest happiness.

What jubilation there was when the great helper in need appeared in the Ladscheiders' house and poured out his treasure on the table. Twelve eyes shone up at Blasi like the brightest of Christmas stars, and six pairs of lips just would not stop kissing his gnarled old hands. To escape all this danger Blasi quickly beat a retreat and trotted off toward his hut in the forest, singing or

rather, gargling—on the way. Once there, he immediately began to work on his new, great plans for the crib.

And never in his life did the Forest Bear have a happier Christmas time than this year.

SONG FOR A NEW BABY

WORDS & MUSIC, SYLVIA BEELS

who will go in must soft-ly go

Like the shep-herds Long a-go,

for here there sleeps a lit-tle child, Like

Je-sus, un-de-filed.

Who will go in must softly go
Like the shepherds Long ago,
for here there sleeps a Little child,
Like Jesus, undefiled.

Who will go in must humbly go,
Like the wisemen Long ago,
for here a Little baby Lies,
A mystery to the wise.

And who a Loving heart will bring,
brings an offering to a King;
for here a Little child is born,
Like Jesus, Mary's son.

THE CHESS PLAYER

by GER KOOPMAN

t was Christmas Eve. The whole day a cold wind had been blowing and now it had started to snow. Thousands—millions—of snowflakes came out of the sky and slowly covered the little village where Farmer Dyhema lived. They covered his fields, already plowed up for the next sowing; they covered his huge barns, full of hay or corn; they covered the yard, the big stable, and the house.

Old Farmer Dyhema had seen the snow coming down. He was sitting near the open fire in his easy chair. He liked the snow on his fields. It will make a better harvest next year, he thought. It was nice and

warm in his room. On the table stood a chessboard.
All the chessmen stood in their right places, four rows
on the white and black squares of the board. Dyhema
liked playing chess. He was waiting for the minister.
Every Sunday evening the minister came to play chess
with the old farmer, and also at Christmas time. He
would come tonight. Oh, yes, Dyhema liked the game.
He always won. There was nobody in the village who
could play as well as he could. There was nobody in

the village who was as rich as he was. He was the best farmer, the richest farmer, the best chess player; and he was honest and righteous, too. He lived alone with his servants. His wife had died years ago. But this Christmas he was not thinking of his wife. He was always alone, thinking about himself. How good the harvest had been this year! What an important man he was in the village! When he walked through the streets they took their hats off as he passed. When somebody needed help—*he* gave it. When somebody needed work—*he* gave it. If anybody needed money—*he* lent it.

Suddenly the door opened. A servant came in. "It is rather late, Dyhema. Shall I keep the Christmas tart hot in the oven?"

Dyhema looked at the clock. "The minister is late," he said. "Yes, keep the tart hot."

The servant, moving toward the doorway, said, "I am afraid the minister will not come. The snow is very deep."

Dyhema looked cross, but he only said, "I can wait."

When the servant had gone, Dyhema stood up and looked out of the window. "Dear me, what a lot of snow," he said. "I am sure the minister will not come. The snow is very deep." Dyhema looked at the chessboard with longing eyes.

But somebody was coming! The Christ Child!

The whole day the Christ Child had been very busy. Christmas is his time, for then the hearts of people open; and that is what the Christ Child needs: open hearts. People think of their youth, how nice Christmas was at home. They think about their lives, and how things have turned out wrong. They long to change, to start anew. Then the Christ Child comes.

The whole day the Christ Child had been very busy. One thing had still to be done: to go to the old farmer, Dyhema. When God had told him that, he had said, "But his heart is not at all open." But God had only said, "Go. It has been closed and hard for too long. It is time now."

As the Christ Child was walking through the snow, he thought this over. What could he do? But when God says, "It is time," then it is time. And so at once the Christ Child was in the room of the old farmer. Nobody had heard him coming; nobody had seen him, but suddenly he was there. "Good evening, Dyhema," he said, in his beautiful voice.

Dyhema looked, and looked again. "Who are you, little boy, and how did you come in?"

The Christ Child sat down on a chair, opposite Dyhema, near the fire.

"I am the Christ Child."

"The Christ Child? So. What do *you* need?"

"I only want to talk to you."

294

"There is nothing to talk about. I did everything a man can do. I gave five hundred guilders for the Christmas celebration in the church."

"I know," said the Christ Child, "and two hundred and fifty guilders for the Sunday School celebration."

"Yes," said the farmer again, "and five hundred guilders for the poor people in the village; and wherever there are sick people, I send my servants to bring them a parcel."

"I know it all," said the Christ Child, and he sighed. "You are like a king on a throne who gives little presents to all his people. Yet how small these gifts are if you think of the thousands of guilders which you earned this year. And all these gifts were given, not out of love for others, but only out of love to yourself, so that you can sit here, content and satisfied with yourself. Oh, if you only knew the Christmas story!"

"I know it. By heart. 'In the days of the Emperor Augustus...' "

"See, you are quite wrong!"

"Wrong?" Farmer Dyhema took the Bible which was lying near him. "See, here it is. 'In the days of the Emperor Augustus...' "

"Wrong! *I know* the story. *I* am the Christ Child! It was not long, long ago, in the days of Augustus. It happens every year anew. Somewhere every year a child is born, poor and without clothes, waiting to be helped, by you. Sometimes it is a sick child, or a poor man, or a poor woman, waiting to be helped, by you. That is the Christmas story."

"I know that I am a sinner before God," said Dyhema. "Every one is a sinner before God. But as far as I was able I did what I could. I cannot give all my money away, or anything like that. That is just nonsense."

"I do not ask only for money. I ask for much more than money. I ask for love! You said that you did everything you could? What about your daughter Bouke?"

The old farmer stood up angrily. "Bouke is dead. She is dead for me! If you were really the Christ Child you would know that ten years ago she married against my will. She married an artist, a musician, against my will. Children should obey their parents. No, do not speak about Bouke."

"She is poor. She has a son."

"I know. It is her own fault. Not mine!"

The Christ Child looked at the clock. Half past seven. And at eight o'clock—at eight o'clock Bouke was to come here with her son. He had been to the place where she lived, and he had told her to go back to her father. He had said that everything would be all right when she came. And now there was only half an hour left, and the heart of the old farmer was harder than ever before. But he was not dismayed. God had sent him. He even smiled and said, "Let us play chess!"

"Can you play?"

"A little bit."

"Come on. That is better than all this talking."

They started. It seemed that the Christ Child was not a very good player. After ten minutes he had already lost two castles and a knight. Dyhema rubbed his hands. He would win the game. That was certain. When the Christ Child had lost nearly half his pieces, he suddenly spoke. "Imagine for a minute that your daughter came to you this Christmas Eve with your grandson. Would you receive them?"

"Stop that nonsense. Look at your game. You have nearly lost. And why should they come?"

"I have almost lost. Well, perhaps. But suppose I should win the game before eight o'clock, would you receive them?"

The old farmer laughed. "I would, because it is impossible."

The Christ Child smiled, too. It was one minute to eight. The Christ Child had only his king, queen and one bishop. Dyhema had almost all his men. Dyhema looked at the clock. "Eight o'clock," he said.

"Eight o'clock. And I think it's checkmate," said the Christ Child.

"Checkmate?" Dyhema looked at the board. His eyes

widened. "Oh? Wait a minute. You have changed the positions of all my men. No, no! But what has happened?"

The Christ Child smiled again. "That is what happens in life," he said. Then he looked very earnest. "Often people think they are lost. They think that nothing in the world can help them. And then God looks and says, 'It is time.' And all at once everything looks different. Everything comes into a different light, and all at once you see that all is not lost, but won. Remember this, Dyhema! All is not lost in His eyes. The lowly shall be lifted up—the first shall be last." And then he was gone.

Dyhema stood up. He sat down in his chair near the fire. He closed his eyes. He would think this over.

Suddenly he awoke. Somebody had knocked at the door. He rubbed his eyes. I have been sleeping, he thought. I had a wonderful dream about the Christ Child. He looked at the table. There was the chessboard. The two rows of white men and the two rows of black men stood neatly on opposite sides of the board. Yes, it had been a dream. "Come in," he said. A servant came in.

"Dyhema, here is a little boy. He says..."

Dyhema stood up in astonishment. "A little boy with his mother?"

"No, he is alone. But he says his mother had an accident. She has sprained her ankle. She is waiting in the snow about half a mile away. She sent the boy for help."

Dyhema laughed. He thought, of course it is not my daughter. And then he said, "Send the servants out with the horse and cart. Make a room ready and bring her here. Send for the doctor. Bring the boy here."

The servant went out. A moment later a boy of about nine came in. Dyhema stood up. He was strangely moved. The boy looked—yes, he looked just as he himself must have looked long, long ago. "What is your name?"

"Sigurd," said the boy.

Dyhema sank back into his chair. He closed his eyes. Sigurd, that was *his* name. His daughter had called her son after him. But what about the Christ Child? It was a dream, of course. But dreams are lies, nonsense. But still there was the boy. His grandson. No. He would not receive his daughter. He stood up and went to the kitchen. Only one old servant was there. "Where are the others?" he asked.

"They are all with their families, of course, and two have gone out to fetch the poor woman," she said.

"I do not want her here! They must take her somewhere else!"

"Dyhema! On Christmas Eve you are going to refuse a poor woman your house! Very well. You are responsible. But I cannot go out and through the snow. Who will tell them?"

"As soon as they are here, call me. But don't let the woman come into the house."

Dyhema went back to the living room. The boy sat near the fireplace. When Dyhema came in he stood up and, going to him, the boy said, "Are you my grandfather?"

"Of course not," Dyhema said angrily.

The boy looked sad. "Then I have come to the wrong farm. You know, Mummy said, when she fell down, 'That light over there is the farm. Run over there and ask for help.' But it does not matter. When Mummy comes here she can tell you where she wanted to go. She was born in this village, you know. My granddad is the richest farmer in the village. My mummy said, 'He is like a little king. Everyone asks for his advice. He is very clever, you know.' "

Dyhema suddenly said, "Why are you going to your grandfather?"

"Mummy said that the Christ Child had told her to

go. We have never been there. We are very poor, you
know. My daddy is dead. We had no money, but Mummy always said, 'I will not take the first step.' And then
all at once she told me that the Christ Child had told
her to go."

"Did she see the Christ Child?"

"I don't know. Afterwards she said it was a dream.
And on the journey she was very uncertain. She said to
me, once, 'Do not be surprised if we only stay for a
short time.' "

Dyhema said nothing. He looked into the fire. Suddenly the boy saw the chessboard. He went to the table.
"My granddad can play chess! He always wins, my
mummy says! Can you play? I can. Mummy says that
I play so well because I got it from my granddad. Shall
we play? Do you know, I am hungry. We had no supper."

Dyhema looked up. "Can you really play? Such a
small child?"

"I am not small. And I often win."

"Come on, let us try," Dyhema said.

After a short time Dyhema understood that the boy
really could play. Almost without thinking he made the
right moves. After half an hour Dyhema became restless. The boy was winning! Really, the small boy seemed
to be a better player than he was. And what annoyed
him most was that while he did his utmost to win, the
boy just played, without thinking it over. If Dyhema

made a move, after a long time of consideration, the boy followed immediately, and it was always the right move. Perhaps it was because Dyhema was so annoyed that he suddenly made a wrong move. The boy smiled. "That is a bad move," he said. "You had better take it back."

"No. What I have done, I have done!"

The boy looked at him. Why was this old man so angry? He could not help it, could he? Was it because he could not win the game? A lot of people grew angry if they could not win. It was interesting. You learned

302

most in a game that you lost. But this was an old man. Perhaps...

Suddenly the old servant came in. "Dyhema, what about the Christmas tart? Can I bring it in now?"

Dyhema looked very angry. "Go away with your tart!"

What a pity, the boy thought. He was so hungry. How angry the old man was. Was that only because he was not winning? Suddenly he said, "I should like to have some tart. I had no supper, you know."

Dyhema only said, "Your turn to play."

Sigurd sighed. Then he had an idea. He would let the old man win. He would make a bad move. It was not easy to do that. He sighed. It is Christmas Eve, he thought, I will do it. And he made his move.

Dyhema laughed. "A bad move. See, I can take your queen. Oh, I knew I could win. I have never yet lost a game!"

Sigurd blushed. This was not fair. He had always been told not to be sad if he lost, and not to be proud if he won. Suddenly he smiled. If I can cheer him up, let him win, he thought, and he said, "You can never be sure who wins before it is checkmate."

All the time Dyhema had looked at the boy. He had seen the tears come into his eyes after he had spoken. And he had seen the change, the smile. And then the words of the boy. It was as if he saw the Christ Child again. He remembered the words of the Christ Child, "Sometimes you think all is lost." He stood up. He walked up and down the room. The boy looked at him in surprise. Dyhema saw his life—his long life—in a new light. No mistakes? Open and right? There was a fault, a great fault. How could he have been so blind? My heart has been cold and unmoved, yet I've always thought I was such a good man, with all my good deeds. What a wretched old man I am. All this he felt deep in his heart and he saw his dream again, heard the words of the Christ Child, "God comes. He brings something new into life. *Love!*" That was it. Love!

Dyhema went to the boy. He put his hand on his shoulder. "You have won," he said, "you and the Christ Child."

The boy looked at him in astonishment. "What do you mean?"

Old Farmer Dyhema smiled. "It does not matter, my son," he said. "It does not matter. But remember this: the Christ Child brings new life, yet all seemed so lost to man when Jesus was born. Born in a stable, poor and cold. All seemed to have been utterly lost in the end, my son. A cross was the end. We must remember, Sigurd, remember the moment when God looked and said, 'It is the time.' And it was! The cross was not the end. And even today the Christ Child still comes to warm the hearts of men."

There was a hard knocking, and the door opened. The old servant said, "Tell me, Dyhema, where must I send this woman? She is here now."

"Bring her in here, of course."

"But you said…"

"It is my daughter! Didn't you know that? Bring her in here at once! It is Bouke! Quick! And bring the Christmas tart. Quick, it is Christmas!"

how far is it to bethlehem?

how far is it to bethlehem?
    not very far.
shall we find the stable-room
    lit by a star?

can we see the little child,
    is he within?
if we lift the wooden latch
    may we go in?

may we stroke the creatures there,
    ox, ass, or sheep?
may we peep like them and see
    jesus asleep?

if we touch his tiny hand
    will he awake?
will he know we've come so far
    just for his sake?

great kings have precious gifts
    and we have naught,
little smiles and little tears
    are all we brought.

for all weary children
    mary must weep.
here, on his bed of straw
    sleep, children, sleep.

god in his mother's arms,
    babes in the byre,
sleep, as they sleep who find
    their heart's desire.

FRANCES CHESTERTON

306

THE CRIBMAKER'S TRIP TO HEAVEN

by REIMMICHL

 illibald Krautmann and Christmas—these two things belonged together like a door and its hinges, like a clock and its face, like a bell and its tower. The whole year round Willibald Krautmann thought, dreamed and prepared things for Christmas. During his whole lifetime, Krautmann had carved more than a thousand crib figures, he had built sixty manger scenes, he had been present at every cribmakers' conference in Innsbruck in Tyrol.

Willibald Krautmann had a small, round, stocky figure, which was much too small for his ambitious soul. Often his soul would inflate itself mightily, climb up over his head and whisper into his ear: "Willibald, after all you are the greatest artist and cribmaster throughout the whole land, there is nobody who can be compared with you. And so there will be hardly a single soul who is so highly respected in heaven as you. When you go up to heaven some day, they will fling all the gates wide open and lead you in in triumph." He was sure that in heaven a palace would be prepared for him. To such whisperings the little fat man was always willing to lend an ear.

Now it happened that Willibald Krautmann died and just on the night before Christmas Eve. He passed away peacefully, and now he was energetically trotting up the steep road to heaven, and soon began talking to himself.

"Do you see, my dear old Willibald, how the Christ Child honors those whom he wants to honor? He is having you fetched just on Christmas Eve, for the most beautiful feastday in heaven. Perhaps they are calling you up there just so that you can fix the heaven crib scene for them. But for that they called him rather late! I would say on short notice! Well, well, we will see...."

When Willibald thought about making a crib in heaven, it came over him like a fever, and his progress seemed to him much too slow. The road was long, and it was winter time, and cold. Often the wanderer to heaven slipped off the icy path and slid back a few steps. This annoyed him, and he soon began to grumble properly.

If they really wanted him in heaven, they could at least send a carriage to get him. That wouldn't be asking too much. It wouldn't need to be a coach-and-twelve exactly, he would be satisfied with a coach-and-four just as well. And what are all those angels in heaven doing, that not a single one is coming to meet him here, Willibald Krautmann? Certainly he doesn't demand that the whole legion of angels comes along to accompany him, but at least a couple of dozen of the most distinguished kind could give him an escort; that would be only proper. Willibald Krautmann, after all, is no mere travelling worker, *that* they should know by now.

But in spite of all his muttering and grumbling, no escort of angels appeared, no heavenly coach with team of four or twelve either, and there was nothing Willibald Krautmann could do but walk wearily onward. For a long time he continued walking on in silence; darkness fell, moon and stars rose, and the tired wanderer's strength all but failed him. He sat down on a large rock. Then in the distance he suddenly saw the heavenly Jerusalem, the wonderful city. It lay on a hill of purest silver, and the walls, the houses, the churches, the palaces and towers were of solid genuine gold. Inside the city a wonderful fine light was shining, a thousand times brighter than the sun, yet much milder and softer. The windows in the golden house fronts shimmered red, blue, green and a hundred other colors. Willibald Krautmann looked and looked.

But isn't anybody ever coming? Perhaps they are not yet finished with the preparations for his reception— or they believe he is still far off and have no idea that he is already there. Let's let them hear from us!

He stood up on a star and waved his big hat and shouted with all the might of his voice: "Halloo!" Then a little angel in a white gown fluttered up over the golden city, looked out quickly and disappeared again in a jiffy....

...Ah, now it's going to begin, now all the bells are going to ring at once and the cannons will shoot.

But a quarter of an hour went by and nothing moved. Only a few fine, soft bells rang, like the chimes in the cathedral at Salzburg. He heard "Silent Night" but that was far far back in heaven. Krautmann shook his head. What does that mean?

But now it dawns on him. They want to prepare him a surprise. He is supposed to approach quite close to heaven, and then when he is close the gates will fling wide open and the whole heavenly splendor will stream out and the choirs of angels and archangels will sing for Willibald Krautmann. Yes, yes, that is how it will be, that's the only way. To be sure, in lifetime Willibald Krautmann never liked surprises, but if they just enjoy such surprises in heaven, then in the name of goodness he will let them have the joy....

In high spirits Willibald Krautmann now marched towards the silver mountain and before long he was standing before the gate of heaven. But the gate did not spring open, and no music crashed out into his face, and nothing streamed out, but everything remained quiet, just as if nobody was there.

Good heavens, how am I to take that?

—But now Willibald Krautmann gets the idea: the angels are little rascals, they want to have their fun with him and play hide-and-seek with him. Why, he himself had often amused himself with his angel figures. Afterwards, when they have fooled him a bit, the joy will be all the greater. But Krautmann isn't going to let them get away with just anything. A joke that goes too far is no joke any more. And the angels are not allowed to imagine that he will stand in front of heaven's door like a beggar and ask for shelter. No, it hasn't come to that yet, he doesn't need that—he, Willibald Krautmann, who worked all his life for Christmas. If they can wait there in heaven, I can wait too. Let's see who is the first one who gives up his patience!

Right away the cribmaker turned to the left and sat down on a stone a hundred paces away from the gate of heaven, supported his head on both hands and went into a sulk. It didn't take long before he perceived many fine, high, jubilant little voices behind the arch of the gate, and now the gate of heaven was opening and an enormous crowd of angels was pressing outwards. At the threshold of the gate stood Peter, speaking to the angels in a deep voice and giving them directions.

Willibald Krautmann stood off on one side of heaven's gate and since they didn't notice him he gave a couple of loud coughs so as to draw the angels' attention to him. But not a single one glanced at him, nor did they

have any time at all to pay any attention to the cougher. Now he was really at a loss.

Have they forgotten altogether that he is arriving? Is it perhaps that in all their Christmas activity they forgot to announce that Willibald Krautmann is coming to heaven? Then he himself will have to make himself noticed.

In a few jumps Master Krautmann was again at the gate of heaven, and immediately he hung with his whole little body on the bell-pull. Inside, the shrill sound of a bell rang. And there Peter was sticking his head out through the window.

"Who's pulling our gate bell out of its post?

313

What kind of a ruffian are you out there anyway?"

"I, Willibald Krautmann, well-known artist, carver of Christmas figures," replied the cribmaker.

"Willibald Krautmann," said Peter, "what an odd name! It is *not* known to us. I suppose you want to ask for lodgings with us?"

"Of course. I've been waiting out here for an hour already."

"That is not a matter of course at all. Let's see what is written about you in the Book."

Peter disappeared and left the man standing there, eyes and mouth wide open.

...."Well, thanks a lot for your friendly welcome! They don't even know him up here in heaven, me, Willibald Krautmann, and they first have to go and look whether he is written in a book! The world pays with ingratitude but I would not have thought that it was like *that* in heaven too...."

Now Peter returned and he turned to the Book. He took a long, long time. "Yes, yes, that's right. Willibald Krautmann. But you cannot enter."

"I, I cannot enter! I'd just like to ask for good cause and reason."

"You may hear those. Just listen! You have been arrogant and vain, and proud of your own works. You have considered others worthless in comparison to yourself and thought that nobody made such fine things as you."

314

"All right Mr. Heavenly Gateman, then you are making a fuss over such trifles? You used to be a fisher, and a catcher of fish like you just has no idea what an artist feels. And you don't say anything about other things. In my lifetime I have set up more than a half a hundred Christmas cribs. I have awakened many thoughts of heaven in human hearts, have caused much Christmas joy, and people could take a good example from my figures."

"Yes, that is true. It says more, too. I mean your arrogance, and I can't scratch that out."

"Yes, yes, every human being has some fault, and I'm not so conceited as to think that I am one of the greatest saints; but really one shouldn't make such a to-do about petty trifles."

"My good fellow, there are still other things written down here. You have been lacking in patience. When a piece of work wasn't going smoothly under your hands, you broke out in rude anger...."

"Mr. Gatekeeper, that was holy anger," Willibald Krautmann interrupted Peter; "the evil one could not stand my work and often hid my tools or pushed over my crib scene, so that all the figures rolled over in a heap—then certainly a righteous anger came over me."

"But the things you said then were anything but quick prayers."

"For goodness' sake, who thinks about what he says

in anger? You can't put that sort of thing on the golden scales. And I have never done damage in anger, like other people. I never struck an ear off anybody."

"Well, it seems as if you are trying to start a lawsuit with me," said Peter sharply, "then you ought to be looking around for an advocate or defender."

"Fine, all right. Just let me hop into heaven and I will have an advocate."

"Nothing that's impure can enter. You have to look down on earth for someone to speak for you."

"On earth? No, I unfortunately know no one on earth. I had no time for other people."

"Yes, yes, there you have it, that's just what you don't have. And now I'm going to read out to you the heaviest debt you have on your account. You have had far too little love for your neighbor; you have neglected to gain a friend or an advocate for yourself in heaven through a work of mercy."

"Heavens, I had to use my dollars for the Christmas work I did."

"No Christmas expenses mean so much as a warm-hearted gift of love to people in need."

"Sure—if one only had it.... I always did a little bit."

"Yes, a little bit, but it was too little. Last year, on Christmas Eve itself, you turned away a widow with three hungry children."

"Well, goodness—last year I had to make a new

design for the three kings and a new design for the wedding at Cana, and I had to gild the framing over. Those things cost money, and our money isn't worth anything. These are times when everything is sinfully expensive."

"Just the same, after all that outlay, you had enough left over to go out for a drink on Christmas Eve, a drink that was more than just to quench your thirst."

"Gracious, that was just a little joyful celebration, a very small one and that because of Christmas. These cheap wines one buys nowadays are so bad that you only have to drink one little glass, and it right away goes to your head."

"What? Are you lying as well? Those were two bottles of the most expensive kind. You won't get far with lying, that's something I really detest."

"Dear St. Peter, don't take it ill!" begged Willibald hypocritically. "Little white lies like that often come over the best people. Once I read about one who lied his way out of his need three times before the cock crowed twice."

"But he wept for it his whole life long, while you cover up and soften all your sins," thundered the heavenly gatekeeper at him. "That's the end of my patience. Now go where you belong."

So Peter, saying this, slammed the little window shut and went back into his gate house. Now for the first time Willibald Krautmann realized that this was in earnest, in bitter earnest. He knocked quite humbly on the window, and begged and whined like a poor soul for the gatekeeper to open up again and let him talk a little. But Peter did not listen to him. A dozen times the cribmaker pulled on the gate bell, but it didn't make a sound any more, and inside everything was as quiet as a mouse. There was nothing left for the poor man than to be outside. He looked for some place there near heaven where he could lie down and sleep.

Anxiously Willibald Krautmann tripped around the walls of heaven, and suddenly he saw a little window out of which a bright light was shining. He hurried up to it and looked curiously through the window. Dear God—there inside was the celebration of heaven. Now he looked into heaven and he saw light and more and more light and he noticed right away that this light meant unending love that delights heart and soul. He had not yet looked at a thousandth part of it all when a million voices began to sing: Gloria in excelsis Deo— Glory to God in the highest and on earth peace to men of good will. No one on earth has any idea that there can even be such music. Then Willibald Krautmann's breast began to feel hot, it pinched and it pressed and burned in his breast as if he had fire in his heart. It was an enormous longing, a pain so great that he felt he would have to die again. He wanted to speak but could

not, even less was he able to call out, so he only cried
down in the bottom of his heart:

"Forgive me my sin;
never again will I do it—
I beg thee!"

And now he began to weep, softly at first, then louder
and then quite loudly, yelling and howling. He pressed
his head against the windowpane so that the glass got
wet from his tears.... Suddenly there was a crack; the
window fell to pieces; Willibald Krautmann got a bad
fright; something terribly heavy was pulling and tearing
at his feet; he could no longer keep his footing and
plunged down and down....

And now he heard a well-known voice:

"What's the matter? What's going on, for heaven's
sake?"

He opened his eyes. There he lay in his room, in the
warm bed, and beside him stood his wife, still shaking
him by the shoulder. Now it became clear to him that
he was being awakened from a deep dream.

"What's the matter with you, you silly fool?" cried
his wife. "You are groaning and whimpering as if you
had at least one of your ears cut off."

"Oh, I have been in heaven," he replied.

"A fine heaven where you have to yell and gasp like
that."

"Quiet, woman, you don't understand. I will tell you all about it."

But Willibald Krautmann only told his wife half of what he had experienced. Instead he became more and more thoughtful; and during the Christmas holidays he lost a big sum of money—at least his wife believed he had lost it. He became friendly with everybody and no longer spoke impatiently. But he told a neighbor that this year he had had an especially wonderful and blessed Christmas. He also revealed to the neighbor, who was his best friend, the whole story of his trip to heaven.

People, Look East

People, look east. The time is near
Of the crowning of the year.
Make your house fair as you are able,
Trim the hearth, and set the table.
    People, look east, and sing today:
    Love the guest is on the way.

Furrows, be glad. Though earth is bare,
One more seed is planted there:
Give up your strength the seed to nourish,
That in course the flower may flourish.
    People, look east, and sing today:
    Love the rose is on the way.

Birds, though ye long have ceased to build,
Guard the nest that must be filled.
Even the hour when wings are frozen
He for fledgling-time has chosen.
    People, look east, and sing today:
    Love the bird is on the way.

Stars, keep the watch. When night is dim
One more light the bowl shall brim,
Shining beyond the frosty weather,
Bright as sun and moon together.
    People, look east, and sing today:
    Love the star is on the way.

Angels, announce to man and beast
Him who cometh from the east.
Set ev'ry peak and valley humming
With the word, the Lord is coming.
    People, look east, and sing today:
    Love the Lord is on the way.

ELEANOR FARJEON

JOURNEY TO CHRISTMAS

by B. J. CHUTE

he world had never been so deep in snow.

Rom swore at the little donkey when it stumbled into a drift of the wicked whiteness, and it shook its head and looked back at him sorrowfully as if its master ought to know it was doing its best.

"Get up, you beast," said Rom between his teeth. They were making such a slow way that it would be evening at least before they reached the great town, and, by that time, someone else might have laid claim to the miserly bit of a job that Rom was after.

"Get up, you beast," he said again and glared about him fiercely, hating the fields that lay so still and bound, the fields that had panted and scorched all summer long under the cruelest sun he had ever known in his eighteen years.

There had been bad times before, when the flour bin was scraped to its bottom and potatoes and old cabbages did for a daily diet, but there had never been bad times like this in the memory of the oldest. Now it was every man for himself in a world that had once seemed loving, and if he could only reach the great town in time, he would slit the throat of any man who came to take the bare promise of work away from him.

He looked at the donkey's sides, caved in like a broken barrel, and all he could think of was how slow its little hard hooves plodded. Months since the animal had known the treat of a carrot or even good hay under its nose, and there would be none tomorrow, the next day nor the long day after.

Only, tomorrow was Christmas Day.

"God's curse on it," said Rom, and the sound of the words was quick and dreadful in his ears but he could not take them back. His eyes stung with the tears whipped up by the icy wind, and he shook the stinging away and looked up the long road ahead.

Someone was walking the middle of it, someone shapeless as a huge bundle of blown rags and plodding even slower than the donkey. The thin jingle of harness must have reached the walker, and the haystacky figure turned heavily and watched the cart come.

324

It was the peddler woman that he remembered from childhood, thinner by pounds than when he had seen her last but still as broad as an oak beam. She threw up one hand out of her tatters, the other clutching a worn brown sack, and cried a greeting as if she was met up with a saint.

He pulled the donkey up alongside her, grudging even the moment of delay. She grabbed at the bridle rein, and the donkey put its nose on her shoulder, nuzzling hopefully.

"God be praised," said the peddler woman. "All the other carts are traveling east. You'll take me where I'm going." She trundled around to the side of the cart and leaned on the high wheel. "Give me a hand up, lad. I'm that bent with the crippling."

He had an impulse to push her away, but it would take as long to argue as it would to let her clamber on. "I'm following the road straight to the great town," he said sharply. "I'll not turn an instant off it, not for the Devil himself. Lay that to your mind."

She gave a short laugh and heaved her bulk up the step which creaked its protest. "The Devil'd not be walking in this weather," she said. "I'm going to the Kestery house."

"Not by me you're not going," he told her. "I'll take you to the crossroads because it's on my journey, but you'll walk the rest of the distance in your own two

325

shoes." He slapped the reins across the donkey's back, and the cart lurched ahead.

The peddler woman gave him no heed, grumbling and settling herself about. "Been going there for a month's time," she said, a little pleasanter now she was in the cart. "Each day I've put it off, telling myself there'd be tomorrow and I'd not walk so lame and the snow and cold would go. I might have known for myself that nothing good like that would happen this year."

"I'll take you to the crossroads," said Rom again.

"We'll talk that between us when I get my breath back." She went right on. "There's a doll in my sack for the little Kestery girl," she said, "the first doll she'll ever be having. They'd promised it to her from the day she was born, I think. Not born natural, she wasn't, you know. Her arm withered, poor mite, like a bird with one wing, though she's quicker than most, even so. Word came to me through the preacher that the Kesterys had the money all laid by, and I've had the doll for them since autumn. Would you like to see the doll, lad?" She fumbled at the sack's drawstrings, mumbling to the knots.

"No," said Rom. "I would not." Money for dolls, some had, money to throw away even in the bad times with not two coins to rub together for most. With the doll money in her pocket, the peddler woman would be

able to see a little ahead, if only around the next corner.

"I can draw breath easier for a bit," she said, reading his thoughts. "Wood on the fire, at least, and a bit of food without fighting for it, and maybe an extra or two."

"You're fat enough," said Rom.

She did not take it in bad part. "I'm not so bad off as your donkey," she admitted. "Poor beast. It'll lie down where it walks one day, by the looks of it."

"It's not laid down yet," said Rom grimly.

The peddler woman shrugged and looked at the sky, half-closing her eyes. "There's another storm up in there. It'll be a bad Christmas Day if the clouds mean anything."

"There'll be no Christmas this year," said Rom.

"God's truth," said the woman heavily. "Do you mind how it was other years, the lights in the windows and the little trees inside with their glitters on them? People buying my trinkets wherever I went, and the churches with their warm stoves and the pine boughs and the singing. They were fine, the churches were, before the bad times. The floors are so cold for kneeling now, it reaches up through your bones and into your heart."

"The Lord's not so long remembering as He was once," Rom said bitterly.

"That's blasphemy for a lad to think," said the peddler woman.

328

"I'll think it and I'll say it," said Rom. "There's precious little good left in the world."

The woman sighed heavily and fell silent. The cart jogged and lurched on its journey, turning wheels muffled by thick snow. The little sharp donkey-hooves shushed through it, and the road unwound, white and with no seeming end.

When they came at last to the crossroads, Rom pulled the donkey up. It stopped and stood with its legs spread and its head drooping, as it had stood in the oven of summer, under a sky like metal. Rom spoke over his shoulder. "This is your turning-place," he said. "I'm going on."

There was no answer, and he glanced back. The old fat bundle of rags had fallen into sleep on the floor of the cart, hand still clutching the sack. He leaned from his seat and shook her by the shoulder. "Get up and get out," he said. "This is as far as you go."

She woke with a cry, and it took her a moment to find where she was. Then she looked about and up the road she would have to travel alone, the snow not even broken along it. She gave a whimper. "It's a long ways yet," she said, "and I'm that crippled—"

"Your feet carried you to where I found you," said Rom coldly. "They can carry you again. Get out, and don't be keeping me. There's work waiting for me in the great town, and I'll not be kept from it."

"I'll fall," she said, sitting up and swaying back and forth. "I'll fall, and the snow will cover my bones."

"You'll not fall, a great lump like you. Get out."

"No," said the peddler woman, making a rock of herself.

Anger swelled up inside Rom. He could taste it bitter on his tongue, and he almost liked the taste of it. "Get out!" he said.

She held herself tight in her own arms, against the cold and his voice. "With the cart it's only a bit of a way to the Kestery house. I'll stumble forever and never get there."

"It's time out of my road coming and going," said Rom fiercely, "and I could lose what I must be having if I'm late to the town. The way's been slow enough. Get out of my cart!" He raised his hand, almost as if he would strike her.

She scrambled to her feet and climbed over the cart side and down into the snow. She stood so, for a long moment, staring at him, and then she drew in a long sigh and turned away.

He watched her. She was getting along all right, and she did not look back, thanks be for that. He muttered a curse and turned back to the donkey. It was still standing, patient as the eternal, its head down but one long ear pointed back to listen for the voice that would tell it to go on.

"Poor beast," said Rom suddenly and shook the reins. The little donkey must be aching for rest, but it moved forward without question. Rom had a quick memory of it, all through the hot summer and the dry autumn and the icy days. Its belly had not been filled in a long time and its fur was patchy with bad feeding and the rub of the harness, but it never even asked to rest a moment longer. It was old, too, old donkey, and tired half to death. Like the peddler woman.

Rom hunched himself up and pushed away the thought. The peddler woman would reach the Kestery house and there was money waiting for her there, money saved up and put aside for the child's doll. She had more ahead of her, she and the child both, than he could even hope for. The road was not so long but the old woman would reach the money.

"Who ever eased *my* way?" said Rom aloud, angry, and then he looked at the donkey.

He told himself not to be a fool. Just because a poor bag of donkey bones served him so willingly, that was no reason to risk his hope in the great town ahead. Others could look after themselves, others could—

"Ah, the Devil take it!" Rom cried out suddenly, and he pulled hard on the reins, turning the donkey about in its tracks. The donkey ears waved as if the creature was surprised, but the cart circled.

"It's God's own fool I am," said Rom despairingly,

and he slapped the reins across the donkey's back so that it broke into a shambling trot.

The peddler woman was plodding along up ahead, bent over against the pain in her back and the bite of the wind, but she heard them coming and faced about. From the look on her face, the donkey cart might have been a gold chariot and six white horses. "Get in," said Rom. "Get in, and be still. I'm a fool."

She looked at him queerly and got in, and there was not a word out of her until they came in sight of the Kestery chimney. Then Rom stopped the cart once more and she climbed heavily over the side. She started to speak but Rom would not listen, so she only gave him a look before she turned away.

But it was such a look that it stayed with him as the cart rolled him back down the road, and it seemed as if the wind was a little less cold after all.

Mrs. Kestery had seen the cart and came running out of the small house. The cart was gone before she reached it, and there was only the peddler woman, standing still.

She was a little body, Mrs. Kestery, young and once-pretty, but the bad times had put the scar of lines on her face and her eyes were too big. She said, "Come inside, come out of the cold," and led the way back into the small house, with the peddler woman lumbering behind.

"It's a wonder I'm here at all," said the peddler woman, spreading her bulk on a chair and puffing with relief. "But today it had to be, or never, with Christmas Day almost upon us. I got your message from the preacher in the autumn, and I'd have come sooner, only—"

Mrs. Kestery put the back of her hand to her forehead as if she had lost something in her mind. "The preacher?"

"Surely, the preacher." The peddler woman looked suddenly canny and glanced around her. "The little one's about?"

"In her bed," said Mrs. Kestery, and her own glance darted like a bird toward the closed door. "She's warmer so."

"Ah, then, we'll do our business at once and I'll be off, and the little one will never know how it came." She undid the string of the sack lying on her lap and put her hand inside. "The doll," she said proudly and pulled it out.

Mrs. Kestery gave a small cry and held out her hands like a child herself, wanting to touch and stroke the pretty thing.

"I found you the best," said the peddler woman proudly. "See—the dress and the little shoes." She

333

held the doll in the air, twirling it around gently, and then suddenly she looked at Mrs. Kestery. "What is it? What's wrong?"

Mrs. Kestery stood there, twisting her hands inside her apron and looking everywhere in the room except at the peddler woman. "I can't—" she said. "We can't—" She looked at the doll with terrible longing and said, fast and quick, "We can't buy the doll. I'm sorry you've had the journey."

The peddler woman sat the doll up on her lap and blew out her breath in a great puff. "What's this nonsense?" she said. "The preacher himself gave me your message, and I went to get the doll at once. It was not my fault I was so late coming, and even so I'm not too late. The child will have her doll on Christmas Day, that's what you wanted." She looked sharply at the mother. "You've not been and bought another doll?"

"No, no, it's not that." Her apron was all screwed tight in her hands.

"Well, then." The peddler woman sighed her relief and danced the doll on her knee. "The preacher said you'd laid the money by before you sent your message, and—"

"The money's gone," said Mrs. Kestery, very low.

The peddler woman gaped at her. "Gone?"

Mrs. Kestery's hands dropped the tormented apron, and she lifted them to hide her face. "I thought from day to day things would be better," she said, very close to the edge of tears, "and then, when it got so near to Christmas and you not come, I made certain you knew—"

"But the money! The preacher said you had the money."

"Oh, we had it all right. We put it away in the brown teapot for the child's Christmas, and we'd take it out at times and smile at it, my husband and me, thinking how the little one would care for the doll. She's been planning a home for it all year—Oh, dearie, dearie," she said and sobbed outright, letting all the held-back tears spill over the drought of her grief.

"You had the money," said the peddler woman dully, "you must have it still. The preacher said it was all laid by and would not be touched." She got to her feet, suddenly outraged. "You wasted it. You wasted the money for the child's doll that I came all this way through the snow to bring her! And all the weary way back to go and—" She stopped. And nothing at the end of it for herself, except the fireplace without enough wood and the cupboard without enough food and the bad times grinning at her from every shelf and cranny. "Oh!" she said. "You could not have wasted the money so!"

Mrs. Kestery raised her head, and suddenly she began to dart about the kitchen like a little mad creature. For a moment the peddler woman thought her brain was turned, but all Mrs. Kestery was doing was to throw open bins and cupboard doors and even the door of the oven itself.

"Look," Mrs. Kestery said. "Look there, and there. Not enough to get us through the cold days, not enough of anything. See, there's so little flour left in the bin, it's no more than a scraping. I made the last loaves yesterday and how will they last all the while we need them? Cabbages and potatoes, half of them gone bad, and never a bit of meat anywhere. You don't know what it's been."

The peddler woman shook her head, not able to believe. "But you had the money," she said again, and again. "The preacher said you had the money. Your man was working and doing well. I know it's bad times for most, but you were able to set money by for such a thing as a doll without fretting. The preacher said you had done it."

"My man's got no work," said Mrs. Kestery, her hands fallen loose to her sides. "The fever came on him, and the blood in him went bad. That was how the money went, the money we'd saved for the doll, and all the money we scraped up later. The medicine and the doctor and all the things. We prayed the bad times would end—"

"No money," said the peddler woman, seeing only

the reflection of her own money lost to her. You couldn't use a doll for food or heat.

"He's out gathering wood now, my husband is," said Mrs. Kestery, suddenly timid, looking at her pitifully. "When he comes back, he'll tell you how it was. We should have got a message to you, but I put it off and kept hoping. She wants the doll so, she's talked of nothing else, and this year we were so sure—Oh, I'm sorry you've had the long journey." She made a gesture. "If there's anything I could offer—"

The peddler woman got to her feet, her mouth set tight. The long journey, indeed! And all the way back. And none of the little extra things to look forward to, to be bought with the money that would have carried her ahead for a little while. She looked down at the doll in her hand, and a counting look came into her eyes. If she went to the great town now, surely there would be someone wanting a doll. And there would be carts coming back from the town to bring her home. It would not be like hoping for someone to take her up the road to the Kestery house. Perhaps she could get more, even, for the doll in the great town.

"Well," she said at last, "it's not so bad but it might be worse. I'll find someone to take the doll and make my money from them. But another time you might take more thought to others," she added sourly.

"I'm sorry you had the journey," Mrs. Kestery whispered, her eyes on the doll. Suddenly she stretched out her hand. "May I hold it for a moment?" she said and, without waiting for an answer, she took the doll into her hands.

The peddler woman reached to snatch it back and then paused, struck by something odd in the way the doll was held. Crooked in one arm, instead of cradled in two. She frowned for a moment, and then it came to her. The mother held the doll as the child would have held it, one arm withered. Poor wounded wing.

"Give it me," said the peddler woman sharply and reached out her hand.

For just a moment Mrs. Kestery laid her cheek against the doll's cheek. "It's so sweet," she said. "Such a little love it would have been for our baby to hold. I wish I'd never told her it was going to be Christmas Day tomorrow."

"There's no Christmas this year," said the peddler woman grimly and took the doll, gave it a quick shake to straighten its dress and thrust it into the sack. "There's no Christmas for anyone, and I've miles to go. I hope to God there's a traveler on the road who'll go my way." She turned, stumping toward the door. "I'll be off before the child wakes."

"Yes," said Mrs. Kestery.

The peddler woman pulled her cloak tight about her shoulders and, without looking back again, she went out. She hoped she would not meet up with Kestery himself coming back from the search for firewood. She hoped she would not meet up with anyone unless it was another cart going her way which led toward the great town. She would do better selling the doll there, no doubt of that.

It would be a sore Christmas for the Kestery child, but there was Christmas for none this year and no helping it. Time taught you not to expect good things. Who ever did a kindness for an old peddler woman?

Then she remembered the lad in the donkey cart, it coming into her mind without her asking it. Well, she admitted, that had been a kindness. He'd chanced his job for her, and now it was all for nothing, since the doll was still to be sold.

She braced herself stolidly. Sold it would be, then, and some other young one would be well-pleased with the world at sun-up. Not a young one with a wounded wing, but someone.

"He turned off his way for me," said the peddler woman aloud.

"It was not so much to do," she said. "Only a mile or so."

She walked ten paces very briskly. She walked another ten.

But he had risked his job, had he not?

She stopped. She opened her sack and took out the

doll and stood looking at it very fiercely. She shook it a little as if it had done something wrong to her, but it only looked back calmly out of blue china eyes.

"I'm a fool," said the peddler woman, and she turned about in her steps and marched back to the house, opening the door without a knock or a by-your-leave. Mrs. Kestery was sitting at the table, just sitting, her hands idle.

"Here," said the peddler woman and thrust the doll into her hands. "Give it to the child in the morning. You can pay me when there's money again, and Christmas again, and the bad times over. If that day ever comes."

She turned and was gone, off again down the road she had come by. The snow was not quite so deep perhaps as she had remembered it.

It was past dark when the knock came at the Kestery door. Husband and wife, sitting together by a faint glimmer of light so as not to waste the lamp, looked up startled, each from private thoughts. The little one was sleeping, her last awake words of the doll she would have in the morning. Kestery had been greeted with the news of the doll the instant he came back from the woods, and the slow smile that had not shown for months broke across his face.

The doll lay on the table between them now, and the

joy of it had lasted through twilight. But they had spent the time since in trying to see ahead, and there was little to see that was not darker than the night itself. With carefulness, their food would last a few weeks, not more. The bread baked with the last of the flour would be gone in a week's time.

"If the spring would come early," said Kestery heavily, "and I would be stronger."

"You're mending," his wife said as she had said it so often, but she felt a pain in her heart, knowing so well what he meant. The rising sap, and the summer birds coming back, and the sky blue again, they would be healing. He could look for work. But, if the winter held, how long would it be before their little girl would shrink and pinch and pale beyond saving?

"The times have never been so bad," Kestery said hopelessly, and then there was the knock at the door.

Mrs. Kestery went to open it, and the small skinny creature that stood there grinned ingratiatingly, mouth stretched over skeleton jaw. She knew him at once— Barren the Mean Man, come to beg. There was nothing for him in this house, and she all but got the door shut in his face before he slipped inside.

"There's nothing for you here," she said.

He stood, still grinning, so thin his clothes hardly touched him at all, looking like a shivering dog. "I'm hungry."

342

Kestery rose to his feet. "Get out. There's nothing to share."

"I'm starving," said Barren, whining but telling little less than the truth.

"The world's starving with you," said Kestery.

"You've food."

"None to spare."

"A rind—a scrap of bread—all the doors have been closed in my face. Tomorrow is Christmas. In the sweet name of Jesus—"

They knew Barren from years back, he had never said thanks to anyone and he had never reached out a hand to a person in the world. If he died, no one would be poorer, and if he lived, no one would be richer. The name of Jesus had never lain in a mouth that treasured it less.

"Get out!" said Kestery again, and raised his hand.

Barren shrank back. "Only a little crust, only a moment's help—"

"There's none has helped us," said Kestery.

Barren's eyes ran to the doll on the table. Mrs. Kestery reached out and tried to cover it away from his look and make it safe. "It took money to buy that," said Barren.

"It was left us in kindness," said Mrs. Kestery quickly, and then she put her hand to her breast and looked sideways at her husband. Then, "It's God's truth, there was one who helped us, there was the peddler woman," she murmured. "I could give him a crust."

"Not while I stand here," said her husband, but he looked at the doll too.

"If I'd strength to get to the great town," Barren whined, "I'd go there and beg. But without food, I'll fall in the snow."

"Fall then," said Kestery. "There's none will miss you." But he could not take his eyes from the doll or his mind from the thought of the peddler woman's kindness. She had been going to sell the doll in the great town, that was what his wife had told him, but she had left it behind. And the man Barren was skin and bones.

He jerked his shoulders as if something lay on them heavy, and he made a gesture with his hand. "Give it him then," he said. "Give him the crust."

Barren said "Aaaah" hungrily.

Mrs. Kestery went to the place where the bread lay hidden away and took out a round loaf and the knife to cut it. She laid the bread on the table and she measured her knife's edge just against the heel of the loaf. Then she looked up at her husband. "Like this?" she said.

He nodded, and she was about to draw the knife across when suddenly he came over and took it out of

344

her hand. Barren sucked in his breath with sudden fear that he was to go empty-handed after all.

But Kestery had set the knife to the very center of the loaf and cut it into two equal parts. He lifted the one half in his big hand and held it out to the beggar.

"Here," he said. "Take it and be on your way." He hardly dared to look at his wife for shame of the fool's thing he had done, but when he did look he found he need not have been anxious. Her eyes were so full of love.

Barren the Mean Man never stayed to say his thanks. He scuttled to the door and was out faster than a thieving rat, and he ran into the snow and away from the house before they could change their minds, the half-loaf held to his chest like a dear thing.

Not until he was safe in the woods did he stop running, and then he sat down on a log, his breath coming fast and the loaf clutched tight. "Slowly," he said, "slowly," and broke off a corner and stuffed it into his mouth and tasted the sweet taste of grain.

The wind had died down, and the woods were quiet. The storm clouds had gone over, and the moon was up. There were stars in the sky, one of them so bright in the darkness that its rays were like torchlight. A great fir tree stood in the center of the space where Barren had come, its boughs friendly and wide and sweeping

346

down to the ground. One year such a tree had stood in the square at Christmas time, with tinsel and glitter and a huge star at the top made of something silvery. There had been singing of carols, and even Barren the Mean Man had not been turned away. That was back in the time when Christmas was real.

Now all that was real was the half-loaf of bread, and Barren tore off another chunk and chewed it slowly, savoring the smallest crumb. Bit by bit, bit by bit, the hunger dying in him a little.

It was then that the birds came.

Perhaps they had been already there, and he had not noticed them in his hunger, but likely not. Birds coming out at night made a strange sight, and Barren looked twice before he made sure his eyes were not tricking him. Small handfuls of feather and beak, scrawny as plucked chickens, all of them. What seeds or scraps lay about for birds in bad times?

Barren looked at them very cunningly and held the loaf tighter. "There'll be no crumbs," he said maliciously and laughed to himself because all the crumbs were his. The birds came a bit closer. He had never seen birds by moonlight before; birds were day-walkers, except the owls and such.

They pecked at the snow and gave little cries and fluttered their wings, hopping toward him and then away. He waved his hand and shouted angrily, and

347

some flew off, but even those came back to the near branches of the fir tree and watched him.

"Get out, get away," said Barren furiously, wishing the moon would find a cloud to hide behind so he could not see his strange audience.

They would not go, and the moon would not either. And the star had grown so terribly bright that he almost covered his eyes against it. "There's scarce enough for one," said Barren to the birds, "let alone all you things. Get away!"

Still they would not go, though he half-rose, threatening, and then he pulled off another chunk of bread to thrust it in his mouth and show them he would have it all.

They watched him with their bright eyes, and they pecked at the empty snow. "The Devil take you!" Barren shouted. He made a sudden move and hid the bread away from them, under his coat where they could not see it, though he wanted to hold it in his hands and eat and eat.

One little sparrow came closer. It was so thin a man could take it up and crush it like a handful of tiny twigs. Barren huddled himself around his half-loaf of bread, as if a little bird would tear it away from him, and anger shook him like wind.

Why should the little birds come begging to Barren?

Barren the Mean Man—he knew very well how they named him. Begging to him, the birds were, as if he ought to do for birds what no man had ever done for him, share of his very life.

And then the memory of Kestery came to him clear with the knife in his hand, and he remembered how the promised crust had grown under that knife and become half a loaf of bread. There had been precious little to share in the Kestery house, a beggar's eye had told Barren that.

The sparrow pecked snow, and it might better have pecked air for all the food it got.

Slowly, Barren drew the loaf out from under his rags. He nipped a tiny crumb off between thumb and finger and flicked it toward the sparrow. The bird moved so quickly it scarcely seemed to move at all, but it was on the crumb in an instant and the crumb was gone. A flutter ran through all the birds, and a little talking asking noise like a cry.

He pulled off another crumb and then another, and then, before he could stop his hand from what it was doing, he had torn off a great hunk of his bread and was crumbling it up in his fingers and scattering the bits all over the snow.

"I'm a fool," said Barren, half sobbing it. "God's truth, I'm a fool if there ever was one."

349

It seemed as if he could not stop himself. The fir tree was all at once alive with more birds and such a singing of carols that it was like the old days in the square.

Barren looked up, his eyes going from wide branch to wide branch, until they came to the top branch of all. Caught there at the very tip, blazing against the sky, the great star shone with its rays streaming down to the earth.

He could not know it, having no way to tell the hour, but midnight had just gone by and it was the morning of Christmas. He stood still, holding what was left of his half-loaf of bread, and something stirred inside him as if a hand had been laid on his heart.

No one ever knew afterwards just when the bad times had passed. But pass they did that winter as if they had never been, and that was God's truth, and no one ever rightly knew why.

ADVENT

the sky is deep above the hill,
the silent stars, the frozen tree,
the world so still!

builder of stars beyond our sight,
touch our hearts that are so cold
with fire and light

that fire may leap from heart to heart
across the reaches of the dark!
shatter the night!

one master and one lasting home!
awake and kindle, rise to praise!

the Lord will come!

JANE T. CLEMENT

ACKNOWLEDGMENTS

The editor and the publisher have made every effort to trace the ownership of all material contained in this book and to obtain permission from publishers, authors, and authorized agents. In the event of inadvertent errors, the publisher will be happy to make necessary corrections in future editions of this book.

BERG, Maria, "Hallelu-nein," copyright by L. Berchtenbreiter. Published in Germany by Berchtenbreiter Verlag, Rosenheim, Bayern. Translated and printed by permission of the publisher.

CHRISTALLER, Helene, "Bruder Räuber," ("Brother Robber") copyright by Friedrich Reinhardt AG Verlag, Basel. First published in *Lichter im Strom* by Helene Christaller and is now included in *Aus Assisis Grossen Tagen*, published by Friedrich Reinhardt AG, the publisher of all her German works, who has given permission for this publication in English.

CHUTE, B. J., *Journey to Christmas*, reprinted in its entirety by permission of E. P. Dutton & Co., Inc. Text, Copyright © 1955 by B. J. Chute. This story first appeared in *Good Housekeeping Magazine* under the title "The Year There Was No Christmas."

GOUDGE, Elizabeth, "The Well of the Star," reprinted by permission of Coward-McCann, Inc. Copyright 1941 by Elizabeth Goudge.

KOOPMAN, Ger, "The Chess Player," printed and published by permission of the author.

LAGERLÖF, Selma, "The Legend of the Christmas Rose," from *The Girl from the Marsh Croft* by Selma Lagerlöf. Copyright 1910 by Doubleday & Company, Inc. Reprinted by permission of the publisher.

ONNEN, Marie, "The Angel's Song," was given to the Bruderhof communities in England one Christmas many years ago by Marie Onnen, a member. It was one of her favorite stories, but whether one she had been told as a child or one she made up herself, we have no way of knowing now. Marie came to the Bruderhof from Holland when she was already over eighty years old.

PHILLIPS, J. B., "The Angels' Point of View," reprinted with permission of The

354

Macmillan Company from *New Testament Christianity* by J. B. Phillips. Copyright © J. B. Phillips 1956.

PICKTHALL, Marjorie, "The Worker in Sandalwood," from *Christmas Stories and Legends* published by Meigs Publishing Company, Indianapolis, Indiana. Copyright 1916 by Meigs Publishing Co. Reprinted by permission of the publisher.

REIMMICHL, "Krippenmachers Himmelgang," (The Cribmaker's Trip to Heaven"), and "Der Waldbär," (The Forest Bear"), from *Weihnacht in Tirol,* by Reimmichl, published by Verlagsanstalt Tyrolia, Gesellschaft M. B. H. Innsbruck. Translated and printed by permission of the publisher.

SAWYER, Ruth, "The Shepherds" and "Words from an Old Spanish Carol" from *The Long Christmas,* copyright 1941 by Ruth Sawyer. Reprinted by permission of The Viking Press, Inc.

WIECHERT, Ernst, "Der Kinderkreuzzug," (The Children's Crusade"), from *Am Himmelstreif ein Stern.* Translated and printed by permission of Verlag Kurt Desch G. M. B. H. Munich.

"Der Armen Kinder Weihnacht," ("The Poor Children's Christmas"), from *Märchen* by Ernst Wiechert. Translated and printed by permission of the Rascher Verlag, Zurich.

"Behold that Star," by Thomas W. Talley, from Walter Ehret and George Evans, *The International Book of Christmas Songs.* Copyright © 1963. Reprinted by permission of Prentice-Hall, Inc. and authors.

"Heaven's Gate Has Opened." Reprinted with permission of Cooperative Recreation Service, Inc., Delaware, OH, from *The Little Book of Carols.* "How Far Is It to Bethlehem?" by Frances Chesterton, "Mid-Winter," by Christina Rossetti, "People, Look East," by Eleanor Farjeon, "The Christ-Child Lay on Mary's Lap," by G. K. Chesterton, "Poverty Carol," translated by K. E. Roberts. All reprinted by permission of Oxford University Press from *The Oxford Book of Carols.*

The Plough Publishing House, publishers and booksellers since 1920, carries a wide variety of books on spirituality, social transformation, radical Christianity, community – and last, but certainly not least – books, songbooks, and cassettes for children. See selected titles below:

THE SHEPHERD'S PIPE
Songs from the Holy Night
Poems by Georg J. Gick
Music by Marlys Swinger

Simple enough for anyone to sing, yet rich enough for the accomplished, Marlys Swinger's best-loved cantata contains unusual Christmas poetry set to music that is at once modal and contemporary. Ideal for family enjoyment, as well as for school or church use. The vocal scoring ranges from unison to three-part harmony (SSA), with piano and optional string quartet accompaniment. Includes suggestions for performance as a pageant.

Music Ministry
Emphasizes with deeply moving piety the response of the hearts to the coming of the Christ Child...Annual performances of *The Shepherd's Pipe* may well become a treasured tradition.

The Messenger
Understated, hauntingly beautiful music to recall the "night of all nights." Poetry of wisdom and joy.

Shepherd's Pipe choral edition
0-87486-011-3, softcover

Shepherd's Pipe cassette
45 minutes, 0-87486-049-0

THE SPARROW
And Other Stories
Jane T. Clement
Illustrated by Kathy Mow

Here are the stories from a mother who has written the kind of tales she wished she could have found for her own children: tales that renew and refresh, that quietly remind us that love, purity, and self-sacrifice are still precious.

Clement's stories, which include a whimsical fairy tale, a legend, and a richly historical piece, demonstrate how meaningless lives can find new purpose. All are bound together by a sense of expectancy, a belief that something new is on the way. No stilted moralism here!

For older children, for adults to read aloud to their children – or for their own enjoyment.

Friends Journal
Clement writes with simplicity and directness, gentle, probing insistence, and conviction. One lays down the book in thought, and with a thankful heart.
0-87486-009-1, softcover

SING THROUGH THE DAY
Ninety Songs for Younger Children
Edited by the Bruderhof
Music arranged by Marlys Swinger

A time-honored collection of songs that reflect children's love of daily life, friends, pets, weather, and special events; appropriate for singing throughout the day, from waking to sleeping. The melodies – simple, folk-like tunes that children will easily pick up – are filled out with piano accompaniment and guitar chords. Includes illustrations too! Ideal for the home as well as for kindergarten and early elementary school classes.
0-87486-107-1, hardcover,

Sing through the Day **cassette**
Forty-seven songs from the book
0-87486-047-4, 61 minutes

SING THROUGH THE SEASONS
Ninety-nine Songs for Children
Edited by the Bruderhof
Music arranged by Marlys Swinger

A companion to *Sing through the Day*, this volume celebrates the seasonal round and its joys, from sleds and snowmen to sandbuckets and ice cream; robins and crocuses to pumpkins and falling leaves. Many of the melodies are new settings of tried-and-true poems by well-loved writers like Eleanor Farjeon, Elizabeth Coatsworth, Aileen Fisher, and Ivy O. Eastwick. Like *Sing through the Day*, a perennial favorite.
0-87486-006-7, hardcover,

Sing through the Seasons **cassette**
Thirty-one songs from the book
0-87486-048-2, 48 minutes

FOR A COMPLETE CATALOG, WRITE OR CALL

The Plough Publishing House
Spring Valley Bruderhof
Route 381 N
Farmington PA 15437, USA
Toll-free: 1-800-521-8011
or: 412-329-1100

The Plough Publishing House
Darvell Bruderhof
Robertsbridge E. Sussex
TN32 5DR, UK
Free phone UK: 0-800-269-048
or +44(0)1580-881-003